CREAT
CREATION

J.R.GAGNE

WE MAKE WORLDS LLC.

ISBN: 978-1-7371216-0-2 E-Book

ISBN: 978-1-7371216-1-9 Paperback

CONTENTS

This book is dedicated to all the people in this world who just need an escape from reality. Come visit when you need to unwind and let me guide you on this wonderful journey.

CHAPTER ONE
BIRTH

In the distance a dark-robed figure stood atop the hill, looking down on the quaint little town of Addleberry as the storm grew in the sky above him. A spiderweb of brilliant light weaved across the night sky as the lightning annunciated the storm's presence. One bolt lit the tiny hamlet for a short time, creating an eerie silhouette. The grass swayed on the hillside, appearing like waves rolling across an ocean of water as the wind continued to howl. The figure looked down at the town with an icy gaze as the relentless rain continued to pelt him. His right hand was outstretched, clutching a red staff that was covered in intricate glyphs up to the orange-colored stone embedded at the top. A low glow emanated from the stone, giving the man an eldritch appearance. Thunder clapped as another bolt of lightning streaked across the sky. Without moving, the robed figure's eyes studied the town as if searching for something. "Ahhh, there it is," he announced. With a nod, he walked down from the hillside towards the town.

The streets of Addleberry were deserted this time of night, and only a few homes still shone candlelight through rain-pelted windows. He passed a handful of run-down homes, as well as the market and the blacksmith. Without warning, he stopped at one very shabby home and turned towards the door. "Yes, this is the one, I can feel her presence." A wide grin shown on his bearded face as he silently opened the door and walked in. It was dark inside and the occupant was fast asleep. He walked forward slowly, passing by a small table with two chairs to his right and a smoldering fireplace to his left. He moved silently, like a ghost, as he approached a middle-aged woman. Her long black hair framed her face beautifully as she slumbered in a small, uncomfortable-looking bed. "Today will be the beginning of a new era for this world, my queen, and I am here to welcome you to your kingdom," he whispered. With a crack, the butt of the staff struck the floor, waking the slumbering woman. The orange stone ignited in a blinding light, turning the darkness into day. "Helnum, zemilio, barda," the words hissed from his mouth.

The woman struggled but could not move. "What have you done?" she shouted, struggling as some unseen force held her fast to the bed. Cries could be heard from the woman as she wept in fear. "Please let me go," she pleaded.

"Not before I have delivered her." He whispered, "Sulap," and the blankets were ripped off the bed.

"I am with child, please don't hurt us." Her swollen abdomen was now clearly visible.

"Yes, this is what I came for," the robed figure spoke while staring at her stomach.

"Please don't hurt my baby," the woman begged as tears rolled freely down her face.

"I wouldn't dream of hurting the child, quite the opposite. I'm here to save her!" With that, he tipped his staff towards the woman. He muttered the word, "Expel," and she exploded into a bloody haze. The bed, walls, and floor were now covered with the blood and gore of human remains. As he stepped closer to the bed, the squishing of the woman's flesh under his black leather boots broke the silence. In the center of the bed, where the woman once lay, a womb was visible in a pool of blood. Slowly and very gently after such a horrific act, he took his left hand and with his razor, sharp fingernails, sliced open the sack. The amniotic fluid spilled out, revealing a baby girl inside. The tiny bundle did not cry, but instead gazed at this robed man. Her icy-blue eyes stared up at him as he reached down and scooped up the child with one hand. He placed his staff on the bed and pulled out a golden-handled knife from inside his robe. Immediately he sliced the child's life cord and knotted it. "Magnificent, together we will shape this world and rule over all that are in it." His smile was wide as he tucked the child into his robe. After placing the knife back in its sheath, he picked up his staff.

With all the commotion, he failed to notice the figure standing in the home's doorway. A crackling bolt of lightning shot across the room and hit the black-robed figure. Within inches of making contact, the lightning bolt shattered into hundreds of smaller sparks as it struck the invisible shield around the mage repelling the attack. The force of the blow was still strong enough though to knock him to his knees.

The figure in the doorway spoke with authority. "Give me the child, Valin, or I will destroy you!"

Valin responded with a low menacing laugh, "My old friend, Ezra, is that you?"

"I won't ask you again, Valin. Leave the child and maybe I will let you live."

"Tsk, tsk, tsk, you're too late, Ezra. I have her and there's nothing you or anyone can do about it." Effortlessly, Valin stood back onto his feet. "You see, Ezra, I have had a premonition that led me to this child so I can protect and guide her on her journey to shape this world. I have seen magnificent things in this vision. Join us, Ezra, or you will be swept away like so many leaves in the storm that is about to come."

A look of disgust bloomed on Ezra's thin, pale face. "Valin, I too have had a similar vision. But in mine, this child was compassionate and brought prosperity to this new world. You will poison that child with your hunger for power, and doom this land to despair and strife!"

In that instant, Valin attacked with a blinding light from his staff.

"Ahhh!" Ezra screamed, covering his eyes. As his vision slowly returned, he found Valin had fled. "No, I let him escape! I have to find him and recover that child."

Slowly, he walked further into the room where the remains of the woman were. "This horrific act is just the first of many if Valin has his way," Ezra said. He turned around to leave, but the slightest movement from the bed caught his eye. He cocked his head slightly to the right and approached the bed; he could see something moving from the supposedly empty sack. "What do we have here?" he asked himself as he pulled a dagger from his belt to lift the flap of skin and look inside. What he saw made his heart race. "My god, there were two!"

Ezra wiped his dagger and placed it back in its sheath hanging from his leather belt. Reaching inside the still lukewarm remains, he pulled forth a little baby boy. Ezra smiled and chuckled as a tear rolled down his cheek. Elation that he had not completely failed washed over him. This boy had the deepest green eyes Ezra had ever seen as their gaze met. Finding some unsoiled linens in the kitchen, he quickly cleaned and wrapped the child tightly. "That ought to do it."

The storm was passing now, its thunder fading in the distance. The rain had all but stopped and only the remaining water running off the roof could be heard splashing on the ground. Ezra cradled the boy in his arms, left the home, and vanished into the night.

CHAPTER TWO
LUCIOUS DRAKE

It was a midsummer's day on the farthest outskirts of Addleberry. Lush fields of green grass stretched to the north and south. Forests ran along the east and west sides of town, as did a small river. Close to that river, a young man, about six feet tall with a thin muscular build, laid in the grass, quizzically watching a red cannon beetle sunning itself on a large rock. Every living thing seemed to captivate him, and he often spent considerable time inspecting and analyzing whatever creature crossed his path. His focus at the moment is a shiny red and black beetle with six legs and a tube-shaped proboscis protruding from its forehead. *I wonder what that's for*, he thought. *The beetle hasn't moved; I wonder if it's dead?*

Lucious pushed himself up off the grass before moving closer to the specimen for a more thorough examination. He angled his face down, trying to detect any sign of life. He stretched out his right pointer finger to touch the beetle, and in that second, a horrible red fluid shot from the tube on the beetle's head and hit him squarely in the face. With great speed, he jumped back and began gagging from the stench. After sprinting to the riverside, he began splashing water on his face to rid himself of the horrible fluid. Breathing heavily, with water dripping from his head, he now realized what the tube was for. Lucious chuckled at himself as he stood up from the riverbank. His white, stained shirt was now soaking wet as the water ran from his thick blond hair. Brushing himself off, he walked back to the flat rock where he had been so rudely assaulted. The beetle was no longer there. "Little guy must have run away after he sprayed me. What an amazing defense mechanism."

"Lucious," someone yelled from in the distance.

He recognized the voice as his father's, and judging by how late in the day it was, he guessed it must be time for dinner. "Coming, father," he shouted as he headed east, toward their home. The sound of the rushing river was ever so calming as Lucious walked beside it. Looking toward town, Lucious saw Mr. Lother hammering a bit of steel at his smithy. Lucious waved to him as he passed by, but Mr. Lother just gave a simple nod and continued molding that piece of red-hot metal with his tools. *I wonder what he's making today*, Lucious thought. *Horseshoes maybe, or a knife, or maybe even something more exciting, like a sword or shield?* He couldn't wait to visit tomorrow and see what beautiful item would be finished. Lucious liked the idea of knights with pristine armor and ornate, well-crafted swords defending the defenseless and upholding order. His father was always telling him the most amazing stories of battles that had been fought in the past.

Lucious finally arrived at his family's small but modest home. He could see a bit of smoke from the hearth coming out the chimney. The smell hit his nose as he reached for the door. *Oh, that smells wonderful. We must be having cabbage and fish stew tonight*, he thought, as he pushed open the door and went inside. "Hello, Father. Dinner smells delicious and I'm absolutely starving!"

Ezra stood tending to a large cooking pot that was hanging just above the flames in the hearth. "Tidy yourself up, Lucious. There's fresh water in the basin and the dishes are ready to be placed on the table when you're clean." Ezra pulled the ladle out of the pot and tasted the stew. "Mmmm, that's just right."

He put the ladle back in the pot and pulled the whole thing off the fire. As he stepped over to the old wooden table, he could see Lucious setting the bowls and spoons out in their usual spots. With precision, he scooped out two massive servings of stew and filled the bowls. Ezra placed the pot on a flat stone to protect the wood from the heat. Lucious and his father sat down and ate.

"Lucious, my boy, did you get all of your chores done like I asked you?"

Lucious swallowed a mouthful of stew, then replied, "Yes, I took care of feeding and watering the livestock this morning, as well as chopping all the firewood."

"That's very good, Lucious. After dinner, I would like you to help me clean up and then it will be time to study your spell-craft."

Lucious smiled from ear to ear. He loved learning about spell-craft almost as much as he liked swordsmanship training. The two carried on with the meal. Lucious had a second bowl and would have had a third if his father hadn't stopped him.

"Son, I know you're at that age where you're becoming a young man and you need to feed that growing body, but you don't want to overdo it and get sick."

"All right, but after spell-craft, can I have some honey cakes for dessert?"

"We'll see how it goes. If you practice hard, then just maybe we can both have a little treat."

Hurriedly, Lucious cleared the table and washed up the dishes in a pail of dishwater in the small kitchen. After they had dried, he put the bowls and spoons away and walked to his father's room where the bookshelf was located. A bed and table were in the room, along with his father's clothes. On the bookshelf were nearly twenty books of all shapes, sizes, and various thicknesses.

"Let's see, which one was it?" Lucious wondered as he ran a finger down the spine of the first row of books, "Ah, there it is." His finger stopped on a light blue book titled *Light Arcana*; its intricate letters were written in gold. This book was for novice mages to teach the basics of light magic. Lucious enjoyed using this book, but it was mainly used for creating a flash to blind a foe, or a light to see in the dark when a lantern or torch were not available. Lucious walked back to the dining table and sat down with the book. "Father, these spells are fun and all, but they do little. Not like the fire spell book with its exploding orbs, or the lightning book with its arch bolt. When do we get to finish with the Light Arcana?"

"The light spells do little you say, huh?"

Poof! A blinding flash exploded at the table, completely stunning Lucious. His eyes hurt and there was something cold pressed against his throat. He reached his hand up and found it was his father's dagger that was gently pressed against him.

"You see son, the most basic of spells, like the blinding light spell, can incapacitate your enemy, giving you the chance to move in for the kill or retreat to safety."

Lucious swallowed hard and nodded his head. "Yes sir, I understand."

His father sheathed his knife and sat back down. "All right, you may begin with the guiding light spell on page thirty-five."

With that, Lucious opened the book and flipped to the page Ezra instructed him to start with. For the next few hours, the two sat across from each other, one the student, the other the teacher. Most of the spells were extremely easy for Lucious, as he was attuned to it.

"Father, why is it that everyone doesn't use this amazing force of nature?"

His father put a hand to his chin and thought for a long moment before he spoke. "Well, you see, Lucious, the essence of magic flows around us all endlessly, like the breeze that moves clouds across the sky. It doesn't belong to you and I, but to all living creatures. The catch, my boy, is that for a special few like you and myself, we can harness this energy, which manifests as magic. True mages are attuned to it and can cast spells with a simple gesture or word. Now it is possible to harness this power without this connection, but it requires the use of rare stones and runes, as well as ancient words of invocation. Getting it this way is unnatural, to say the least!"

"I understand," replied Lucious, and closed the book. By this time, it was dark outside and almost his bedtime. Sliding his chair back, he picked up the book and headed back into his father's room. "There we go," he said, placing Light Arcana back on the bookshelf. He then walked back to the table and stood next to his father. "Can I have the honey cakes now?"

"You did very well with your training, Lucious. I think you deserve it, don't you?"

"Yes, sir," Lucious said, a grin on his face. He took a few steps to the kitchen and pulled down a gray jar with a black crow painted on it. Lifting off the lid revealed his prize. In the jar's bottom were three small, round honey cakes. He walked to the table with the jar and divided up the spoils between them. The two made quick work of the desserts, leaving not even a crumb to waste.

"Why don't you put the jar back and get yourself ready for bed. It's getting late and there'll be plenty of work to do tomorrow."

Lucious did as he was instructed, closing the jar, and placing it back where it belonged. "Good night, father," he said, and off to bed he went.

It was a fitful night for Lucious, as his dreams had continued to become more vivid and disturbing over the previous few months. Creatures the likes of which didn't even exist were tearing man, woman, and child to pieces.

War ravaged the land, and everything burned. Black-robed figures followed behind a lone, armor-clad young woman. A long sword hung at her hip, still coated with blood from countless foes. It always ended the same way, with the woman stopping and slowly turning her head towards him.

"Ahhh!" he yelled as he sat bolt upright in his bed, covered in sweat, with his heart beating so hard he could hear it in his ears. *Why do I keep dreaming of her every night? I can feel her gaze burn right into my very soul.*

Lucious didn't sleep anymore that night. He pitched his legs over the side of the bed and sat for a moment while his pulse slowed. "Whew, I guess I better get to my chores."

The sun was just peeking through his room window. Lucious threw on his clothes and headed outside to tend to the animals. The rooster cocked as he always did at sunrise, and chickens exited the coop for breakfast. Lucious grabbed his bucket full of feed and spread it on the ground for the chickens to eat. Into the coop he went to gather the freshly laid eggs. Gently, he placed them in the empty feed bucket and dropped them off inside the front door of the cabin.

"All right, let's see," Lucious began. "Chickens are done, now the horses and then the goats." He walked over to the gate, entered the corral, and proceeded to the makeshift barn. From inside, he could hear the horses and goats making quite the ruckus. "All right, all right. I'm coming, you guys."

As Lucious placed a hand on the barn door handle, he noticed something wasn't quite right. There was a hole to the left of the door, as if an animal had dug under the wall to get inside. "Oh no, I hope a fox didn't get in here!" Quickly sliding the large door open, the animals that were desperate to escape almost trampled him. "Whoa, whoa. What's got you guys all spooked?"

The horses and goats ran past him to the other end of the corral. A wave of uneasiness washed over him, and the hairs on the back of his neck stood up. Cautiously, he slowly opened the right barn door and walked inside. His eyes scanned back and forth, searching for the intruder. The horse stalls looked fine, besides the usual piles of manure.

What was that? Lucious cocked his head to get a better listen. It was coming from over by the goat pens. It sounded like something was being torn apart. Moving towards the noise, Lucious walked as quietly as possible. He grabbed the pitchfork he used for cleanup and gripped it tightly in both hands with the four sharp tines pointing forward. Peering around the corner to the goat pens, he could now see what the noise was from. His eyes fixed on a creature about the size of a fox as it ripped into the flesh of one of the goats. Lucious studied the creature, as it was unlike anything he had ever seen or heard of. It was dark purple, almost black, with a row of spines like that of a porcupine running the length of its back and on through to its tail. Its paws were tipped with razor-sharp claws. The creature paused for a moment at the interruption before lifting its head from the goat carcass. Growling, it turned towards him. Its muzzle pulled back in anger as it showed a mouth full of sharp, blood-stained teeth. Adrenaline pumped throughout Lucious' body, causing him to shake. *I can't run, or this thing will surely catch me before I can get help. I have to get out of here.* Carefully backing up the way he came, Lucious never took his eyes off the creature. Slowly, it turned itself to face him, its spines now standing on end in an aggressive posture. This was bad, for he knew the attack would come quickly.

The two faced off, sizing each other up. Lucious was still walking backwards towards the door with his pitchfork facing the beast. A mere six feet separated the two. His next step would have been fatal, as he slipped on horse manure and fell backwards. As Lucious fell, he could hear the creature's snarls. It lunged forward and attempted to jump on him. There was a flash of light and a crack so loud it made his ears ring as he hit the ground. Looking towards the entrance, he saw his father; Ezra stood there with his right arm extended in Lucious' direction. His face was rigid and focused, as if it were chiseled in stone. Lucious had never seen his father so formidable looking. Quickly, he scrambled to his feet, looking back for the creature. It was dead, its smoldering remains in chunks strewn about the ground. He hurried to his father and threw his arms around him, burying his face in his chest.

Ezra could feel Lucious shaking and sobbing as he held him for a few moments. "There, there, my boy. You're safe."

After a few moments, Lucious calmed down and let go of his father. "What . . . what was that?" Lucious stammered, shaking his head from side to side. "I've never seen an animal like that before. Have you?"

"No, I have not," Ezra replied, walking by Lucious to grab a shovel and broom. "Come, let's get this mess cleaned up so we can have breakfast and figure this out." The two set about gathering all the remains, piling them up outside the corralled area and lighting them on fire. "Now, let's get some food," said Lucious' father. They walked into the cabin, closing the door behind them.

The two of them combined their efforts to prepare breakfast. Fresh eggs and some leftover salted strips of bacon sizzled in the pan over the still-hot coals of the fireplace. The air was full of the delightful smells, but Lucious' mind was elsewhere; he was thinking about what had just happened. Breakfast was cooked and served up at the table. Chewing a mouthful of egg and bacon, he asked, "Where would something like that have come from, Father?"

"I'm not sure, Lucious, but it was definitely not from around here."

"Any normal animal would have fled when I approached it with that pitchfork, but it never hesitated," said Lucious. "It seemed as if it would attack anything that crossed its path. I saw such hatred in its eyes when it attacked me." Just the memory gave him the chills.

"I think it best if you don't wander too far from home today unless I'm with you."

Lucious nodded in agreement. "Yes, Father."

Once they finished eating, Lucious cleaned up the dishes while his father pulled out a small wooden pipe and packed it with some tilly leaves. This was his usual morning routine: first breakfast and then a smoke. He snapped his fingers and the leaves ignited. Lucious finished up and went out front to continue with his chores. He glanced back at his father, who was deep in thought, puffing on his pipe while still sitting at the table.

Lucious spent the remainder of the morning splitting wood, cleaning around the cabin, and tending to the animals. Lucious hadn't seen his father since breakfast and was wondering if the man had fallen asleep at the table. Opening the door, he soon realized that was not the case. Standing in the doorway, he could see his father looking down at multiple books opened up across the table. He was flipping pages and circling the table from one book to the next, searching for something. "What's going on?" Lucious asked. Without even looking up, his father continued to pore over the scriptures. "Can I help you find something?"

His father stopped with a finger on the page of a blood-red colored book. "There you are," he muttered, and looked up at his son. "Look here, this is a barrier spell I think we can use to alert us of any more intruders."

Lucious looked down at where his father's finger was on the page. The word "Trammels" was written there, with instructions on how to cast the spell. It required placing runes along with an incantation around their farm. With book in hand, Lucious and his father started setting up the spell. They drew runes on the ground roughly every ten paces, as instructed. Finishing back at the cabin, they found they had placed one hundred and sixty-three runes around the entire perimeter, which included the cabin, barn, and corralled pasture. The next step was the incantation to activate the runes. "Pronum, protecto, trammels," his father spoke. One by one, a blue flash sparked as each rune lit up and vanished. In seconds, the spell was complete.

"Father, do you expect to see more of those things here?"

With a somber look, Ezra said, "Lucious, let's go inside. It's time I told you the truth."

Standing there with a puzzled look on his face, Lucious asked, "The truth?"

What does he mean by the truth? he thought as he headed inside after his father and closed the door behind them.

Inside, his father was picking up the books from the table and returning them to the shelves in his room. "Have a seat," he called out. Lucious did as he was instructed and sat in his chair at the dining table. He folded his hands in front of him as the anxiety built, his right leg rocking frantically up and down as an outlet for his stress. His father came back from his room with the pipe in one hand and a small book in the other. Sitting in his chair, he opened the book and slid it across the table with his right hand. Lighting his pipe, he took a deep drag of the tilly leaf and exhaled a large cloud of smoke.

"That book you see in front of you is the journal I wrote some eighteen years ago. I wrote it after having a vision of things to come—a premonition, if you will. In that vision, was a child of unimaginable power who would shape our world and change life as we know it." Lucious' eyes were wide as he listened to what his father was telling him. "You see, Lucious, there is good and evil in this world and an infinite number of levels between the two. I was not the only one gifted with this vision. An evil mage named Valin was also shown it. We both traveled a great distance to the place where this child was to be born. It was in the town we now live on the outskirts of."

"Addleberry," left Lucious' lips in a whisper.

"Quite right, my boy. By the time I arrived at the home where your mother was, Valin had already killed her and taken the child, a baby girl. I thought I was too late. But what the vision didn't show was that there wasn't just one child, but two! You are the twin to that little girl who was stolen away."

Lucious' jaw dropped, leaving his mouth wide open. He sat speechless. The information coming at him was overloading his young mind. He could only mutter a single question. "I have a sister?"

CHAPTER THREE

ARAIN DRAKE

F ar to the west, in the Moorlands, his sister was raised in the citadel of the banished. This massive citadel was roughly the size of a castle, with enormous stone walls and twelve spires around its perimeter. Two large wooden doors bound in steel were at its entrance. The inner structure was chambered to house and train the mages who preferred the dark arts of death, chaos, and destruction. Orbs of magic fire hung in the air every ten feet, to light the grounds, as black-robed figures walked about performing daily tasks, experiments, and purchasing reagents from the local merchants that had shops setup in the courtyard.

It was dusk and the moons were just now on the rise. A cool breeze blew about the courtyard as everything went completely silent. Everyone had stopped to kneel and bow their heads. Valin had just entered the front gates, and to his right was a slender woman cloaked in black. Her icy-blue eyes were visible from across the courtyard, and behind her walked a massive gray wolf. The three of them strode in as if it were their personal home, which it was. Arain Drake commanded all who lived at the citadel, and any of them would gladly die for their queen. When Valin arrived here with this child all those years ago, they were told of his vision and the future that she would bring them. A future of wealth and power; a future full of amazing creatures and magical creations; a future where the banished ruled all, and the good and just served as their slaves.

Arain had always been raised with the notion that it was better to be the ruler instead of the ruled. *Take what you want when you want it. Rule others with fear and force, not love and kindness*, was what Valin always told her. Power was absolute, and to gain it, everything and everyone was expendable. Valin had made sure from early on that every confrontation, every situation, had to be dealt with using these morals. When Arain was ten years old, a little boy had made fun of her and pushed her to the ground. Valin stood by, watching. "Arain," he spoke, looking at her on the ground with tears in her eyes. Like a switch flicking to release a trap, she grabbed one of the many fist-sized rocks on the ground and sprang to her feet. Without pausing, Arain pummeled the boy across the head. His head shot back and he dropped to the ground, unconscious. "Good, exceptionally good, my child. Come now." Valin turned to walk away, but he could see she was standing over the boy with the bloody rock still in her hand. He watched with delight as she continued the onslaught, smashing the boy until his brains lay on the ground next to his head. Only then did she drop the crimson-covered rock and look up with a blood-spotted smile.

"He won't do that again, father." Carrying on, she stepped over the corpse and grabbed her father's hand as the two of them continued on their way. Little did she know, Valin had paid the boy to provoke a fight, just to see what she would do. He was very pleased with the result, very pleased indeed.

As the years passed, Arain Drake continued her training in various disciplines. Her father taught her all she knew about magic and the dark arts. She picked up spells quickly, as she was also one of the attuned few, like her brother, Lucious. She absorbed knowledge like a sponge, constantly searching to learn more. Ichi Tori of the assassin's guild handled her training with blades, stealth, and the making and use of poisons. By the time she reached her current age of seventeen, she was a deadly, fine-tuned fighting instrument. Arain had amassed dozens of kills in minor battles and skirmishes in the area surrounding the Moorlands, and word spread of her conquests.

Arain and Valin walked through the courtyard and into the citadel's great hall. Inside, it was bright and clean, with two massive rows of columns running across the entire hall from one end to the other. As they walked toward the far end of the hall, multiple doors leading off to the other areas of the citadel came into view. One of these doors led to Arain's room and another to Valin's. "Good night, Father," she said, and entered the room on the left.

"Rest well, my child," Valin replied as he headed into his chambers.

The large gray wolf followed Arain everywhere, and her bedchamber was no exception. "That was a wonderful day, wouldn't you agree, Timber?"

The wolf sat down and gazed at her. His tail measured over four feet long as it bounced up and down on the floor.

Inside Arain's room was a giant, luxurious bed covered with the absolute best in linens. Across from the bed, some thirty feet away, was a fireplace with a river-stone mantel and chimney. Over towards the far corner was a lavish bathing tub made of gold and silver, which two servants were busy filling for her bath. Another maid was tending to Timber with an entire pot full of meaty stew and a basin of fresh drinking water. "Your highness," she addressed Arain with head bowed. "Will there be anything else?"

"Yes, bring me some dinner and a tankard of mead for after my bath."

"Yes, your highness," said the maid, and left the room with a quick bow.

By this time, the bath was full and trails of steam emanated from its surface. The remaining two maids walked to Arain and removed her armor and clothing. Piece by piece, they placed the garments on a mannequin designed to hold armor. One servant gathered the soiled undergarments and left the room to have them cleaned. Without a word, Arain silently walked across the room to the bathing tub, stepped in, and submerged all but her head and shoulders. The servant walked behind her and began her duties of washing her mistress.

Timber took his eyes off Arain for only a few seconds at a time while he devoured the entire pot of food and lapped up all the water. When satisfied, he walked over and laid down in front of the fireplace, all while keeping a watchful eye on his master and the woman cleaning her. "Good boy, Timber," Arain said, giving him a smile.

Arain finished her bath and dried off, dressing in a beautiful red silk gown. A knock rapped on the door, and Timber's gaze turned to it.

"Supper, your highness," the servant called out.

"Come in and put it over on the dinner table by the fireplace."

The other servant continued with her duties, cleaning up after the bath, while the food was brought in and placed on the table along with the tankard Arain had requested. While bowing her head again, the maid asked, "Anything else, your highness?"

"Finish helping the other one clean up and then you two can go."

In a matter of minutes, the place was clean, and the two maids had left her room. Arain sat at the small table and ate the meal of grouse and potatoes while sipping on the sweet mead. The fire crackled as she sat there, enjoying the warmth with Timber at her feet. "Tomorrow will be my eighteenth birthday, and I have a feeling it will be unforgettable." Reaching down, she caressed the soft gray fur on his head. Pure joy shone on the wolf's face and his front canines protruded over his bottom lip. "Bedtime, boy," she told him, and off they went to sleep.

Chapter Four

Coming of Age

The sun was rising across the land on another beautiful day. Today, the twins both turned eighteen and it would forever change their lives, as it would that of every living creature in the world of Tauro.

Lucious slowly opened his eyes, staring at the old wooden beams on the ceiling. With a couple of yawns and a stretch, he tossed off his warm blankets. *I feel amazing*, he thought as he started getting dressed. He put on his pants, shirt, and boots. Exhaling deeply, he said, "Guess I might as well get the chores done." With that, he walked out of his room and headed for the front door. He was startled to find his father standing there, waiting.

"Good morning, Father. You're up early."

His father stood there looking at him. "Good morning, Lucious, and happy birthday. I have a gift for you." Ezra held a slender object about three feet long wrapped in burlap. Smiling, Lucious took the gift and unwrapped it. In his hands, he held a beautiful sword in a black leather scabbard adorned with gold stitching in intricate patterns. The hilt gleamed with gold, and tight leather bindings wound up the pommel. With almost no effort, Lucious removed the sword from the scabbard with his right hand. The blade was exquisitely crafted and polished to a mirror finish. Various magical glyphs were etched down the middle of both faces.

"Thank you so much; this is more than I could have ever hoped for." He sheathed the sword before he wrapped his arms around his father and hugged him. "You shouldn't have, Father. It must have cost a fortune."

Ezra looked into Lucious' eyes. "You are becoming a man now and you will need a proper sword for what lies ahead."

He let go of Lucious and strolled over to the kitchen table. Before Lucious could speak, what felt like a lightning bolt struck him in the head. Lucious hovered above the floor as bolts of energy encircled him, passing in and out of his body. His eyes turned white and his body convulsed. *What is this?* he thought.

Images flooded his mind of past, present, and what he assumed would be future events. Suddenly he was floating high in the sky, higher than any bird ever dreamed of flying. The entire continent was beneath him, and the impenetrable fog that completely bordered the entire landmass shimmered as if alive. Tauro continued to shrink the further up he floated. From this distance, he could see that the known world was just a small piece of a much larger planet. In an instant, he was even farther away and could see the sun and many other planets circling one another. It was beautiful beyond anything he had ever seen. With that thought, he was whisked away, and abruptly found himself submerged in the darkest shadows. A person was walking towards him.

"Hello, who are you?"

The figure continued to advance, and Lucious could now see it was a slender young woman with the most stunning blue eyes. She stopped roughly ten feet away and studied him. Lucious impulsively did the same. "Who are you, and why am I here?" he asked.

"My name is Arain Drake, and I would like to ask you the same thing."

His heart skipped a beat as he gasped. "I'm Lucious Drake, your brother!"

Arain knew in her heart that he spoke the truth. Valin had told her she had a twin brother taken at birth. For a moment, the two just stared at each other, trying to process everything that was happening. Tears of happiness welled up in Lucious' eyes, and he walked forward with arms wide open to hug his sister. He had only just reached her when a right hook knocked him to the ground. With his head reeling, he held his jaw. "What the hell did you do that for?"

Hatred burned in her eyes. "I have no need for your affections, Brother. This world and all the others are mine!" Arain now clearly agitated, clenched her fists as though she would strike him again. "There is nothing you or anyone can do to stop me!"

What a pathetic weakling, she thought, looking down at Lucious. "I will give you a choice, Brother: you can serve at my feet, or be buried beneath them." Turning, she began walking back the way she came. "Lucious, that will be your one and only offer." With those last, spiteful words, she vanished.

Lucious' consciousness slammed back into his body and he crumpled to the floor. Ezra ran to his son and knelt by his side. A look of genuine concern showed on his face. "Lucious, are you okay?" he asked, trying to comfort him.

A few moments later, Lucious' eyes opened and he groaned as he sat up. *I cannot believe how hard she can punch*, he thought as he clutched his jaw. His head was still fuzzy from the blow.

Ezra rose from beside him. "Let's get you up and into a chair." He grabbed his son's hand and hoisted him up with ease. "Come now." Ezra gently assisted Lucious over to the dining table.

Lucious pulled out the old wooden chair and sat down, placing his elbows on the table and his hands on his head. Ezra grabbed a cup and filled it with water from the drinking pail in the kitchen. "Here you go, drink some water and try to rest." He placed a metallic drinking cup on the table next to Lucious. Swiftly, like the wind, Ezra walked into his bedroom, then returned to the table to sit down. "Here we are," he said as he placed a leather-bound journal to his left and a quill and pot of ink to his right. "Now, Lucious, when you can, I need you to tell me everything that just happened." Ezra opened the journal and dipped the quill into the black ink.

Lucious removed his hands from his head, grabbed the cup, and drank the entire glass of water his father had given him. His head was still reeling from whatever that was, and his scalp was sore, like he had been burned. Pulling his bangs out of his face, he asked, "Father, can you see anything wrong?"

Ezra's eyes were wide as he reached out a hand and pointed back at Lucious' head. "Your forehead, it's marked, like the band of a crown."

Lucious ran his fingers over it, and could make out a one-inch band encircling his head at temple height. From the feel of it, there were very intricate lines in this band, like pictures and symbols. "What is all of this? The floating, the light, the markings. I was high above the world, past the clouds and into the black sky, looking down at everything. I met my sister who threatened me with death or servitude, and I saw our world beyond the mist borders."

The whole time, Ezra never spoke; he just listened closely and feverishly wrote in the journal as Lucious recalled the entire incident. When he finished, Lucious simply sat there, going over everything in his head repeatedly as he tried to process it all. Ezra finished writing and put the quill in the ink pot and left it there. Leaning back in his chair, he closed the journal and let out a heavy sigh. He stared across the table at his son for a minute or two before he spoke. "Lucious, I believe events are now set in motion that will change our lives forever."

Lucious' eyes fixed on his father. "I fear you are right, and my sister's thirst for conquest will change the lives of everyone else."

On the other side of the continent, Arain was sitting up in her lavish bed. Her head was still spinning from the awakening. In that instant, Valin burst through the door with one of her chambermaids in tow. A look of anticipation was written on his face as he approached her bedside. "Are you all right, my dear? Your chambermaid, Ulta, was hysterical when she witnessed you levitating off the bed with bolts of light coming from you."

With her head still hung down towards Timber, Arain spoke. "Valin, I saw him!"

A wave of anticipation washed over him as he stooped his head lower towards her. "Saw who, your grace?"

Arain lifted her head to meet his gaze. "I saw my brother, Lucious." Valin stood erect, never breaking eye contact. "I also saw much of what you have told me of your vision you had eighteen years ago."

Valin grabbed a small mirror from Arain's nightstand and handed it to her. Puzzled, she took the mirror. With great satisfaction in his voice, "Look, you now wear the crown of a true ruler." She looked in the mirror and pulled her hair back to reveal a band etched into her forehead just below the hairline.

Turning her head slowly from left to right, she examined the markings. "What do these markings mean, Valin?"

"I think they mean it's time to start your reign!" As he spoke those words, he turned and left Arain's bedroom.

Timber was by his master's side throughout the entire experience and walked over to make sure she was all right. He nudged his soft gray muzzle under her hand. "I'm fine, boy," she told him, patting his head before she got out of bed. She walked across the room to her dresser and armor stand, where she pulled out black leather breeches and a gray tunic. After quickly dressing, she pulled on a pair of black boots and strapped on her belt with a scabbard containing a twelve-inch-long ornate dagger with an ivory handle. *No need for armor just yet*, she thought, as she grabbed her shimmering black cloak and placed it over her shoulders. Satisfied, she left her room and headed to the council room. Timber followed silently behind her.

CHAPTER FIVE
A QUEST

I t had been a little more than a day since his awakening, and Lucious was just now coming to grips with it all. When he walked out the front door, he saw Ezra and farmer Wumblum talking. The two shook hands, and Mr. Wumblum turned and headed back towards his home.

"Father, what was that about?"

Ezra gently grabbed Lucious by both shoulders and looked him in the eyes.

"Son, we must leave in a day's time and head to Westlin to request an audience with King Elrick. Mr. Wumblum's eldest son, Chester, and wife, Winnie, will stay here and tend to the farm while we are away. We must inform the king of what is coming. King Elrick has a mighty army that we will need if we are to stand a chance against your sister." Releasing his grip, he added, "Come now, we have a lot to prepare before we head off." With that, Ezra headed inside to pack for their quest.

Lucious took care of the animals, feeding and watering them as he always did. "Let's see," he whispered as he walked into the barn. "We'll need our saddles for sure, and bits for the horses."

Lucious grabbed two well-worn brown leather saddles and hung them over the section of corral next to the gate. He walked in and out of the barn many times, bringing with him everything needed to prepare the two horses for the long journey ahead. When he finished, he stood in front of the barn and looked out towards the horizon, thinking about what lay ahead. He had never ridden more than a day in any direction in his entire life. The thought of this quest was exciting and terrifying to him at the same time.

The morning quickly turned to afternoon, and before long, the sun was getting low on the horizon. When he walked into the cabin, Lucious saw four full packs sitting in a row on the floor. "Do you think you're bringing enough, Father?" A smile stretched across his face as he peered over to see Ezra making the last dinner they would have in this home for some time. With a skillet in hand, Ezra stood at the hearth, frying up some eggs, bacon, and potatoes. The smell was heavenly as the ingredients snapped and sizzled together.

Ezra stood up from the fire and rubbed his hands together while looking at Lucious. "Well, my boy, I could pack more, but we don't want to kill our horses from exhaustion on the first day, do we?"

Lucious shook his head and went to the kitchen to fetch the plates and utensils, as he always did for meals. "You're right, Father, that would make this journey even harder than it has to be if we walked the whole way." Coming from the kitchen, Lucious carried the dishes and set them on the table. Satisfied with his settings, he headed off to get cleaned up for dinner.

Ezra used a long wooden spoon to push the contents of the frying pan around so nothing burned. He bent over and looked in the pan. "Yes, yes, I believe that is ready to serve." Wrapping a kitchen rag around the handle, he pulled the pan from the flames. By then, Lucious had walked back to the table and sat in his chair. Ezra divvied up the contents onto both plates and put the empty pan into a wash bucket in the kitchen. Pulling out his chair, he sat down at the table across from Lucious. Sitting up tall and straight, Ezra grabbed his fork and gave the nod that it was okay to eat.

Lucious used a technique more akin to shoveling as he ate. "This is amazing, Father," he mumbled with his mouth half full.

Ezra was a bit more reserved when he ate, taking his time to enjoy each bite. "Slow down, Son, before you choke," he said, but Lucious already finished the entire plate of food.

Lucious leaned back in the chair with his hands on his stomach. "That was one of the best meals I think you have ever cooked."

Ezra nodded his head and took another bite. "I do believe I have outdone myself," he agreed, looking completely satisfied. Ezra finished his meal and placed the fork down on the side of his plate. He thought now was a perfect time to chat. Sitting back in his chair with hands folded on his lap, he looked across the table at his motionless son. "How are you feeling today, Lucious? You look much better than just a day ago. Does your forehead still burn from those markings?"

Lucious sat up in his chair and opened his eyes. "I feel pretty good and my head has no remnants of pain whatsoever." As he spoke the words, his right hand went to his forehead and his fingers touched the markings from one side to the other. Lucious let out a little laugh. "You know, with being so busy all day, I almost forgot about it." He placed his hand on the table, pushed the chair back, and stood up. "I'll take care of the dishes, Father. Why don't you have one last pipe?" Lucious walked around the small wooden dinner table, picked up all the dishes, and headed to the kitchen to wash them.

Ezra slid his chair back from the dinner table and stood up. Walking over to the mantle above the hearth, he picked up his pipe and the metal container that held his tilly weed. "Ah yes, nothing better than a good smoke after dinner." He went back to the dinner table and sat down. *Tap, tap, tap.* The sound rang out as he hit the wooden pipe to clear out any leftover weed. A few small burnt chunks fell out onto the table and he quickly brushed them to the floor. Satisfied the pipe was clean, he set it upright and grabbed the metal can. Off came the top and onto the table it clanged. Reaching in with his right hand, he pinched some of the weed and packed it into the pipe. By the time Lucious had returned, Ezra was sitting back in his chair, relaxing with almost perfect circular smoke rings rising in the air above his head.

Lucious sat back down across from his father and folded his hands on the dinner table in front of him. "So, I have everything ready outside for Red Cloud and Mirage." These were the two horses they would ride on their way to Westlin the next morning. Red Cloud was a large, white horse with reddish brown markings that looked like little clouds. Mirage was about the same size, but was pure black from muzzle to hindquarters.

"Good," spoke Ezra, looking over towards the full bags sitting on the floor. "I think I have everything we'll need." He pointed to the first bag while taking another puff of his pipe. "That bag has my journal, some spell books for your training, and a pot of ink and two quills for taking notes along the way." Moving down the line, he rattled off what was in each bag. The second one had clothing for both of them. The third held a pan, two plates, and some utensils for mealtimes. The fourth bag contained water skins, goat jerky, dried fish, spices, and apples.

Lucious nodded his head in approval. "It looks like we should be all set then, Father." Getting up from the table, Lucious grabbed his sheathed sword and dagger, along with a faded brown leather belt, and set them next to the bags. He turned towards his father while he stood by the bags; he wanted to ask some questions about the journey.

"So, how long do you think it will take to get to the castle in Westlin?"

Ezra pulled the pipe from his mouth. "It should take seven days, give or take, depending on the weather and any other unforeseen issues."

"Unforeseen issues?" Lucious blurted out. "What kind of unforeseen issues might we encounter?"

Ezra slid his chair backward from the table and rose. "Not to worry, my boy, I just meant things like the trail being washed out, or the stray bandit or thief harassing us. I'm sure we can handle whatever comes our way." Ezra walked back to the hearth and dumped the smoldering ashes from his pipe into the fire. Placing the pipe and weed tin back on the mantle, he turned to face Lucious, who was still standing there, thinking about the potential hazards tomorrow might bring. Ezra grinned and put a hand on his son's shoulder. "Don't worry about it, Lucious," he spoke in a soothing tone. "Come, we should get some sleep, tomorrow we start our quest!" Ezra headed off to his bedroom and disappeared.

Lucious stoked the fire and added a few more pieces of wood to keep it burning throughout the night. Putting his hands on his knees, he pushed himself up from the hearth. *Well, I guess he's right. I better try to get some rest*, he thought, and off he went to his room.

CHAPTER SIX
UNINVITED GUESTS

It was the dead of night as the fire in the hearth crackled sending little embers floating up the chimney on the hot, rising air. Insects and frogs chattered and croaked outside their home. The sound of nature was always very soothing to Lucious, and it helped him sleep. His eyes slowly closed as he lay in bed, waiting for sleep to claim him once more. He was almost at the tipping point, when suddenly every creature outside fell silent in an instant; it was like an invisible switch being flipped to shut off all sound. Lucious became very uneasy as he slowly sat up, listening. Complete silence surrounded him. There was absolutely no noise as he cocked his ear towards the window. *Something is very wrong*, he thought as he rolled over and out of the bed. He was about to yell when his father startled him, coming to stand next to his bed. Ezra's quick reflexes let him cover the boy's mouth, silencing any screams. His heart was beating so fast it sounded like drumming in his ears. Ezra removed his hand from Lucious' mouth and put a finger up to his lips, signaling for him to be quiet.

Ezra moved closer to his son so he could whisper, "Lucious, I think we're in trouble. I want you to get dressed, collect your things, and meet me by the fire. Whatever you do, don't make any noise." As quickly as he appeared, Ezra vanished, disappearing back to his room to gather his weapons.

Lucious, as quietly as he could, stepped down onto the cold wooden floor and got out of bed. As quickly as possible, he slipped on his britches and boots. With his shirt pulled halfway over his head, he froze. Turning his head towards the window, he could hear a low-pitched growl. As his eyes adjusted to the darkness, he could see something move past it. Panic gripped him, and he rushed out to the fireplace while he finished pulling on his tunic. Hastily, he grabbed his belt, dagger, and sword he had placed next to the packs just a few hours prior, and put them on.

Grrrrr.

He could hear the growling again, but now there were multiple points the noise was coming from. He stood by the hearth and panned his head around, trying to pinpoint the noise. They sounded as if they were moving around the perimeter of the house.

Ezra showed up next to him as quietly as a cat. This time, though, he was fully dressed, and he brandished a sword in his right hand. It was father's enchanted sword, Masmune; a long sword with a mirror-like finish and a razor-sharp edge on either side. Down the center were black symbols etched into the steel, signifying the spells imbued into the weapon. The hilt wore silver embellishments, with the pommel ending in a beautiful green stone. Ezra faced Lucious. The look of concern on his father's face was something Lucious had only seen a handful of times in his life, but it always meant the same thing, dangerous things were about to happen.

"Lucious, you need to get out of here and head north towards Westlin. I will stay behind and cover your escape." Lucious objected, but was silenced as the front door splintered into a thousand pieces. Next, the sound of shattered glass hitting the floor echoed in the kitchen to their left. The blood-curdling growls were very loud now. Both stood with the fireplace to their back, waiting to see what made that horrible sound. Ezra had Masmune raised in front of him, ready for an imminent attack, and Lucious unsheathed his sword as well. "No, Son, you must make it to Westlin to warn the king of what is coming."

"I won't leave you to die, Father!"

Ezra looked over at Lucious and gave a grin. "I don't plan on dying anytime soon, my boy."

Then, as if the darkness of night were alive, a large black creature stepped into the light of the room. A moment later, the same could be seen coming from the kitchen. These beasts were massive, roughly the size of a bear. Their bodies shimmered ever so slightly, and wisps of black haze emanated from their skin. Five long, razor-sharp claws tipped each of their paws, and their eyes reflected like a cat's would in the moonlight. Their head was the thing of nightmares, with rows of long, sharp teeth inside gaping jaws. Slowly and methodically, they inched closer to the two men.

"When I tell you to, run out the back as fast as you can and don't look back!" Ezra raised his left hand. "NOW!"

Lucious turned and bolted for the back door as a burst of light flashed. The beasts shrieked in pain as the light's intensity blinded them. Ezra used this advantage and leapt at the creature at the front entrance. Masmune cut through the beast with great ease, dropping it to the floor in a massive pool of its own black blood. Quickly, he turned to face the second one, only to narrowly miss getting gouged by one of those massive claws as the creature attacked. In one fluid motion, he stepped to the side and brought the blade down on the back of the creature's neck, sending its head away from the arterial spray of its body on the floor. Ezra stood there, taking a moment to catch his breath. The tip of his sword was resting on the blood-soaked floor. For a second, he thought it was over, but then came more growls. Ezra raised his sword as three more shimmering black figures entered the room in front of him.

Lucious burst out the back door as fast as he could run and headed north into the forest. He could hear the battle as he ran further away towards the old wooden bridge. His heart was racing as he ran as quickly as his legs would carry him. Moments later, he reached the bridge that led over the river and into Rennit Forest. Lucious stopped there for a minute to catch his breath and looked back at his home. Just then, it exploded into a massive fireball. Burning timber flew some fifty feet in all directions, and the framework blazed bright red. The hot ash floating down from the sky looked like orange snowflakes. Lucious leaned against one of the bridge posts with his face frozen in a look of pure disbelief. He shook his head as tears filled his eyes. *No, no, no, this can't be. How am I supposed to go on without you, Father?* The moment had to be cut short; Lucious looked back at the burning structure to see more of those creatures reflecting in its light. Crouching down behind the post he was leaning on, he silently headed across the bridge and into the forest.

Once Lucious reached the cover of the woods, he flicked his right pointer finger and conjured a small, white floating orb. He made sure to keep the size small and brightness low so he could just barely make out the path ahead and not give away his position to those things. *That should do it, he thought, and* continued on the path heading north. His mind was feverishly trying to grasp what had just happened as he ran deeper and deeper into Rennit Forest.

Many hours passed while he traveled the dirt path. There was no sign of his assailants, and the only sounds were that of crickets, frogs, and other small critters of the forest. He could hear the occasional owl as well. Over time, his pace slowed and his eyelids began to feel extremely heavy. Lucious stopped and stretched, letting out an enormous yawn. The faint white orb floated next to him, just a few feet away. Cocking his head, he listened intently in all directions for signs of danger. Nothing sounded out of place, though. Looking around at the ground near him, he whispered, "I guess this is as good a spot as any to set up camp." He took off his pack, setting it on the ground. Next, he gathered some sticks and branches, staying as close to the trail as possible. Within minutes, he had enough to make his campfire and neatly arranged the wood in a cone shape. After standing up and stepping back, he motioned to the pile, and it ignited. The flames danced about the wood as it crackled every so often. Lucious laid down on the ground next to the small fire and placed his pack under his head for a somewhat-lumpy makeshift pillow. Thinking to himself how good the warmth of the fire felt, he slowly drifted off to sleep.

CHAPTER SEVEN
CONQUEST

A rain strode through the many corridors and rooms of the citadel on her way to the council room. The inhabitants were abuzz, rushing this way and that in a manner Arain had never seen. News of the awakening had spread like wildfire throughout the complex, signaling the start of the conquest they had all been training for these many years. Seeing this, she smiled and looked down at Timber. "Here we go, boy," she said, and the two continued on into the council chamber.

They stepped into a large room with lofty ceilings and a large square table in the middle. She could see most of the council members already assembled and sitting in their designated places. There were twelve members, including Valin, and each one was to prepare for a distinct part of the upcoming conquest. The thirteenth seat was the queens. Guards lined the room, spaced apart every ten feet or so. They were clad in black plate armor, with a shield in one hand and a lance in the other. Standing there, motionless, they watched over those in attendance. Arain walked around the table to her seat. Valin was standing there, and pulled out her chair as she approached.

"My queen," he spoke with a nod of his head. Arain sat down as Valin pushed her up to the table. Timber sat next to her and began scanning the room for threats to his master. Valin sat to Arain's left, and now all members were present.

Valin looked around the table before speaking. "Members of the war council, it is my honor to announce to you all that the awakening has begun!"

A deafening roar of applause and cheering erupted from all who were present. The atmosphere in the room was electric, as everyone knew the years of preparation were now coming to fruition.

Arain raised a hand and all members quickly quieted back down, waiting for her to speak. Sitting in her chair, composed, cold, and calculating, she began while looking around the table as she spoke. "You all have worked tirelessly for this day, and now I will lead you in claiming this world. No longer will our kind be cast out to live in the shadows!" Arain's voice raised with every word she spoke. Standing up from her chair, she exuded an aura of complete, unwavering conviction for her cause. "From this day forth, we eradicate all who do not bow before me and this empire!" As the last word left her lips, she slammed her fist onto the table with such force the wood fractured. Simultaneously, the room erupted with cheers of support for their queen. When she turned towards Valin, she could see nothing but complete approval on his face. Arain once again raised a hand in the air and the council silenced. "I have laid the plans out with my first in command." She turned back towards the council. "Valin will brief every commander here with a specific mission that is to be completed before rejoining me at Castle Kragg." With that, she handed the council over to Valin and exited the chamber with Timber in tow.

Arain was still drained from the awakening that morning and the recent war council finished what little energy she had left. It took all she had to make it back to her bedchamber where she collapsed on her bed, still fully dressed. Timber jumped onto the bed and curled up beside her, and within minutes they were asleep. For the rest of the morning and into the late afternoon, she laid there motionless, but her mind was hard at work. As she dreamed, her thoughts drifted towards her newfound brother, Lucious. She was standing in front of him on a battlefield. War raged all around them as the two faced off. Dead bodies of man and creature alike were strewn as far as the eye could see. The ground was so saturated with the blood of the fallen that it turned red. Something was different, though. This Lucious that stood across from her was not the same weak boy she had met earlier. No, this was a battle-hardened, matured version of him that looked fully capable of challenging her. She knew at that moment he would need to be dealt with as soon as possible. Standing there, Arain became infuriated at this realization. She stared Lucious in the eye, then she spoke. "You will not get in my way, brother!" Lucious stood there, motionless, not saying a word. Arain raised her left gauntlet hand and squeezed a fist so hard the metal creaked. "Kill him, my Morlocks!" she shouted.

At that moment, her eyes shot open to see Timber looking down at her. Arain sat up in her bed and swung her legs over the side. *I still feel drained*, she thought, as her head hung so low that her chin rested on her chest.

Drip, drip, drip, one drop came after another. Small droplets of crimson dripped from her nose and splashed onto her legs. *What is this?* she wondered, raising a hand to her nose. The bleeding stopped as suddenly as it started. Using the back of her hand, she wiped the remaining blood away. Sitting on the edge of her bed, Arain could feel the tiredness subside as she recounted the dream she had just had. As she sat there, she couldn't help but notice how charged and filled with energy she felt. *Powerful* was the word that came to her mind as she stood up from the bed. Arain looked over at Timber. "It's time we get started!"

Timber jumped off the bed and the two headed out of her room.

CHAPTER EIGHT
DYING

Time passed slowly as Lucious lay asleep on the ground next to the fading coals of the fire. His body shivered, waking him from a less than restful slumber. Slowly sitting up, he pulled his tunic close to his body and rubbed his arms, trying to generate some heat. *It's the coldest night in months,* he thought to himself. Reaching over to his side, he grabbed a pile of sticks that he had collected earlier and put them onto the hot coals. The fire slowly crackled back to life.

Looking up, he could see the sky was clear and the two moons glowed in the night. *Crack!* A branch snapped in the forest just a little ways off to his left. Eyes wide, Lucious scanned the area where the noise came from. Anxiously he waited, sitting there silently. Even with the moonlight, it was still too dark to see far into the trees. *Snap! Crack!* came the sounds again, but this time it was further forward, indicating whatever it was to be circling him. His pulse raced as he stood as quiet as possible. His hand went instinctively to the pommel of his sword. Lucious hoped that it was just a forest animal on the hunt for its breakfast and not one of those things like back at his house. He slowly started to relax when he saw it. Yes, there was definitely something there.

Standing, waiting some twenty feet away, the same black mass he saw at the farmhouse was now staring at him, its eyes glinting from the moonlight. Lucious stood motionless, as if the creature wouldn't notice him. His heart raced as the beast walked towards him. The walk turned into a full-on sprint as the creature attacked. Lucious pulled his sword from its scabbard and plunged it into the beast's neck. The creature let out a scream before slumping to the ground, its blood pooling rapidly around its body from the open wound. Lucious barely composed himself in time before a second one jumped from the shadows. In the distance, he could hear the howls as more of the creatures signaled, they had found the prey. Lucious stood steady with both hands on his sword. His mind raced. He could handle one or two of these things, but not if more kept coming. He knew he had to come up with a plan quickly, or this was going to be the end of his journey.

The second creature lunged forward at Lucious, who sidestepped to dodge most of the blow. But its razor-sharp claws contacted his left arm, leaving four deep cuts. He winced in pain and countered with an upward swing of his sword that connected with the midsection of the beast. The creature's entrails spewed onto the ground, along with its lifeless corpse. Lucious grabbed his pack and ran north along the trail as fast as his legs would carry him. He ran for some time, only looking back every so often to see if he was being chased. After a while, he no longer heard any howling, and hoped his assailants had given up.

Unable to run any further, Lucious collapsed to his knees, heaving for air to fill his lungs. His left arm was numb and cold, and sweat poured off of his forehead. Quickly, he cast the light orb spell and examined his wounds for the first time. To his surprise, the four gashes didn't look nearly as bad as he thought they would, and it looked like the bleeding was all but stopped. Lucious, still on his knees and breathing heavily, didn't hear the beast until it was on him. He sprawled to the ground on his stomach, and white-hot pain shot through his entire body as the weight of the beast pinned him down. In seconds, it tore at his flesh. His vision was fading as he began losing consciousness. The last thing he screamed through the flashes of agony was, "HELP!"

CHAPTER NINE
NEW FRIENDS

Am I dead? Everything is black, but I feel no more pain, Lucious realized. A great calm washed over him as he floated in nothingness. *Maybe this is a dream, a bad dream I just haven't woken up from yet,* he thought. Lucious closed his eyes and opened them again, but this time instead of blackness, his gaze met that of a humanoid creature staring back at him. The creature jumped back, startled. Lucious was lying on his back, covered with a blanket, and positioned next to a fire. He could now see the full shape of this new humanoid-looking creature. It stood on two legs, but that was where all similarities ended. It stood approximately six feet tall, with greenish-blue scales covering its body. It was apparent from its figure that this was a female of the species. Her eyes were bright blue and she had long black hair. Sharp, pointy nails tipped each one of her ten fingers and she wore a light leather tunic and breeches. In his eighteen years of life, Lucious hadn't seen or heard of such a creature. It was strange that he didn't feel scared like he should; instead, she made him feel safe. Lucious pulled off the covers and sat up on the ground. His body now racked with pain, as if a bear had mauled him.

The female creature slowly walked over to Lucious and knelt beside him. "How are you feeling?" she asked in a surprisingly beautiful voice, with a genuine look of concern in her eyes as she awaited his response.

Lucious' mind was still foggy as to what exactly was going on. "My back is sore, and my head is throbbing, but I'm alive, and I feel like I have you to thank for that." Only a foot was between the two of them as they stared at each other in silence.

The female bowed her head as she spoke. "It was my honor to protect you, my king."

Lucious sat there silently for a moment, processing what she had said. "King? Why are you calling me your king?"

She got off her knees and sat down next to Lucious. "I called you king because that's what you are, my king."

Lucious shook his head. "I don't understand what's going on. The last thing I can remember is being attacked, and it felt like I died, but now I wake up alive. Then I am tended to by a being that doesn't exist anywhere in Tauro!"

A smile crossed her face, "That is because until now, we haven't existed . . ."

Lucious pulled his knees to his chest and thought about the situation. "Wait a minute, what do you mean, *we*?" At that moment, two more of these creatures walked out of the woods and sat down near the fire. Shocked, Lucious looked at these two newcomers. "There's more of you?"

The first female he met spoke, "Yes, Lucious, the three of us came into being when you were attacked, but I feel there are more of us in this world. My name is Morgan Hunter, and that big brute over there is my brother, Selim, and his mate, Ulandra. We are all Draconians."

Lucious was still sitting as he examined Selim and Ulandra. Selim was a massive man, standing close to seven feet tall, with a wide chest and large, muscular arms. His scales were a darker shade of green than that of the females, and his eyes were a dark crimson color. Selim also had a more reptilian-shaped head, with two slightly twisted horns coming out of the top, pointing backwards. Ulandra possessed a physique much closer to Morgan's, and her scales were also lighter. She had brown eyes, black hair, and looked to be a little shorter than the other female. They were both wearing clothing similar to what Morgan was dressed in. Each of them had a unique weapon, Lucious noticed. Selim had a large dual-sided battle-axe which lay on the ground beside him. From the black ooze on the surface, it was clear he had used it to fight against those creatures that attacked him. Ulandra had a long dagger sheathed on each hip, and Morgan was wiping off a short sword she had recently used.

Lucious lifted himself to his feet and walked over to Selim. Immediately, all three Draconians went from sitting to kneeling, with heads bowed toward Lucious. "Thank you, all of you, for saving my life."

Selim was the first to speak. "It is our honor and duty to protect you, my king." Lucious stepped forward and placed one hand on Selim and the other on Ulandra. Their scales were smooth and warm to the touch.

"Come now, there is no need to bow. We are equals, and I would very much like to call you, my friends." With that, their heads raised as each one nodded, repeating the word *friends*.

The four new companions sat around the fire and talked while eating some rabbits that Selim had caught. The remaining darkness of night faded as the sun slowly rose. They encountered no more of those previous creatures, other than the corpses that lay just outside the camp. Lucious stretched as he stood up, letting out a yawn. *I feel a lot better than a few hours ago*, he thought. He still wasn't sure how he was even alive, as he knew the wounds should have been fatal. His tunic had seen better days; the creatures badly ripped it on the arm and the back was in shreds. Every little breeze now sent chills up his back. Morgan approached Lucious. "May I have a look at your wounds?"

Lucious nodded and turned around. He could feel her warm, delicate touch as she examined him. Morgan stepped back with a pleased look on her face.

Lucious asked, "Well, how does it look?"

"It's amazing, you only have small scars where just hours ago there were massive gaping wounds!"

Lucious slipped on his cloak to protect his bare flesh and stood facing Morgan. "I'm not entirely sure what's happening to me. I was just a normal young man until my birthday yesterday, and now I have powers I can't explain." Lucious looked at Morgan and shrugged his shoulders. "Honestly, I can't even grasp how I summoned you three!"

Morgan stepped close to Lucious and placed her hand on his shoulder. "You didn't just summon us, you created us and the entire Draconian race." Her words added much weight to an already heavy load on his mind. Morgan turned away and began packing up the rest of the camp, along with Selim and Ulandra. She looked back at Lucious, who was still standing where she left him. He was obviously trying to process everything that was happening. She called to him, "We should probably get moving soon, we still have a long road ahead."

Snapping out of his thoughts, "You're right, we should continue on without further delay." Lucious packed his equipment and strapped on his weapons. The four of them continued north along the trail towards the city of Westlin.

CHAPTER TEN
MORLOCKS

A rain left her bedchamber and headed towards the great hall to get some food for her and Timber. The smells from the kitchen filled the air as the cooks worked round the clock to keep the busy citadel inhabitants fed. Tables were filled with hungry people while servers whisked about, serving up plates of food and flagons of mead. Arain took her usual table in the far corner, where she liked to sit alone with her wolf. No sooner did she sit down when two plates of food were placed on the table, one for her and the other for Timber. A moment later, another server brought over a bowl of water and placed it in front of the wolf. She then provided a cup of brimbale wine for Arain. "Is there anything else I can get for you, my queen?"

Arain leaned over and set Timber's plate of meat stew on the floor for him. "That will be all for now." The servant stepped out of sight, but stayed close enough so she could hear if she were needed again. Timber waited for his master to signal it was okay to eat. "Go ahead, boy," she commanded, and the giant, gray wolf laid down and began eating. Arain took a large swig of wine before starting in on her own plate of food with bread, various cheeses, eggs, and goat meat. Barely halfway through her breakfast, Arain noticed Valin hurriedly heading towards her. She sat back and watched him approach as she finished a mouth full of food. Timber finished his meal first, as usual, and was sitting next to his master.

"There you are, your majesty. We have a situation in the courtyard you may want to come address as soon as you are able."

She looked up at Valin. "What's going on?"

Valin stood before her, a little uneasy, almost excited even. "You're going to want to see this for yourself, my lady."

Slightly annoyed, Arain pushed back from the table and followed Valin to the courtyard. As they walked, she noticed everyone was heading in the same direction as them. Arain's interest was now piqued as they rounded the corner. Hundreds of people stood in a large circle and all were looking at something in the center. The chatter was deafening as she proceeded through the crowd to see what all the commotion was about. The last few black-robed mages stepped aside when they saw her coming. Arain entered the center of the circle of onlookers and could now see what was drawing so much attention. Sitting in front of her were six large, black beasts. Valin was standing to her left and Timber to her right. The wolf's hair rose on its back and he bared his teeth with a snarl. The black creatures took notice and turned her way.

Valin watched with anticipation. "My queen, I believe they are waiting for you."

Arain put a hand down to Timber, gently scratching his head. "Easy boy, they pose no threat to me." She walked towards the closest one, which was by far the biggest of the beasts. All chatter stopped that instant as everyone watched to see what would happen. Arain placed a hand on the creature's head and looked directly into its shimmering eyes. In that instant, she knew they were there to serve her. They felt familiar, almost as if they were an extension of her body. Arain closed her eyes for a moment and then removed her hand from the creature. As she opened her eyes, the creatures bolted out of the courtyard and disappeared from sight.

Valin approached her. "Where did they go, my lady?"

Arain spun about and in passing him, uttered, "To kill my brother."

Arain returned to the citadel to finish preparing, while Valin addressed the group that stood assembled. "Continue with the preparations. We leave at dawn."

The crowd dispersed and continued on with the task at hand. Timber was left sniffing feverishly at the ground where the creatures had just been, and then was off to find his master.

CHAPTER ELEVEN

THE ROAD AHEAD

Lucious, Morgan, Selim, and Ulandra continued on the trail, heading north through Rennit Forest. The morning was fairly uneventful as they traveled, with only the occasional animal crossing their paths. Selim and Ulandra walked together, ahead of Lucious and Morgan, as they conversed about all the new and exciting things they were seeing. Lucious smiled at the two of them as he walked next to Morgan.

"What is it, Lucious?" she asked.

He glanced over at her. "It's just kind of funny. Those two are so big and formidable looking, but they remind me of children seeing things for the first time."

"I see what you mean," said Morgan, noticing what Lucious was picking up on. "I guess we are like children to this unknown world," she remarked as she smiled back at him.

"Morgan, do you mind if we talk?"

"Of course not, my king, you do not need to ask to converse with any of us."

"Please, it's just Lucious, okay?"

"My apologies, Lucious. What is it you would like to talk about?"

A mountain of questions piled in his head, and picking where to begin caused him to pause for a moment. "I guess

I would like to know how it is you think I created you?"

Morgan pondered the question for a moment before answering. "It's a feeling, a connection we felt to you from the moment we came to be. Nobody had to tell me who you were to me, no more than a bird must tell her chicks she's their mother. You just know down to your core that the person in front of you is your reason for being."

Lucious continued walking with Morgan while he wrapped his head around her answer. "If I created a whole new species, how did I do it, and why can't I remember it?"

After a moment, Morgan spoke. "I can't say how you use this power, but I think it triggered subconsciously when you were dying back there."

That answer immediately raised more questions in his head. "I should have been dead back there when that thing was mauling me, don't you think?"

Morgan nodded, "Yes, I think you actually were dead."

His head was aching from trying to process everything. A look of concern crossed Morgan's face as Lucious put his left hand on his forehead, rubbing it. "Are you alright? Would you like to take a break and rest for a little while?"

He dropped his hand back down. "I'm all right. We can go a while longer, and then maybe we can stop and eat."

"Very well, I will let Selim and Ulandra know."

Morgan picked up her pace until she reached the others. "Keep a lookout for a good place to stop and rest for a bit off the trail." Selim nodded, and he and Ulandra went on ahead to secure a location. Morgan dropped back to walk beside Lucious again.

"Where are they off to in such a hurry?" he asked.

"I told them to find a safe place up ahead so we may rest undisturbed." Lucious thanked her, and Morgan bowed her head in acknowledgment.

The two walked for a while longer until they reached Ulandra, who was standing off to the side of the trail. "Follow me," she instructed, heading away from the trail and into the trees. Lucious followed, with Morgan behind him. Through some brimbale bushes and over a small rise, they could see Selim building a small cooking fire. Two old fallen trees were positioned on either side to sit on or lean against if one was inclined to do so. Lucious dropped his pack on the ground and sat on the log facing Selim. "What can I help with?" he asked the massive Draconian who was kneeling, feeding sticks into the fire.

Selim's gaze remained on what he was doing. "You rest and leave everything to us, Lucious. We still have much traveling left today." Lucious noticed Ulandra was gone again, as well as Morgan. Selim looked up at Lucious. "Don't worry, they went to gather food and water. They'll be back shortly. Try to take a nap and I'll take the watch."

I am a little tired, Lucious thought. "Okay, Selim, you win. I'm going to rest for a bit." Lucious removed his sword belt and set it next to him on the soft, leafy ground. He took the blanket from his pack and rolled it into a makeshift pillow to prop his head up. He closed his eyes and took a nap next to the campfire. Lucious fell into a deep sleep and dreamed of the past few days' events. He dreamed about his childhood home exploding, losing his father, Ezra, and today's travel along the road to Westlin. Then he dreamed he was floating high in the sky again. He could see mountains to the north and a great city with a massive castle at its center. To the west was the City of Knowledge, with its enormous white towers and sprawling establishments. Further to the west, at the continent's edge, was Castle Kragg, an equally massive, obsidian black castle. Its back was to a mountain with swamp and marshland on the remaining three sides. For the most part, it was how he remembered seeing it during his awakening, the continent of Tauro encircled in the impenetrable ice fog. It was almost the same, but he could tell something had changed. Far to the southwest of his hometown of Addleberry, he could see the fog had dissipated in an area, revealing a new island. *What in the world made the fog recede in that location?* Lucious focused on this new island and began descending from his vantage point in the sky. Closer and closer he got, and just when he could start making out structures on its surface, he woke from his sleep. Lying there on the ground, he took a moment to clear the cobwebs from his head. He looked over and could see Morgan cooking something over the small campfire. Ulandra was sitting on the opposing log, sipping from a water-skin. Selim was out of sight at the moment.

Morgan smiled as she looked over at Lucious, who was getting his bearings after such a deep sleep. "Did you rest well, Lucious?"

He sat up while stretching and let out a yawn. "Actually, I slept very well. I did, however, have the most vivid dreams. It was like before, where I was floating above everything looking down on the known world. But this time something was different. There was a new island to the southwest that the fog was hiding this whole time."

"That sounds like a very intense dream," replied Morgan as she pulled some freshly cooked meat from the fire and served it to Lucious.

"Aren't you two going to eat?" he asked.

"We have already eaten and did not wish to wake you," replied Ulandra. Morgan was already going about cleaning up the campsite and extinguishing the fire. Just then, Selim walked out from behind the log that Lucious was leaning against.

"I've scouted ahead and doubled back a ways and everything looks clear, no humans or other creatures." Selim leaned his ax down against the log Ulandra was sitting at and pulled out a water-skin to have a drink. Once finished, he looked over at Lucious, who was devouring the meat Morgan had given him.

"When you're finished, we should get going, if that's all right with you."

Lucious swallowed a mouthful. "Yes, by all means, we still have a long way to go." He finished his meal and packed his blanket back into his pack. Strapping on his belt and weapons, he faced the group. "I'm all set, let's get going," he said, and they continued their journey towards Westlin.

Chapter Twelve
A Growing Threat

The citadel was abuzz throughout the night, as Arain's commanders delegated tasks to be completed. They brought horses from the stables and outfitted them with packs full of supplies, along with saddles and bits. One by one, small groups of black mages, mercenaries, and assassin guild members departed from the citadel's courtyard, vanishing into the night.

Arain Drake had finished preparing for her own departure come sunrise. Her ornate black plate armor was fully polished and placed on the stand. It was beautiful and sleek, with silver accents on the breastplate and gauntlets. As plate mail went, this was a tiny and custom fitted set of armor unlike the large, bulky plate of the guards. She sat in her nightclothes at the table by the fireplace and ran a whetstone down one side of her sword and then the other until it had a razor-sharp edge. This was the sword her father, Valin, had made specially for her. It was a beautiful mirror-finished longsword, with red characters down the middle on both sides and a cross-shaped pommel and hand guard. Its name was Bloodletter, and it was indeed enchanted. Arain set the stone on the table and wiped the residue off the blade with a rag. Tilting it this way and that, she eyed the weapon carefully, making sure it was perfect. *Yes, I think you're ready,* she thought as she looked at the blade. Standing up, she walked over to where her armor was placed and picked up a black scabbard, sliding the sword into it with a satisfying *snick* sound. She stood there a moment, taking a mental inventory of everything.

"Good. I think we are ready to go, Timber," she informed the wolf, who was lying on the bed staring at her. Arain walked over to the bed and climbed in. She covered herself with the soft blankets and moved herself up against the enormous wolf for warmth. For a while, she lay there thinking back on the day. She was especially thinking about those black hounds she had somehow summoned. *Morlocks, that's a fitting name,* she thought. She wondered if that dream were related to the new power she now possessed, and if so, how she could use it again.

A brief time passed as she slowly fell into a deep slumber. Timber laid his muzzle on her abdomen and drifted off to sleep as well. The fire crackled in the hearth and all was quiet in her bedchamber.

Valin was still awake, checking over his equipment and making sure he had the correct tomes and other magical necessities for the journey. His black robes and magical staff were placed with his things to take in the morning. He sat in his room for a bit, going over the plans that Arain and he had laid out over the past few years. Everything looked to be in order, but one thing was nagging at him. It was the news that her brother was alive and well across the other side of the continent. *What part would he play in this conquest? Did he have similar gifts like Arain?* His thoughts trailed off on the subject. *He'll probably be dead I suppose, once those creatures get to him.* He smiled at the thought and decided it best that he get some sleep before they depart. With that, Valin crawled into his bed and went to sleep.

Arain dreamed of the world in flames. Cities, villages, and castles lay in ruins, and a massive black army covered the land like a plague. She could see herself sitting atop a gold and obsidian throne, with Timber to her left and Valin to her right. As far as she could see, humans and creatures alike were bending the knee, worshiping her. Arain felt like a god, sitting there above all others. After a few moments, a man walked out from the endless sea of worshipers and began climbing the steps towards her throne. She recognized the armor he wore, and as he moved closer, she could see that it was her brother again.

"STOP!" she shouted as she bolted up from her throne. Lucious was only ten steps away when he did just that. The twins stared at each other menacingly. "What do you want, brother?"

Lucious did not reply, but stood there silently. He raised his right arm and made a sweeping motion. As he did, the horde of worshipers burst into flames. Their ashes blew away. Arain's eyes were wide with rage, and she clenched her jaw so hard the flexed muscles were visible from where Lucious was standing.

"How dare you interfere with my plans!" she shouted. In a split second, she drew Bloodletter from its sheath and lunged at him, driving the sword clean through the front of his armor and out the back. The blade hissed as the inscription along its surface glowed. Arain was face to face with Lucious, still holding the sword that was plunged into him. Quickly, her anger turned to disbelief as Lucious stood there and smiled.

Arain's eyes shot open, and she was in her bed staring at the ceiling. "That felt so real," she spoke aloud. She laid there for a while, dissecting the dream she had just had. One thing she knew for certain was that Lucious was going to be a problem if her Morlocks didn't dispose of him. Arain rolled her head to the side and looked down at Timber, who was watching her with his head resting on her thigh. "It's time, boy," she said as she sat up and petted his head.

———◦———

It was dawn, and the first faint rays of sunlight entered her bedroom window. Timber lifted his head and faced the door with a low-pitched growl. A few moments later, there was a knock on the door. "Your grace, it's morning," announced one of her maids. "We have breakfast for the both of you, may we come in?"

"Enter," she replied as she left her warm bed and headed over to the table by the fireplace. Its blaze was gone, but the embers still glowed red, emitting plenty of heat. Arain sat down and two chambermaids entered with the food they had promised. After eating, Arain got dressed and donned her armor and weapons. Two soldiers carried her packs as they escorted her to the courtyard, where her primary force of about two hundred soldiers, mages, and assassins were waiting for their queen. Arain approached Valin, who was sitting atop a brown and white horse. Even with the armor and weapons, she was almost silent as she walked. Valin knew what she wanted, and so he briefed her.

"Your highness, good morning. Everyone is assembled and accounted for. With your permission, we can start on our way to Castle Kragg."

She looked up at him atop his horse. "Let us begin."

Valin signaled to his captain to begin the journey, and with that, the assembled army filed out of the courtyard. They brought Arain her black warhorse, Bane. With no effort, she mounted the horse and gave him the command to follow the others. Timber ran ahead to scout the area, while she and Valin rode out after the army.

CHAPTER THIRTEEN

THIEF

It was a beautiful day as the party of four walked along the trail through Rennit Forest. Birds chirped, squirrels scampered here and there, and the occasional deer wandered in the distance. For a moment, Lucious felt like everything was normal in the world. However, a quick glance at his companions dispelled any further thoughts of normality. The group had been walking for hours, and from his best guess, Lucious figured it was going to get dark soon. "Morgan," he called to her, some twenty steps ahead of him.

Looking over her shoulder, Morgan replied, "Yes, what is it?"

"We should think about finding a place to camp soon, don't you think?"

Morgan stopped and looked at the sky. "I think you're right, we might as well get settled before nightfall." Morgan, as usual, took charge and gave orders to Selim and Ulandra. "Selim, you stay with Lucious. Ulandra and I will scout further off the trail for a suitable place to set up camp."

It amazed him how silently these Draconians could move through the forest when they wanted to. In an instant, the two women faded from sight. Selim and Lucious stood there on the trail as the awkward silence set in. Lucious looked up at Selim. This creature was an intimidating sight. "So, if you were just created a day ago, do you have memories of your childhood?"

Selim's reptilian face showed he was trying to recall any memories. "I can't say I do," he finally responded in a somewhat raspy voice.

"How old do you think you are, Selim?"

"Again, I am uncertain, but I would guess I'm a young adult like the others." His tail curled back and forth on the dirt road, reminding Lucious of an impatient child that couldn't sit still. "May I ask how old you are, Lucious?"

"I'm also a young adult. I just turned eighteen the other day, and that's when all this crazy stuff started happening." The thought of Ezra and those creatures came to the forefront of his mind. Lucious' head slumped downwards as tears welled up in his eyes. *So much has happened in so little time that I haven't had time to mourn the loss of my father*, he thought.

Selim looked concerned at the sudden change in Lucious' posture. "Are you alright?"

Lucious wiped away the tears. "Yes, I'll be fine, Selim. Thanks for asking." *By looking at him, I can't believe that this formidable-looking creature is also very compassionate*, he reflected.

As quickly and silently as she left, Morgan walked out of the woods and over to Lucious and Selim. "This way, you two," she said, gesturing for them to follow her.

"Hey, where is Ulandra?" Lucious asked.

"I sent her to look for food. She should be back shortly." A little farther down the trail, they reached a flat area between a group of large pine trees. The ground was a carpet of old fallen needles and pine cones. Morgan already had her pack on the ground, leaning against one of the trees. She turned to Selim. "Go gather some wood so we can make a fire and Lucious and I will gather these pine cones for kindling and clear a soft spot to sleep." Selim dropped his pack and pulled the large ax from his back, where he kept it for travel. Without wasting a moment, he began looking for downed trees he could use. It didn't take long to find enough wood to last them through the night. Lucious dropped his pack as well and began helping Morgan collect pine cones. Before long, they had a fire burning in the center of their makeshift camp.

Ulandra showed back up as night crept in. From the looks of it, she didn't have any luck hunting, but instead had a sack full of wild berries. She gave the sack to Morgan, who was tending the fire. "No luck with any wild game, I'm afraid."

Morgan took the berries and put them in a pot she carried in her pack. Some left-over rabbit meat and some wild herbs she picked earlier in the day all went into the pot. Morgan poured in some water from her water-skin and placed the concoction on the fire. Lucious pulled some bread from his pack and handed it to Morgan, who divvied it up between the four of them. It didn't take long for the stew to cook on the fire, and just like the bread, Morgan gave equal portions to each one of them.

Lucious sat on the soft bed of pine needles and took a deep breath of the aromatic, fruity stew. "Wow, Morgan, this smells amazing."

She responded with a smile, "I hope you like it."

The four of them sat around the fire, enjoying the meal. Not one complaint was heard as they devoured the stew in short order. Lucious looked over at Morgan as he sat there with a full belly. The firelight danced beautifully off of her soft green scales. Her tail was curled around the bottom of her feet as she sat there soaking up the heat. Her beauty mesmerized Lucious. Morgan, noticing the attention, looked his way. "Are you alright?"

Realizing she caught him staring, he quickly diverted his gaze to the fire. "Fine, just fine. I was thinking about something."

"And what was that?" She was not letting him off so easily.

Lucious cleared his throat and sat up a little straighter. "I was just thinking how fortunate I am to be here with the three of you on this journey. By myself, I would be in terrible shape if I didn't have you all help me hunt and gather food or find safe places to rest and set camp. I appreciate all your help." Lucious looked at each of them as he spoke.

Selim, Ulandra, and Morgan all nodded in agreement. Morgan replied, "Lucious, I'm not sure where the journey will lead us, but we will be by your side till its end."

"Thank you." Pulling his blanket from his pack, Lucious laid down and settled in for the night. For some time, he lay there, looking up through the pines and into the star-filled sky. His thoughts went back to his newfound abilities. Laying there, he thought to himself, *when I created the Draconian, I was so afraid and in pain, wishing for someone to help me as the black beast tore me to shreds. What part of that situation triggered this power? I don't think it was the excruciating pain. It doesn't feel like it was the cause. I don't think fear was the catalyst, either. It had to be something to do with needing or wanting help so badly.* It wasn't much longer until Lucious drifted off to sleep.

Morgan prepped her spot on the ground near him. She looked over at Selim, who was prodding the fire with a stick, "You take first watch, Ulandra second, and I'll take the last." Selim threw the stick into the fire and stood up, grabbing his ax. He walked away from the campsite as he patrolled the area surrounding them. Ulandra and Morgan laid down and quickly drifted off to sleep. The night was uneventful as the watchers all took their turns as instructed. Morgan, being the last of the watch, was awakened by Ulandra. No words needed to be exchanged, just a gentle shaking of the shoulder, and she was up, putting on her weapons and rolling her blanket to stow it back into the sack she carried. Ulandra wasted no time getting back to sleep. Morgan began her watch through the waning hours of nightfall. She walked the perimeter like the others before her. The path they made was easy to follow, even in the dark. Morgan's reptilian eyes gave her excellent vision during the day and even better vision at night.

Crunch, crunch, crunch.

Lucious, lying on his side, opened his eyes slowly.

Crunch, crunch, crunch. Sitting there, just a short distance away, was a weasel devouring a piece of bread. *Crunch, crunch.*

That's odd, Lucious thought. *Where did that little guy get bread from?*

Lucious snapped wide awake and yelled, "That's our bread, you little thief," as he lunged forward to grab the animal. Lucious was too slow, and the weasel scurried out of reach and vanished into the forest.

Morgan stepped into the light of the fire next to him. "What's wrong?"

"Did you see that little weasel steal the bread from my pack while I was sleeping and then have the nerve to sit there and crunch away on it, waking me up?"

Morgan smiled and let out a little laugh. "Sneaky little creature. Should I track it down for you?"

Lucious laid back down. "No, he robbed me fair and square . . . let the weasel enjoy his spoils. I think I'm going to stay awake to see if he comes back, though."

It was already getting light, and soon they would be packing up to leave, anyway.

CHAPTER FOURTEEN

GROWING STRONGER

The first two days of travel from the citadel towards Castle Kragg were harsh, as the weather was anything but nice. It was almost as if the dark clouds, gusting winds, and downpours were following her. Riding atop her horse, Arain had lots of time to think about everything. The Morlocks were on her mind at the moment, or more to the point, how she had summoned them. *A power like this will be put to great use if I can master it*, she thought.

Valin was still riding next to her and could see she was deep in thought. "What troubles you, my dear?" he asked, trying to sound like a caring father.

Rain pelted down, dripping off the hood of Arain's cloak. "I'm just thinking about the Morlocks I created the other day and trying to figure out how I did it. I think I called for them in the dream I had that same night."

Valin put a hand up to his face and stroked his beard. "It is amazing, to say the least. What can you recall happened in this dream right before they appeared?"

Arain recounted the dream in its entirety to Valin. "I just remember being so furious at Lucious and full of rage."

The two rode silently for a while as they pondered what the trigger was. Valin spoke. "I think your powerful emotion triggers your power to create. It's the only thing that makes any kind of sense."

Arain cocked her head and looked across at Valin. "So, the rage I felt flowed out of me and manifested into living creatures?"

Valin shrugged his shoulders. "It's merely an educated guess, my dear, but I am certain it relates to your emotions. You should practice while we travel and see if you can use it again."

Arain nodded her head. "Yes, I think you're right, it would be wise to practice until I can do it at will."

"Very well, I'll leave you to it, then." With that, Valin headed towards the front of the convoy.

For the rest of the day, Arain tried to focus on her emotions and create something, but had no luck. Just as she was getting frustrated, she saw Timber come out of the brush alongside her. She looked down at him and asked, "Did you have fun scouting?"

The large, gray wolf looked up at her as if he understood what she was saying, and to some extent, he did. A few moments later, Timber disappeared into the vegetation again and Arain went back to the task at hand. She closed her eyes and concentrated, trying to focus on an object in her mind. *I should try something simple and small*, she thought to herself. In her mind, she formed a picture of a red ruby, about the size of a small coin. The red was so vibrant and deep that it was almost impossible to see through it. Arain could see herself holding the gem in her mind and in the flesh. The stone was cupped in her right mail-covered hand and she focused solely on it until she felt a burning in her chest. She opened her eyes and looked into her cupped hand. *I did it*, she thought, as her hand was indeed filled with something red.

Arain, still in a trance-like state, moved her hand closer to her face to examine it. She turned her hand over, and the red liquid fell out onto the horse's neck. *That's not a ruby.* Snapping back into the present, she could clearly see that it was blood she held and there was an arrow sticking out of her chest. The warm crimson was running down its shaft and falling onto her plated arm. Arain looked around for an attacker as another arrow came from the brush and went clean through her neck. She grasped her throat and fell from the horse onto the soaked, muddy ground. Her plate clunked from the impact. Arain stared up at the sky as rain pelted her in the face.

Is this how it ends? she thought, *I am to die before I even get started?* She felt cold and her vision faded. Nearby, she could hear Timber attacking someone and the sound of men on horseback closing in on her position. Then everything went black. Arain's body laid still in a pool of bloody mud as the rain continued to fall. A minor battle raged on around her for only a few minutes or so before her small but skilled army obliterated the would-be bandits.

The best healers Arain had were desperately trying to revive her. Valin looked on from a short distance away. It disgusted him that Arain would die so easily and that now he would have to continue on with their plans alone.

"Sir, we have captured the remaining bandits," said a black armor-clad soldier reporting to Valin.

"Where are they, soldier?"

"Follow me sir, we have them secured over here." The soldier walked away from the site where Arain's body lay. Valin followed him as they walked off the road and towards the brush line to the two men clad in brown leather armor, bound, and guarded. Valin's gaze was fixed as he approached the would-be robbers that so drastically affected his plans.

Valin was going over in his head the many ways these two were going to suffer long before he granted them death. He stepped in front of the two battered and bloodied men caked with mud from head to toe. He began to open his mouth to question them when a wave of crimson splashed him in the face, blinding him for a moment. Defensively, Valin stepped back and tried to wipe the blood from his eyes. He could hear screams of agony mixed with the commotion of panicked soldiers. When his vision cleared, the sight before him was nothing short of terror. He stood there in shock as both men lay completely eviscerated. Entrails strewn about the ground, along with a torso here and a leg there. In the center of the carnage stood a massive creature, some sixteen feet tall, with rippling muscles and stone-colored skin. Its eyes were an orange hue and its head was completely bald. In its huge hands was the torso of one of the bandits, and it was crunching away delightfully on what used to be his head. The skull cracking in the giant's mouth sent chills down Valin's spine, just before it put the biggest smile on his face.

Valin turned back towards Arain, who was propping herself up out of the mud with her hands. The rage in her eyes warmed his heart, and any thoughts of her being dispatched so easily disappeared. The two healers were helping her up as she collapsed from the tremendous strain of creating such a gigantic creature. Blood streaks ran from her ears and nose. Valin signaled the company captain, Seget, over to discuss matters. He was a tall, slender man in his forties, with brown hair and eyes. He was a master at arms serving under King Malik before the two of them had a falling out of sorts. Now he led the small army of Arain Drake. Seget dismounted his horse and strode over to talk with Valin. His plate mail was gray with red and black highlights.

"You wish to speak with me, sir?" he asked, waiting attentively for a response.

Valin, now more composed, began giving orders to the captain. "We need to set up camp here, as the queen requires time to rest. Have her quarters set up immediately. Break off a group to gather wood and build fires while the rest set up the remaining tents and begin preparing food."

Seget looked past Valin at the giant who was devouring the remaining pieces of the bandits. "What do we do with that, sir?"

Valin looked back at the monster and then to Seget. "Tell the men to keep clear and not provoke it. When her majesty awakens, she can deal with it."

Seget acknowledged the commands and hastily turned about and mounted his horse. Off he rode to meet with the division leaders to hand out the orders.

CHAPTER FIFTEEN

CHAMELEON

Lucious and company walked a better part of the morning before they reached the edge of the forest. Standing before them were grassy hills stretching out as far as the eye could see. They could barely make out the faintest shape of mountains in the distance. The sun was out all morning, but the weather was changing as gray clouds filled the sky and a cool wind picked up, making the tall grass dance back and forth. "Well, I guess there goes the pleasant weather," replied Ulandra.

Lucious looked across the group. "Why don't we all take a brief break before we continue on? I imagine we all could use some food and water."

Everyone agreed and dropped their packs before sitting on the ground. Morgan opened her pack and pulled out some dried meat, which she distributed between the group. Lucious opened his pack and reached for the leftover bread, only to remember the weasel stole it the night before. He ripped off a chunk of the dried meat and looked over at Morgan. "I guess we're going to need to find some more supplies soon." Lucious told the group about a small village between Addleberry and Westlin that Ezra had talked about. "I think it's called Belrose, if I remember correctly. We should be able to buy what we need there."

"That sounds good, Lucious," Morgan replied. "How far do you think it is from here?"

"I don't know, maybe another day until we reach it." Lucious honestly did not know how far away it was, being that he was secluded to his hometown for the entirety of his life.

Selim finished his allotment and voiced his opinion on the situation. "It's best if we only travel a while longer so we have time to gather food and water to get us to Belrose." His armored tail flicked on the ground.

"Very well then, let's get moving," said Ulandra as she swung her pack over her shoulder and headed away from the forest and into the fields ahead. It was pretty clear that the road upon which they walked was the same one used by the merchants and villagers that occasionally traveled between villages and cities, bringing supplies and goods for sale. Selim followed close behind Ulandra, and as usual, Morgan and Lucious walked together in the back. It was monotonous, and most of their time was spent walking up and down countless hills. Occasionally the scattered tree popped into view, which helped break up the mesmerizing sea of grass.

Lucious kicked a rock along the path as he walked next to Morgan. "Is there anything you can tell me about yourself or your race?"

A long silence followed as Morgan thought about his question. She herself was unsure, she could just recall some random memories. "I know very little, I'm afraid." A wave of disappointment washed over her face. "I know we are a kind, loyal, yet fierce species and are all attuned to the flow of magic." She opened a hand so her palm was facing up, and a small flame appeared. It danced there for a moment before she closed her hand and extinguished it.

"That's amazing, Morgan. You have only been here for three days and you can cast minor spells so easily. Huh, it took me weeks to get that flame spell down. You are truly amazing."

Morgan bowed her head a bit to hide her blushing face. "I'm glad you think so, Lucious. After all, it was your will that created us, so how could we not be amazing? Your gift is one surely only a god would possess. Not to mention your ability to heal."

His brow lifted a bit and his eyes widened as he contemplated what she had just said. "Yeah, I guess you're right, they are pretty amazing. I only wish I knew how to use them when I'm not about to die." He let out a chuckle, as did Morgan. "With magic, I can read and study and practice, but with this, I don't know what to do."

She looked over at him. "I'm sure you will figure it out, and I will help if I can."

"Thank you, I appreciate it." They continued on for a while longer, chatting along the way.

It was almost time to set up camp and begin looking for food and water to get them through until tomorrow, when up over the next hill came an old wooden wagon drawn by two brown and white horses. Lucious could see Selim and Ulandra were already gone from the road, hiding in the tall grass. Morgan grabbed Lucious and hurried him off into the grass as well. The click-clacking of the horses' hooves rang out as the wagon closed in on them. Lucious could see that Morgan already had a blade drawn, ready to attack if necessary. *She looked so intimidating*, he thought. *I'm sure glad they're with me.*

The wagon slowed as it reached the area where Lucious and Morgan were hiding, then finally came to a complete stop. A gruff-looking old man with white hair and a lengthy beard was sitting at the front of the wagon with a pipe hanging from his lips. It looked like an old woman was sitting next to him with matching white hair.

A low, crackling voice rang out, "Come on out here, we saw you run into the grass from back on that hilltop. We're just two old traders on our way to Addleberry and don't mean you any harm."

Against Morgan's objection, Lucious stood up and stepped out into the open. "Good day to you, sir and ma'am."

"Good day to you as well, young man. What possessed you to run off into the grass like that? You know this is a trade road, don't you?"

"Yes, I do, it's just that we haven't seen anybody in days and suddenly you popped up in front of us, I mean, me."

The little old lady smiled down at Lucious, her face wrinkled with age. "Who's your friend, Sonny?" she asked.

"Um, no one," Lucious backtracked, realizing he made a mistake in saying *we*. His nervousness wasn't helping him convince the old couple that he wasn't lying, either.

"My name is Lucious Drake, and you are?" He hoped he could redirect the couple with some introductions.

The old lady spoke first, her hoarse voice was high-pitched. "I'm Edna Thwis and this old man is my husband, Hensey."

From the corner of his eye, Lucious could see Selim at the back of the wagon with his ax drawn. Lucious shook his head to signal him to back down.

"Oh dear, would you look at that," said Edna, transfixed on something behind Lucious.

Oh no, was it Morgan? he thought as he slowly turned around. To his surprise, a beautiful young woman was standing there with long, golden blonde hair and emerald green eyes. Her skin was as white as milk and she wore a plain blue dress. He stood speechless. The girl smiled and walked past him to converse with the old couple.

"Hello, my name is Morgan Drake and I'm his wife."

The couple obviously taken with the beautiful young woman, stepped down from the wagon to get a closer look.

With both hands, Edna grasped one of Morgan's. "You are absolutely breathtaking, my dear."

Hensey nodded in agreement. "Almost as beautiful as you, my dear," Hensey said, knowing full well he better acknowledge his wife's beauty if he knew what was good for him.

Edna rolled her eyes and smiled. "What on earth are the two of you doing out here? Every so often people get robbed traveling this road."

Morgan walked next to her would-be husband and put her arms around him. "We're on our way to Belrose to visit a friend," she explained, "and don't worry, my husband is quite good with his sword and spells."

"Ahhhh, I see," replied Edna. "In that case, I'd say you were in excellent hands, my dear. Well, I guess we will be off to Addleberry, then. But before we leave, is there anything you might need?" Hensey was tending the horses, giving them some fresh carrots, while Edna hobbled to the rear of the wagon with Morgan and Lucious. "Have a look. We have fresh vegetables, wine, water, dried meat, salted fish, some blankets, and some other stuff as well."

Lucious climbed into the back of the wagon. *It was amazing how much stuff they packed into this thing,* he thought. He grabbed some carrots, radishes, water, salted fish, dried meat, and a silver necklace with a red stone pendant on it. Handing everything to Edna, he jumped out of the wagon and asked, "How much for this?"

Edna was in full saleswoman-mode now. "Let's see," as she calculated the total in her head. "That will be six silver and two coppers for the lot." Lucious removed his pack and rummaged inside for the coin sack that Ezra had put in it. He produced a small brown leather pouch, untied the laces, and counted out what they owed. The coins made a satisfying clinking noise in her hand. Lucious cinched the pouch closed and returned it to his pack along with some supplies he just purchased. He put the rest of the supplies into Morgan's pack. Walking to the front of the wagon,

Morgan and Lucious could see the couple were back in their seats and ready to continue on.

"You two take care of each other, and thanks for the business," replied Edna.

"*Yahh!*" ordered Hensey with a snap of the reigns, and they were off on their way to Addleberry.

As suddenly as they had appeared, the traders were gone. Selim and Ulandra walked over to Morgan and Lucious. All kinds of new questions were floating around in Lucious' head as he looked over to see Morgan back to her reptilian self. "What—how—hold on, you can change your appearance?"

"I guess we can," she remarked. Morgan's response did nothing to quell the astonished human's amazement.

By this point, Lucious felt flustered and a bit overwhelmed. He walked off a short way away from the rest of the group to think. Pacing back and forth with a hand on the back of his head, he questioned himself. "Is this how it's going to be from now on? Every day so far, it's been new amazing revelations of abilities, of new species, species with special abilities. I haven't even wrapped my head around most of this stuff and more keeps piling on top of that." As he continued his one-on-one discussion with himself, Lucious didn't realize that Morgan was standing next to him. On his next pace back, he ran smack right into her and almost knocked both of them down. "I'm so sorry, I didn't see you there," he apologized.

Morgan, who always seemed to be smiling, was again doing just that. "It's all right, I shouldn't have stood so close when you were talking to yourself," she said as a slight chuckle slipped out.

Lucious stood there with his hands on his hips, laughing. "I guess I was having a pleasant talk with myself."

Morgan stepped closer, facing him, and placed a hand on his shoulder. "I am sorry for causing you any more confusion, Lucious, but until I changed, I didn't know I could. I was lying there in the grass thinking how helpless I was and that I couldn't help you without revealing myself. Then it just happened, so I came forward and posed as your wife to not raise any suspicions. Luckily, it was just those two elderly traders and not someone dangerous."

Lucious dropped his hands from his hips and hugged Morgan tightly. Her body went rigid for a moment, as she wasn't expecting him to embrace her. However, it felt nice, and she hugged him back.

Selim and Ulandra were close enough that they could see the two holding each other. Ulandra looked up at Selim and asked, "What are they doing?"

Selim shook his head, "I can't say for sure, but I think it's a sign of affection that humans use."

Ulandra looked back at the couple. "You think that's what they're doing, showing affection to one another?"

Selim shrugged his massive shoulders, then reached down to grab Lucious' pack and began to walk over to them. Morgan and Lucious separated, looking into each other's eyes. "Thanks, Morgan," was all he said, and he walked over to Selim to retrieve his pack.

"Well, now that we have supplies, do we keep traveling for a while longer today or should we find a place to camp?" asked Ulandra.

Lucious responded as he slung the pack over his shoulders. "Why don't we continue on a little longer until we come across a good place to stop?"

Everyone agreed with the decision and began traveling again.

CHAPTER SIXTEEN
OGRE

Arain opened her icy blue eyes and gazed up at the roof of her massive tent. She was lying in a bed, but it was not like her luxurious one in the citadel. Thoughts of what happened more than a day ago flowed in like a wave. The dull ache in her chest and neck from the mortal wounds she suffered caused her to put a hand on her neck to rub it. Arain could feel that the wounds were gone, but the imperfections of the skin told her that scars were in their place. Her chest felt the same where the arrow had penetrated her flesh. *I feel like I was dragged behind my horse for a while*, she thought as she pushed herself up into a sitting position. Timber leaped onto the bed and began a greeting of licks to the face. The weight of the wolf pinned her down so she couldn't escape. "Okay, okay, okay, I missed you too, boy," she cried as she pushed his muzzle away with her hands. A few head scratches later, and Timber lay satisfied beside her. Nothing but pure love and devotion shone in his eyes as he stared at her.

Looking around, Arain surveyed her surroundings. A table and two chairs sat in the far corner. There was a fire pit directly in the center of the room with a magical flame blazing inside of it. There were a few light orbs placed around the room towards the ceiling for illumination. Next to her bed was an iron nightstand of sorts, which held a cup with water in it and a wooden dish with a large red ruby in the center. Arain's eyes widened as she gazed at the gem. Reaching out, she picked it up with her right hand and brought it closer to her face to inspect it. She marveled at the sheer beauty of the crimson stone. It was roughly three inches long, faceted on all sides, and it came to a point on both ends.

"I made this," she whispered aloud to herself. "Look at that, Timber," she said as she placed the gem in front of him. The massive wolf sniffed the stone and gave it a quick testing lick. It wasn't food, so he lost interest almost immediately. She placed it back into the dish and went over what had happened in her mind.

They attacked me when I fell behind the rest of the convoy while trying to create that ruby. I remember falling from my horse and hitting the cold mud on the ground. Timber was attacking something when I lost consciousness for a moment. Rage, so much rage, is what I felt when I opened my eyes and saw Valin with those two prisoners. Suddenly, a vision flashed in her head so fast she almost missed it. It was of an ogre, the creature she created to rip them apart. A sinister smile crossed her face as she recalled the men being mutilated and eaten. Getting out of bed, she put on some clothes and walked to the entrance to the tent. Timber was right behind her as she pulled back the opening to reveal the ogre standing guard. The giant creature would give any intruder pause. The ogre bowed his head as she approached.

"Your highness," he greeted her in a low grumbly voice with his head still facing the ground.

"Ogre, I am Arain Drake, your creator and master."

"Yes, your highness," he responded.

"Do you have a name, ogre?"

"Yes, your highness, my name is Grumm the Devourer of the Stone Hammer Clan."

Arain paused for a moment, "What do you mean, *clan*? There are more of your kind?"

Grumm raised his head. "Yes, your highness, there are many clans in the Fenrir Mountains."

"I've never heard of this mountain range before. Where is it located?" Arain asked as her interest peaked.

Grumm, still unsure if he should look at her, turned his focus to the muddy ground. "It's far to the west, your highness, off the coast of Tauro."

"You mean past the fog?"

"Yes, your highness," he responded, standing there like a scolded child holding a stone hammer the size of Arain in his right hand.

Arain now paced back and forth in front of the ogre, thinking of what else she wanted to ask. "How many more of you are there in those mountains?" Growing her force was her top priority at the moment and a bunch of ogres would be a fantastic start.

Grumm put a giant hand to his head as he thought. He knew there was more, but his memory wasn't clear enough to give her an accurate number. "I am sorry, your highness, I can't remember the exact number, but less than two hundred, I would say." Looking up at her, he half-expected to be lashed at for giving her these sparse numbers, but she was not angry, just the opposite.

The thought of a hundred-plus ogres in her army pleased her very much. "Go now and fetch Valin for me, Grumm. I have much to discuss with him."

"Yes, your highness," he answered, bowing his head one more time and then heading off to find Valin. His footsteps left large imprints in the soft mud as he walked away.

Arain noticed two guards now stood on either side of the entrance to her living quarters. She went over to the one on the left. "Send for my maids and get us food and wine immediately."

"Yes, your highness." The guard gave a quick nod and was off. Arain went back into her barracks to make adjustments to her plans.

A short time passed before Valin arrived back at her barracks with Grumm in tow. The ogre resumed his position of standing guard outside the front entrance. Valin pulled back the door flap and entered. Inside he could see Arain was sitting at the table eating while Timber lay next to a fresh, empty bowl. "Your highness, you requested my presence?"

Arain chewed a mouthful of food and chased it with some red wine. "Come, Valin, sit with me. We have much to discuss," as she waved him over to the table.

A few strides took him across the room, and he pulled out the second chair and sat down across from her. Valin sat there with his hands on the table. "It has already been quite a start to this campaign, wouldn't you say, Arain?"

She nodded in agreement. "Yes, it most certainly has. How long have we been camped?"

"This would be our second day. My guess is that the miracles you performed yesterday were quite taxing on your body, my queen."

Arain finished the rest of her meal and sat back in her chair. "Yes, I do believe you are correct. I remember being so drained it felt like I was empty inside."

"Well, I must say you look well rested now. Do you feel as recovered as your appearance suggests?"

Arain took a quick assessment of how she felt. "Besides some soreness in the wound areas, I feel stronger than ever!"

Valin was very pleased to hear this. "So, what was it you wished to discuss, Arain?"

Pushing herself away from the table, she stood up and walked over to grab a map that was hanging from the northern wall. The servants cleared off the table and disappeared out the entrance with the dishes. Walking back over to the table, she laid out the map in front of Valin. With a quick motion of her hand, a white glowing orb materialized overhead to light the area. On the large leather map was the entire known landmass of Tauro. Cities, towns, villages, castles, and other key areas were all labeled in beautiful hand-drawn detail. Standing beside Valin, she traced with her finger the approximate location of where they currently camped. To both of their surprise, part of the map drew itself in. The two looked at each other, not entirely sure of what they had just witnessed. Arain stood straight and placed her right hand on her chin while she paced next to the table. She reflected silently. *Is it possible that this new area was the place Grumm had mentioned earlier? The Fenrir Mountains where my army of ogres awaits?* Walking back to the table and standing next to Valin, who was still seated, she could now clearly see an island comprised mostly of mountains with the name *Fenrir* across the top.

Valin, still clearly confused, looked up at Arain. "What do you know of this, my queen?"

"You see that creature standing guard outside my door?" she said, gesturing to the entrance.

"Yes, it is very hard to miss."

Arain went back to pacing and began educating Valin on the recent development. "That creature I call an ogre, and that particular one is named Grumm the Devourer. I spoke with him earlier and he told me he is from one of many clans in the Fenrir Mountains."

Valin looked back at the map for a moment and then back at her. "You said many clans? How many of those ogres did he say lived on this new landmass?"

Arain stepped closer to Valin. "Almost two hundred was Grumm's guess!"

Valin stood up and placed his hands on her shoulders. "My dear, this is splendid news." The gears were turning in his head as he pieced everything together. He removed his hands and walked a few steps away from her. "So, you created the Morlocks back at the citadel, and now these ogres. Does that mean that in creating these creatures, you also created their homeland?"

"I believe that's exactly what my powers allow me to do."

Valin was awestruck at this revelation. "You are the most powerful being on this planet and I am indeed privileged to serve you, my queen." He bowed while speaking these words.

Timber stood up from his spot by the table and moved to his master's side. Arain began laying out the alternative plan to Valin. "You will take Grumm and as many troops as needed to travel west, to Fenrir. I want as many able-bodied ogres as you can muster. I will continue on with the rest of my forces to Castle Kragg and you will rejoin us there."

Valin watched as Arain decisively laid out what she wanted, leaving no room for question of her total control of the situation. Valin again bowed his head. "It will be done, my queen," he intoned, and walked out of the tent to make preparations.

Arain exited the tent after Valin left, intent on speaking with Grumm. "You will go with Valin to Fenrir to gather the ogres. You will listen to his every command as if it were my own, do you understand?"

Grumm picked up his giant stone hammer. "Yes, my queen, it will be done."

"Good, now go get my ogres!"

Grumm, wasting no time, headed off after Valin, leaving only a trail of large footprints in the mud.

Seeing that the ogre had left, the two guards that were normally posted at her door returned and were placed on either side of the entrance. Arain turned to one guard, "Go find Seget and tell him to be mobilized and ready to leave at first light!"

"Yes, your highness," said the guard, and he headed off to Captain Seget's tent to relay the orders.

Arain looked over to Timber. "I think it's time for a nice hot bath," she told him, and the two of them disappeared into the tent. Not long after, her chamber maids had a steaming hot tub filled and were ready for her.

CHAPTER SEVENTEEN

KING MALIK

Two massive wooden doors embellished in gold led into the throne room. They groaned under their own weight as they were pushed open. Inside the large chamber, guards in dark blue plate-mail lined up about every ten feet. They stood silent and motionless, each with a seven-foot glaive in one hand. The butt of the glaives rested on the floor. Burning sconces in the shape of gargoyles adorned the stone and steel chamber, giving off ample light. At the end of the room were wide steps leading up to a platform where a steel throne adorned with human skulls rested. Each skull had a crown of some sort on top of it. A tall, battle-hardened man sat on the throne with a guard on each side. The man, who was in his forties, had long black hair intermixed with the slightest flecks of gray. His face showed various scars from battles past, and his eyes were as gray as the stone of his chamber floors. He wore finely made clothing that was the same dark blue color as that worn by his knights.

A short, slender person cloaked in black approached the throne. As she reached the first of three steps, this person stopped and knelt down on one knee. "Your highness, I have news of the situation to the south." Pulling her hood down, it became clear this person was a female. She had short blonde hair and brown eyes, and her youthful face was partially tattooed.

Malik shifted on his throne to get more comfortable. "Carry on with your report, Gallena, I'm curious to see what happened with my little surprise."

"Yes, your majesty. As you commanded, I took a handful of nomad warriors south to monitor Arain Drake's advance. We watched her until we found an opportunity to attack, and then the nomads went in. I stayed in the distance to observe, as they cleanly struck her with multiple arrows, piercing her flesh. The fatal blow was an arrow clean through the neck, which toppled her from her horse." Gallena paused for a moment.

Malik leaned forward in his seat towards her. "So, she was dispatched easily?"

Gallena looked up to meet his gaze. "No, she lay there in the mud for a few moments as our men approached her corpse, and then a giant gray wolf came out of nowhere, eviscerating two of them quickly. My attention was drawn to her troops that showed up and who quickly engaged the remaining nomads. The moment I looked back, I couldn't believe what I saw. She wasn't dead. The remaining two warriors began fleeing, but were captured and placed on their knees to be executed. Arain propped herself up and in that instant, a huge ghastly creature appeared and ripped those two to shreds!"

Malik stood from his seat and sauntered down to Gallena, who was still down on the knee. Her heart raced. She had never failed an assassination before, and King Malik was not known for tolerating failure. He stopped as he reached her level.

"Stand, Gallena," he ordered. Without a sound, she was on her feet, standing at attention. Malik, with his hands clasped behind his back, circled behind her. "Are you certain she didn't succumb to her wounds?"

"Most certain, sir. I waited a day and a half until I saw her walk out of her barracks uninjured."

Malik stopped on the opposite side of her. "Do you suppose this could be some form of witchcraft or spell?"

Gallena shook her head, "I couldn't say, sir. I have seen nothing like that before. I am ready for whatever punishment you see fit for my failure, my king." Gallena fully expected to be tortured and possibly even put to death.

Malik stood up on the first step in front of her. "There will be no such punishment. Yes, she's not dead, but the information you have brought me is extremely valuable. I want you to go back and observe her. Take care to note every detail and return here the day before they reach the castle."

"Yes, my king, it shall be done," she promised as she pulled her hood back over her head and headed out of the throne room.

Malik called for one of his guards. "Go gather my generals and inform them there is to be a meeting in my war room, now!"

"Yes, King Malik!" the armor-clad man shouted before leaving to fulfill his orders.

Malik sat back in his throne to think for a short while before he headed out a door in the west wall and proceeded to the war chamber. As he neared the entrance, he could already see his generals arriving. Two guards opened the iron doors to the war room and servants entered with food and drink. They placed the food in front of eight seats on a large black iron table in the shape of an octagon. Each of its sides belonged to one general, and at the head was Malik's slightly more lavish chair. It was a wood and iron high-backed chair with lions carved into the front of the armrests and velvet red cushions on the seat and back. There were maps of Tauro and various other cities and villages hanging on the walls. Some were extremely detailed, showing every trail, road, path, river, and any other notable item deemed important. Others just showed the large-scale locations for reference. The room was lit by magical means to prevent the chance of fire damaging the irreplaceable items in the room.

Malik entered and walked around the table to his seat, which was already pulled out by one of the servants. He sat down and moved himself up to the table. A gold plate with some type of game hen sat in the middle, surrounded by potatoes, carrots, and cabbage, all covered in a rich, brown gravy. To his right was a silver pitcher filled with lingal berry wine, as was his shiny silver goblet. On a smaller gold plate, there sat a steaming hot miniature loaf of bread. The room was filled with all the delicious aromas from the hot food.

One by one, his generals arrived and greeted their king before proceeding to their place at the table. There was Corwin, an average-sized old man with white hair and a long white beard. He was the king's master of magic, as indicated by the black robes he wore. Corwin was chosen from the citadel some twenty-five years ago, and now trained the king's mages in the dark arts.

Next was Hortus, who was by far the largest of the generals. He was some six and a half feet tall, broad-shouldered, and muscular. He was a darker-skinned fellow from the southernmost part of the continent. His hair was short and black, and he wore plate mail of a style similar to the rest of the guards.' Hortus was Malik's hand-to-hand specialist. He handled training and oversaw the guards and foot soldiers. Eleven years ago, Malik was conquering the southern regions and made a deal with Hortus. If Hortus won a duel against him, then his village would be left alone, but if he lost, he would be bound to serve Malik for the rest of his life. After a spirited battle, the victor was Malik.

After him was Vermillion, the king's marksman. This fellow was of average height with a sleek build. He had blond hair and wore a brown silk tunic with green leather breeches and a dark green cloak. Vermillion oversaw anything that had to do with ranged combat. Malik recruited him when he was twelve, after the boy had won an archer's contest the king put on fifteen years ago. People from all over Tauro came to compete, but nobody could match Vermillion. It paid handsomely for his parents to sell their son to Malik.

Ori followed after Vermillion sat down. She was a five-foot tall, thin woman with long black hair tied up in a ponytail. She wore all black clothing and a black facial covering that concealed the lower half of her face. This woman was Malik's master of assassins. She trained a select group of soldiers to be spies, saboteurs, and silent killers. Ori was Gallena's older sister. Malik found the two of them abandoned and alone in a nearby village that was razed by an opposing lord at the time some nineteen years ago. Malik had the girls sent to the dark brotherhood to be trained.

Next to arrive was Pogo, the alchemist. This short, pudgy fellow wore an off-white tunic with brown breeches, small round glasses, and a drab cloak. Pogo was completely bald, with only a small white mustache. He was Malik's alchemist and in charge of making all sorts of concoctions from healing potions to explosive weapons. He oversaw the troops responsible for mass producing these items, as well as unleashing them on objectives. Pogo was being taught alchemy in the City of Knowledge when he accidentally blew his instructor up, along with a portion of the laboratory they were in. They cast him out as a failure, but Malik saw he had immense potential and had him brought to his castle to work for him. That was sixteen years ago.

Clink was the next commander to be seated at the table. This man looked quite ordinary, with short brown hair and hazel-colored eyes. He stood just under six feet tall. He was a fair complexioned man with a mustache and short beard. His clothing was simple, an ivory-colored tunic and brown leather breeches. He was the dirtiest of the generals because he was the king's forge. Clink thought up and built many devices used for war, particularly items used to lay siege and destroy protective walls and ramparts. He trained his men to duplicate his creations and use them in battle. Clink was the only general that grew up in the Kragg with Malik. The two had been friends since childhood.

Last to be seated was Yuni, another female general who was built more like a man with a muscular physique. She had long, braided red hair and green eyes. For a woman, she was quite tall, at about six foot two. She wore light plate armor with the sigil of the healing light on the chest. She was Malik's head healer and was responsible for training and commanding all the clerics, healers, and practitioners of white magic in his kingdom. Yuni grew up being trained in the City of Knowledge until she became injured and left for dead during the King Wars some twenty years ago. That was, until Malik found her and brought her back to the Kragg, where she was nursed back to health. After that, she pledged her life to him.

Malik raised his goblet before speaking. "Let us feast before we discuss the business at hand."

All the generals raised their cups and shouted, "To the KING!"

Everyone began eating and conversed throughout dinner. The servants came and went as they removed finished plates and replaced them with full ones. Drink seemed to be brought in by the barrel just to keep up with the consumption. As time passed and bellies filled, the iron table was cleared and cleaned. When the last servant left the room, the guards outside closed the steel doors. Only the eight were allowed in the war room when matters of the kingdom needed to be discussed.

Malik moved back from the dinner table and went over to the map hanging on the wall. He grabbed it down and brought it back to the table, where he laid it out. The parchment stretched almost ten feet across and six feet wide. It was a detailed rendition of the area between the citadel and the Kragg. Every twist and turn of the road was clearly detailed, along with estimated distance and travel time by horse and on foot. It was mostly swamp and tundra, with some hilly regions throughout. Malik then opened an almost-invisible door built into the table in front of him and all the other generals seats. From inside, he pulled out what looked like forged chess pieces about six inches tall. Most were fashioned to represent troop types and defensive structures. Malik placed a black assassin, mage, and cavalry piece to represent four days' distance from his castle. The generals looked on with great interest. Malik stood in front of his chair, placing his palms on the table as he glanced around at each person.

"I have received word that a small yet skilled army is marching on the Kragg as we speak. They should arrive at our outer walls in four days' time."

Hortus was the first to talk. "How many can we expect, sir?"

"At least four hundred, maybe five."

Hortus scoffed, "Four or five hundred! Beg your pardon, sir, but I could take a thousand of my men and destroy them before they get anywhere near the castle!"

Malik cracked a half smile at Hortus. "I think you may be underestimating this threat, General. What they lack in numbers, they make up for in power. You and your men might defeat them, but between the mages and assassins, they would decimate your troops before they engaged their cavalry and foot soldiers. Chances are, the battle would be lost."

It clearly irritated Hortus at the notion of such a small force posing any real threat. He sat silently, with his arms crossed, looking away from Malik.

Corwin placed his hands on the table and focused on the king before asking his own questions. "Do we know who is leading this army and why they would seek to challenge you, my lord?"

Malik sat back down and settled in for a lengthy session. "What I do know, Corwin, is that a young woman by the name of Arain Drake is leading this army, along with her second in command, a black mage called Valin."

Corwin clearly knew the name and almost choked when it was spoken. "Valin from the citadel? Are you sure my lord?" he asked in an uneasy tone.

Malik's gaze now firmly locked on him. "Yes, Corwin, my spies have confirmed that it is indeed him. What do you know of this mage?"

The old mage took a deep breath before answering. "I trained with Valin at the Black Temple, there at the citadel. He was an amazingly gifted fellow with the dark arts and amazingly vicious as well. There were at least three mages that I know of who in some way or another bothered him, and all three met painful deaths. The last fellow was burned to death from the inside out and then hung over the entrance to the temple. Even the instructor at the time was astonished and disturbed at the level of control it would take to do such a thorough job and still be able to recognize the corpse. Valin was also quite fanatical back then, and he kept going on about a vision he had of a person who would someday change the world forever. *A God on Tauro*, I believe, was the term he kept using."

Now Malik was the one who looked uneasy hearing this revelation, and all the generals noticed. Never had they seen their king worried or fearful of anything or anyone.

Ori spoke next. "Do you think it is her, my king?" As she was the master of assassins, she knew everything that Gallena had already relayed to Malik. Malik sat there silently with his hands clasped together in front of him on the cold, iron table.

"What is it?" asked Vermillion.

Malik straightened up in his chair and cleared his throat. "We have had spies reporting back for years now that Valin had a daughter with him at the citadel, and that the number of mages and assassins being trained and kept there were more than tenfold from the norm. I believe Valin thinks that this young woman is in fact that God on Tauro he was speaking of all those years ago, this woman Arain Drake. I have also just recently put this to the test, as I had sent Gallena with a group of nomads to assassinate her."

Yuni, who was sitting to the king's left, spoke up. "So, she's dead then?" she asked, somewhat confused.

"No, Arain took a lethal arrow to the chest and neck and appeared to have been killed, but she was seen alive, well, and fully healed just a day and a half later."

The war room erupted. The generals couldn't believe what they were hearing.

"We can bring no one back from the dead, not even the best healers in Tauro could accomplish this," remarked Yuni. "A necromancer can reanimate corpses, but back to a normal human?" her words trailed off to her own thoughts on the matter.

Malik motioned for the excited crowd to settle back down. "That's not all," said Malik in a tone so cold that everyone looked at each other with concern in their eyes. "It seems she also has the power to create new forms of life at will."

The silence in the room was deafening.

After a moment, Clink spoke, "What are you talking about? Bugs, birds, snakes?"

"Monsters," was the word King Malik uttered. None of the generals spoke, only the king this time. "Monsters like the ones you read about in children's fairy tales. And this particular monster was three times the size of you, Hortus, and it ate the two nomads that were captured during the assassination attempt after it ripped them apart with its bare hands!"

Their meeting continued on for many hours as the eight discussed possible strategies to subdue this woman and obliterate Valin and the army with as few casualties as possible to their own forces. Malik also informed the council that Gallena would be back in a couple of days to report on her observations of Arain Drake's abilities.

It took until the early morning hours of the next day before they all agreed on the best plan of attack. Every strategy had the same thing in common, to separate Arain Drake from her forces and incapacitate her until they figured out how she could be disposed of. As they finished, the iron doors creaked as the guards reopened them so servants could come in and clean, and the generals could leave and brief their legions on what needed to be done before a much-earned rest was taken. Castle Kragg and its outlying city were bustling as everyone prepared for the upcoming battle.

CHAPTER EIGHTEEN

ROAD TO BELROSE

Lucious, Morgan, Selim, and Ulandra walked until they found a place to stop for the night before continuing on to Belrose. Off to the left, there was a group of spruce trees huddled next to a small river. The group inspected the area and agreed this was where they would make camp. The river meandered and trickled along, giving off a very soothing sound. Lucious dropped his pack at the base of the cluster of trees and walked over to inspect how deep the water was. Morgan, as always, was with him. Lucious looked over the bank, and to his surprise saw how deep this little river was. "Would you look at that, Morgan?" he said, gesturing to the crystal-clear depths. "It has to be at least thirty feet to the bottom!"

Morgan peered over the edge as well. "It is beautiful. And look, Lucious, there are fish down there."

Sure enough, just above the river rock, there were the silhouettes of fish. Lucious looked over at Morgan and asked, "How do you suppose we catch them being so far down? I lost all of my fishing poles in the house fire."

Lucious could see Morgan was already figuring things out. "Let's go back and set up camp. I have an idea on how to get those fish."

Lucious had no doubt that Morgan would catch them. The two walked back to the campsite and saw that Selim and Ulandra had already cleared an area on the ground for a small fire and places to sleep. The mated Draconians moved on to gathering branches and sticks for the fire.

Lucious, with his hands on his hips, faced Morgan. "Well, it looks like they have this taken care of. What are you thinking of using to catch dinner?"

Morgan was staring at the trees, looking for something. Finding what she wanted, she looked back at Lucious. With her usual authoritative voice, she gave him his task. "I want you to empty your pack completely, and I will be right back."

With that, she sprang up the closest tree and vanished into the canopy above. Lucious picked his spot and started the chore of emptying everything out as he was told. By the time he had finished, Morgan was back with a long branch from the trees above. With precision, she used her dagger to knock off all the smaller branches until it left her with a straight rod.

"Hand me the sack, Lucious," she requested.

He could see what she had planned as he handed her the empty leather satchel. Morgan took the items over to her pack and pulled out a small ball of thin rope. Next, she lashed his pack to the one end of the long branch so it would open in the current like a basket. Morgan threw the tool over her shoulder and headed back to the river. Selim and Ulandra were just now starting the fire. It would be dark soon, and Lucious hoped they could catch the fish before nightfall. His stomach started to growl in protest. He followed behind her to help as he could.

They arrived back at the river bank and Morgan handed the makeshift net to Lucious to hold on to. Standing there, it shocked him when Morgan began to undress. *What is she doing?* he thought as things became awkward. He looked away as she disrobed and Morgan looked over at him and smiled. It was clear to see he was blushing.

"It's okay, Lucious, you can look," she assured him. Slowly, his head turned towards her, and to his surprise, she was wearing a loincloth and some sort of short undershirt. Morgan stepped closer to him to lay out the plan. "Okay, Lucious, this is what we're going to do. I want you to slowly lower the net behind the biggest fish so as not to startle it. I will go a little way upstream and swim down to them. When you are in position, I will move closer to the fish and when they turn and bolt, they'll swim right into the bag!"

"Got it," he replied, and stepped to the edge to find the biggest one. Morgan turned and headed upriver. A few minutes later, he had the bag opened about two feet behind his prey. Lucious held it steady, as he could see Morgan approaching from the front. Just as she planned, when the fish bolted to run from her, it swam right into the bag. That was when the plan fell apart. The massive fish panicked in the bag and pushed with enough force against it to knock Lucious off balance and into the water. The water was ice cold, shocking his body and causing him to exhale some of his much-needed air. Panic raced through his mind as he tried to fight the current that was pulling him deeper downriver.

He was an excellent swimmer, spending his summers in the river back outside Addleberry, but this was different. He was still wearing all his clothes and the added weight was exhausting him fast. It felt like forever that he was in the ice-cold water. Lucious made it to the surface a few times to catch some air, but was dragged right back under. Bouncing off the rocky bottom, he wound up in an area of calm water. *That's it*, he thought as he sank to the bottom of the pool with his back to the rocks. *I'm so tired and my lungs are burning for more air.* Lucious was in a state of euphoria as his brain starved. In front of him, he could see a woman swimming towards him. *She is so beautiful*, was the last thing he thought when the woman reached him and pressed her lips against his, blowing her air into him. Now he recognized it wasn't some stranger, but Morgan.

She grabbed him by the collar of his tunic and pushed off of the river bottom with such force that his neck snapped forward, causing him to bite his tongue when his chin hit his chest. A moment later, he was on the surface, being dragged to the shore. Lucious coughed and choked from the water he inhaled. Morgan pulled him onto dry land and fell to her knees, breathing heavily. Swimming for two was strenuous, even for her.

"Are . . . you . . . alright . . . ?" she asked in between deep breaths.

Laying there on the smooth river rocks and in between coughs, he replied, "Yes, I think I'll be okay, thank you."

"Are you two alright?" shouted a voice from the distance. Lucious rolled over and looked up to see Selim stopping from a dead run further up the bank. By that time, Morgan was on her feet and breathing normally.

"We're fine, Selim," she replied. "I need you to take Lucious back to camp and put him in front of that fire to warm up." Lucious stood up, shivering, and dripping wet.

"Where are you going?" he asked.

"I still need to catch us dinner. Do not worry. Go with Selim and I'll be back soon." Lucious felt like a fool for being caught off balance like that.

"Sorry, Morgan," was all he said before walking off with Selim.

A splash was all the two heard, and then she was gone. Selim looked over at him as they walked and asked him with a chuckle, "What happened? Did she push you?"

"No, not exactly. I wasn't expecting that massive fish to pull so hard and I fell into the river. The rest you just saw."

"It happens, my king, nothing to be ashamed of. Morgan was there to assist you, thankfully."

"Yes, she once again saved my life, Selim." He looked over to the hulking Draconian by his side. "And its

Lucious, remember, I'm nobody's king."

"As you wish, Lucious," was all Selim replied.

I'm freezing, he thought as nightfall descended upon them and they continued walking. In the distance, he could see the light from a fire up ahead. *I can't believe how far the current took me*, he thought. "Is that our camp, Selim?" he asked through chattering teeth.

"Yes, we should be there in a few minutes. Would you like me to carry you, Lucious?"

"No thanks. I got myself into this situation, so I will walk. Maybe then I will never forget to expect the unexpected!"

Selim nodded. "That is a good rule to live by, I suppose."

Finally, the torturous walk was over and Lucious collapsed as close to the fire as he could get. Steam rose from his clothing as the water evaporated. Ulandra walked over to Lucious with a blanket in hand. "Take off your clothes," she commanded. Reluctantly, he obliged, shielding his more private areas as best he could. Ulandra wrapped the blanket around his shivering body as fast as she could. "Now sit and I will make you some tea."

The only thought Lucious was having now was how he let Morgan down. *I need to get myself together if I have any hopes of living through this adventure.*

"Here you go," said Ulandra as she handed him a metal cup filled with peppermint tea.

"Thank you," Lucious replied as he took the cup in both hands. Lucious drank the hot tea slowly, and soon could feel the blood returning to his extremities. The adrenaline was all used up and the fire, tea, and blanket were warming him nicely. Exhaustion set in and he dozed off right where he sat.

Ulandra sat next to Selim and asked, "I take it he fell in the river?"

Selim, nodding his head, "Yes, apparently lost his balance while trying to help Morgan catch some fish. It took him a ways down river. Luckily, Morgan was with him."

"Do you suppose I should head back out and see if she needs some help?" Ulandra paused for a moment, looking past the fire at a slumped-over, sleeping Lucious.

"No, she prefers to hunt alone. Let her have some fun while we keep him out of trouble." Ulandra nestled closer to her mate and rested her head on one of his muscular, scaly arms. There the two sat across from Lucious for quite some time.

Eventually Morgan appeared from the darkness with a pack full of fish. "Here, you two, let's get these cleaned and cooked. I'm sure we're all starving." Morgan handed the pack of fish to Ulandra and Selim and immediately went over to examine Lucious. Selim began cutting the fish into fillets while his spouse pulled out the cooking pan and placed it over the fire.

Morgan knelt down beside Lucious, who was still sleeping. She reached out a hand to feel his face. *Good, he's nice and warm again,* she thought, *I'll let him sleep until dinner finishes cooking.* She opened her pack and produced some of the food that they had purchased from Edna and Hensey Thwis earlier that day. She used some of that ball of twine, strung it between two of the trees, and began draping his and her wet clothes over it to dry. Once Selim emptied the pack, Morgan took it with a small block of soap and went to the river to clean it.

Lucious, who was sound asleep, was dreaming of his sister again. He could see Arain covered in blood and mud. People were fighting around her and a giant wolf stood atop a man's chest, ripping his guts out. He looked over to see a horrific creature tearing men apart and eating them. A man's head went into its mouth and the crunch startled him awake. Lucious was sitting in the same spot, breathing short, fast breaths. His heart was racing again from fright. It took a moment to get his bearings as to where he was and what was going on. Morgan had just gotten back from washing the pack and hung it alongside their clothing. She walked over to see what was wrong.

"Are you alright?" she asked in her usual nurturing tone. "You look like you've had a nightmare."

Lucious, catching his breath, replied, "Yeah, a nightmare, you could say that. I dreamed of my sister again and this time she had more creatures." Morgan stood quietly and listened. He looked up at her. "They feel so real. With the sounds and the smells, I feel like I'm right there with her."

Morgan squatted close to him and spoke in a soft voice, "Lucious, maybe these dreams are not dreams at all. Maybe they are some sort of vision or link with your twin?"

"You know, you may be right. Maybe we can tap into each other's thoughts and see what's happening."

Morgan stood up and walked over to fix a plate of fish and vegetables for the both of them. The other two Draconians were already sitting down eating next to each other.

"All right, eat up, you'll need to get some strength back," she said as she handed him the plate and a fork. Morgan sat down right next to him, and the two ate dinner together in front of the fire.

"This is some of the best tasting fish I have ever had," Lucious commented in between mouthfuls of food.

Morgan swallowed before speaking, "Yes, Ulandra is an excellent cook. Give her the simplest of ingredients and she can usually make it into something memorable."

Lucious finished his plate and set it on the ground next to him. He pulled his knees in close to his chest, still wrapped in the blanket. "Morgan, I just want to say thanks again for pulling me from the river and for catching the delicious fish. I am in your debt again and I have a gut feeling it won't be the last time you get me out of a dangerous situation." Lucious reached over to the pile of items he had pulled from his pack and found the necklace he had bought from the Thwis merchants. Turning back over to Morgan, he held out the trinket. "This is for you."

Morgan set down her plate and asked, "What is this for, Lucious?"

He thought for a second before he spoke. "When I hopped in the back of the wagon today to purchase those supplies, I saw this and thought it was beautiful. I think someone just as beautiful should wear it." It was hard to tell, but Lucious thought he could see Morgan's delicate facial scales blush.

She looked down for a moment before speaking, when her eyes coming up to meet his. "Thank you, Lucious, I will treasure it always." With the gentlest touch, she took the necklace and put it on.

Lucious just now noticed the clothesline stretched between the trees with his pack on it. "How in the world did you get that back?"

Morgan looked over at the pack, "Oh, that—well, I didn't want you to have to carry all your stuff by hand, and seeing as I asked to use it, it was only right that I get it back for you."

"Was that evil fish still in it?"

Morgan smiled. "That's what we just ate!"

Lucious could feel a certain amount of satisfaction well up inside him, knowing that fish didn't get away. Selim finished the pot of food over the fire and then began the chore of collecting the metal plates and utensils. Then he and Ulandra headed off to wash them in the river, while Morgan and Lucious sat together by the fire, conversing about what was to come.

Chapter Nineteen
KING ELRICK

T he sun shone over the beautiful Westlin castle with its sprawling city reaching out in front and the magnificent glacial lake wrapping around behind it. Lush forests, crystal-clear rivers and lakes were scattered throughout the region. It was a beautiful place ruled by a just and fair king.

It was early morning when a messenger arrived at the castle with urgent news for the king. The messenger, Sebastian, was an average sized man with black hair and beard. He was a younger fellow in his twenties, with gray eyes, and he was King Elrick's newest royal messenger. Sebastian dismounted his horse and handed the reins to one of the caretakers in the courtyard. He hurried off to the castle entrance, carrying an envelope bearing the seal of the Watch. He encountered the guards on duty, who let him pass. The guards knew who Sebastian was, as he frequented this castle regularly and because he wore leather armor with the kingdom's crest of the gryphon on his chest. Through the main hall, he hastened to the throne room.

The craftsmanship of the castle builders was second to none. Beautiful white marble was used for the walls and a special heat-retaining gray rock known as oxite was used for the floors. The king's banners hung throughout the interior, and sconces were placed in just the right areas to give an abundance of light to every room, hall, and corridor of the castle.

Sebastian passed through the two twenty-foot-tall steel black doors as he entered the throne room. A red carpet, edged in gold stripes on both sides, stretched from the entrance to the throne where the king now sat conducting business with his subjects from throughout his kingdom. King Elrick was a handsome man, in his mid-forties, with blue eyes and mid-length golden hair. He was formidable-looking, as he stood well over six feet tall, with a slim muscular build, and he wore a well-made tunic and breeches. His face looked kind and gentle, as was his tone when dealing with his subjects. Elrick looked up briefly from the man he was conversing with to acknowledge Sebastian's arrival. The messenger waiting his turn to have an audience with the king stood off to the side, as he knew full well that Elrick would hear from every person who showed up to seek his counsel before moving on to him.

Patiently, Sebastian stood there as one after another had their turn and left. The last person to speak was an old farmer who requested the king's help with a group of thieves that continued to steal his crops out by the Buskin River, where his farm was located. The king had no love for thieves, so he immediately ordered for patrols at the man's farm to apprehend them. "I will bring them to justice, my good sir," said the king. As the day's business concluded, Elrick stood and proceeded towards Sebastian. The king hugged him.

"Welcome back. It's wonderful to see you safe and in one piece still." The two separated and went about discussing the report from the southwest. "So, Sebastian, what were you able to find out about this new threat?"

Sebastian cleared his throat. "Well, your highness, I have a letter from spy-master, Rulus himself, that he urged me to get to you with all haste." Sebastian handed the sealed letter over to the king.

Elrick's brow raised as he spoke. "This must truly be of great importance if Rulus himself composed this information." He broke the wax seal and began to read of the recent developments across the continent—how some woman had raised a small army from the citadel and was now marching toward castle Kragg. Rumors and whispers were spreading of how this woman is endowed with unimaginable powers. Some were calling her a messiah, while others were calling her a god. Sebastian stood there silently while Elrick read the letter. He had to admit to himself that it was killing him to know what was in that message. Judging by the king's expression, he knew it had to be some very troubling news. Elrick finished reading and looked up at him. "Sebastian, I need you to go gather Generals Cappell, Erin, and Robert. Have them meet me in the dining room in two hours. Once you carry that out, I want you to get rested and resupplied. You will leave in the morning to deliver a message to the Coven of Elders in the City of Knowledge."

"Yes, your majesty, it will be done." Sebastian turned and started heading out of the throne room when he heard Elrick shout to him to stay safe. "Always your majesty," he replied, and went to find General Cappell.

One of the many servants that was always on hand approached Elrick. He turned to face the young girl. "Marrielle, is it?"

"Yes, your majesty, how may I serve you?"

"Marrielle, my dear, please go inform the kitchen that we will be having dinner in the dining hall two hours from now. After that, would you be so kind and fetch me Joan Leetsal, the cartographer, and have her meet me here?"

Marrielle bowed her head, "Yes, your majesty, right away."

"Thank you," was all Elrick said as he went back to sit on his throne and think about the letter. He sat there with the side of his jaw resting on his fist. *What is this woman hoping to accomplish by provoking Malik?* he thought. *Surely this woman's meager forces have little chance of posing any real threat to his sizable military force? Maybe these special powers she has will make the lack of troops not such a disadvantage.* So many more questions came to mind, but none had any suitable answers. The only thing Elrick knew for sure was that this all made him feel very uneasy.

Elrick knew Malik from fighting him during the king wars, when they were both very young and ambitious. Malik wished to seize all of Tauro for himself, and Elrick was the only king left that stood in his way. It was a long war, with both sides having their victories and defeats, but in the end, it was Elrick who nearly killed Malik in their last battle. The defeated king retreated with his armies to where he had started his conquest, at the Kragg. King Elrick tired of the war and captured back half of the continent before ending his campaign. King Malik was a brilliant tactician and an even better swordsman.

Elrick dropped his arm on the armrest of the wooden, ornately carved throne. He shook his head slightly and thought, *this woman is sure going to have her work cut out for her.*

Ms. Joan Leetsal, a short, gray-haired woman, arrived and entered the room. She adjusted her glasses as she walked up to King Elrick, who was still sitting. "You called for me, your majesty?"

"Ahh, yes, Ms. Leetsal. I will be having a get-together in the dining hall tonight and will need to have the most detailed map you have of the west coast of Tauro, as well as one of the entire continent. We will need to examine roadways, paths, and trails, along with distances between areas. Dinner will be in approximately two hours."

Joan was jotting down notes on a piece of parchment as the king spoke. "Very well, King Elrick, I will have them ready and waiting in the dining hall."

The tapping of small feet echoed on the stone floor as Marrielle approached Elrick. "Sorry to bother you, your highness, but Queen Victoria has asked me to let you know that it's time to start getting ready for dinner."

The king stood up from his throne and stretched his arms over his head. His sheer size made Marrielle look like a child. "Thank you, my dear. I suppose I should get cleaned up and ready."

"Yes, your highness," she spoke while bowing her head slightly. Marrielle headed back to the servants' quarters, as her day's work was over and she herself needed to get washed up and fed. Joan went on to her library where she housed all of her work, and King Elrick exited the throne room and headed to his personal quarters.

When he arrived, the door was already open, and the chambermaids were just getting finished setting up his hot bath. Elrick walked into his bedchamber, gave the women a smile, and thanked them. Shortly after, the three women left and closed the door behind them. His room was spacious, with beautifully crafted furniture throughout. A cobblestone fireplace was at the center of the room and could be viewed from both sides. Windows adorned the exterior wall, stretching from the floor to the ceiling. Green velvet drapes hung on them all, bearing the king's emblem in silver stitching. A luxurious bed and wardrobe were also part of his room. It was very much fit for a king, but not so lavish as to be nonfunctional. To the other side of the room was a large copper tub with clawed feet, and he could see the steam rising from the water. A sultry and seductive voice came from over by the bed. "Good evening, my king, would you like to come over here and pleasure your wife?"

Elrick smiled from ear to ear as his eyes focused on his breathtakingly beautiful wife, Victoria, lying nude across the bed. Elrick undressed as he walked over to the bed and said in a playful tone, "My love, it would be an honor to assist you in your time of need."

It had been almost twenty years since the two met, and she still took his breath away every time he saw her. Victoria felt the same way, as the two were deeply and unquestionably in love with each other more and more every day. By the time Elrick reached the bed, the brown-haired, green-eyed woman stood up on her knees to embrace him. The two kissed passionately as their bodies pressed together. The encounter progressed as expected, with each partner touching, kissing, and caressing every inch of the other's body. Climax after climax sent their bodies into pure ecstasy until both lay there sweaty and exhausted.

Victoria looked over at Elrick lying next to her and whispered, "I love you."

Elrick smiled, "I love you, too. Would you like to accompany me for a hot bath before dinner?"

She nodded, and the two washed each other in the large copper tub. For that moment in time, he thought of nothing but his wife, and all other worries faded from his mind. As the two finished and dressed, they headed off to the dining hall to eat and discuss the kingdom's needs with the generals.

Elrick and Victoria arrived at the dining room, walking hand in hand. In front of them was a long rectangular wooden table with ten seats placed around it. Cappell, Erin, and Robert were as punctual as ever and were already sitting, until the king and queen arrived. Then all three stood at attention and a unanimous greeting of "Good evening your grace," with the ceremonious head bowing was displayed.

Elrick moved to the head of the table and Victoria took her seat to his right. "Come, be seated, friends," he said, and gestured to his three generals. They took their seats once again. Elrick could see two maps rolled up like scrolls at the far end of the table. *Joan may be aging, but she's still the best at her craft,* he thought to himself. A male servant stood in the open doorway of the dining hall. Elrick looked over at him, "You may proceed with dinner," was all he needed to say. The man disappeared and returned with three servers and five large plates of food, along with wine by the pitcher. They set a plate in front of each person along with a fork, knife, and spoon. Next came a cart with a roasted pig on top and then another with a decorative serving pot filled with a creamy soup. The room instantly filled with the delicious aromas. One servant filled bowls with the steaming hot cream of beet soup while another distributed them around the table. Crystal goblets filled with salmon berry wine and the roast pig carved and placed on plates with the roasted vegetables. The three servants left, but the male who was in charge of the dinner stayed to cater to those eating. "Let us enjoy this feast, my friends," said the king, and everyone proceeded to eat and converse amongst each other.

Cappell and Robert sat to the left of Elrick, and Erin sat next to Victoria. The two women had grown up together and were close friends. Erin was a sleek and powerful woman, roughly the same height as Victoria. Her silky black hair framed her face nicely, and she had one green and one blue eye. Erin had gone off to the City of Knowledge to be trained in the healing and protection arts, before returning as an adult to find that her childhood friend had married the king. It took little convincing by Victoria to have Elrick enlist Erin into his army. She would continue to train until the day she was promoted to general and was put in charge of all things to do with magic.

Cappell was an older gentleman in his early sixties, with white hair, beard, and mustache. He was almost identical in proportions to the king and was the weapons master that trained Elrick personally. The two had a brotherly kinship, as they had fought side by side in the King Wars. Cappell had saved his king's life more than once. He was the oldest of them, but was still in superb shape from training the king's soldiers in hand-to-hand and ranged combat daily.

Then there was Robert, a young genius that was kicked out of the City of Knowledge for repeatedly making his teachers look like fools. His talents with engineering and alchemy were second to none. He was barely twenty and had enlisted in the king's army when he was sixteen. He was a brown-haired, blue-eyed lanky kid with a knack for pissing everyone off. They had disciplined him more than once for upstaging his commanders. Elrick saw brilliance in this boy, though, and had a one-on-one chat in a dungeon cell one night and agreed to give Robert an outlet for his skills if he could give respect to his commanding officers. Needless to say, Robert did not desire to spend any more time in those cold, dark cells and agreed to the offer. Only a few years later, he moved through the ranks and became the king's third general in charge of teaching and training the blacksmiths, troops, alchemists, and engineers in the kingdom.

The dinner progressed until all in attendance were full. Hastily, the servants removed all the empty plates and goblets along with the leftover food. "Will there be anything else, my lord?" asked the head servant.

"No, thank you, it was a magnificent meal, and the service was top-notch as usual," replied Elrick, and the other guests seconded the notion as well. "You and the kitchen staff are free to do as you please."

"Thank you, my lord," said the man with a nod. "I will be sure to let them know." He wished them all a good evening and without further discussion, the man turned around and left, closing the doors behind him.

"Well now, since that's out of the way, let us get down to the matter at hand." Elrick stood from his seat and produced the letter from Rulus. "This was delivered earlier today by royal messenger, Sebastian, and it is from Spymaster Rulus himself." Elrick stepped from the table and handed Victoria the letter to read. "Pass this amongst yourselves and see if you come to the same conclusion that I have." They took turns reading the letter, and their facial expressions were nearly identical when the word *god* was reached. Elrick walked to the end of the table, where Joan had carefully placed the maps. He picked them both up and walked back to the head of the table, where he spread out the map of the entire known world. They showed exquisite detail in every river, lake, pond, road, town, and so on. Robert was the last to read the message, and folded it back up and set it down in front of him. Elrick used the four weights that Joan left with the maps and placed one at each corner to keep it from rolling back up. Elrick sat back down and moved in his chair. "So, what are your thoughts on this letter?" Clearly everyone was a little shocked at what they just read.

Victoria was the first to speak up. "Do we have any other information about this young woman and her goal?"

"Not yet," replied Elrick, "but I am sending Sebastian out first thing in the morning to deliver this letter, along with one we draft with our questions, tonight."

Robert was next. "They speak of this woman having unimaginable powers, but what do those look like?"

"What you read is all the information I possess on this subject, my friend," Elrick responded. "This move just happened within the last few days. One thing is clear, she is marching on King Malik at Castle Kragg."

Erin dropped her hands on the table and scoffed. "Well, she must have something planned, because they severely outnumber her."

Cappell spoke up. "I agree with Erin. This woman may have some of the most dangerous assassins and mages with her from the citadel, but the power of your soldiers will only get you so far when they're endlessly attacked by swarms of troops."

Elrick nodded in agreement. "We have so little information at this point," he said, with a hint of disgust in his voice. "I think we need to have the Watch monitor and report back daily while the Council of Elders digs into the history of our new antagonist." All around the table nodded in agreement. "Next we need to plan on lines of defense much closer to the neutral lands outside of Malik's territory so the war isn't fought on our doorstep, endangering the innocent people of Westlin."

All of them pored over the maps and pointed out the most likely paths of enemy troop advancement. Distances and times were calculated, along with prime locations for defensive installations to be placed at choke points and other natural advantages. Victoria walked to a bookshelf along the north wall and picked up some blank parchment and some writing implements. Suggestions, questions, probabilities, and every other observation was written down. It was nearly dawn when all the plans were sorted out and the letter to the council was written. Elrick tasked a squire with delivering the sealed letter to Sebastian for delivery. The five of them, exhausted, sat back in their chairs.

Victoria noticed something not quite right on the map in front of them all. It had bugged her all night, but she just couldn't put her finger on it, until now. She stood from her chair and placed her left finger on the map in one place and a right finger on another. "Pardon me, but am I seeing things, or have these two locations never been there before?"

Erin chuckled and leaned forward over the map. "I think your tired eyes may be playing tricks on you, my queen." But after a closer look, she realized she wasn't seeing things. Erin stood up so fast it startled the others as she examined the two points. "What is going on? Those two landmasses never existed. It was that damn impenetrable fog before." The others all looked on in awe.

Elrick spoke. "I wonder if this is one of those god-like powers she is rumored to possess?"

Erin stepped away from the table shaking her head, "No one can do that, not even the most powerful mage in all of Tauro."

Everyone felt the uneasiness settle into the room. No one spoke, but they were all thinking the same thing. *If this woman can do that, what else is she capable of?* Elrick could see the nerve of his general's waver for just the slightest moment. He stood and took charge like he always had. "Do not be dissuaded, my friends. We have faced many difficult obstacles before and this is just that, another obstacle to be dealt with. Let's depart now and put things into motion, then get some rest."

"Yes, your highness," replied the generals before exiting the dining hall.

Victoria hugged Elrick tightly, putting her head on his broad chest. "I fear we are headed for dark times, my love," she said in a sad tone.

Elrick enveloped her in his arms and rubbed her back. "I believe you may be right, my queen!"

CHAPTER TWENTY

VALIN AND GRUMM

Valin and Grumm split off from the main army and headed west towards the coast and the port town of Warwick. The weather continued to be miserable as they, and the handful of troops, slogged down muddy, rain-drenched trade routes on horseback. Everyone was uncomfortable except for Grumm, for he loved the rain and the mud squishing through his hairy, gnarled toes. The sight of him enjoying himself just irritated Valin that much more. At least he could use a simple shield spell to keep the downpour off him. The others were not magic users, so they would have to suffer.

The ogre led the way, like a dog following a scent he instinctively knew pointed the way home. A home he had cloudy memories of and couldn't actually be sure he had been to before. Valin pushed the group all day with no stops. He looked back at the handful of men with him. "If we are to make it to Fenrir and back in time, we will need to push the pace, men!"

The men were committed to their queen and would do whatever it took to ensure she succeeded. "Yes, Lord Valin," the men replied as they continued on with renewed vigor.

On that first day, they only came across merchants heading from Warwick with their wares and that lasted for the briefest of moments as they turned their horses and wagon around at the sight of Grumm. "Hahahaha, did you see the terror on their faces?" laughed Valin aloud.

Grumm gave a deep-toned chuckle. "I was hoping to have a little snack on the road when I saw 'em," he complained.

Valin rode up next to him. "Don't worry, you'll have plenty of humans to eat before all is said and done." Grumm looked over at Valin with the biggest, toothiest, and creepiest smile he had ever seen. The other men looked at each other, concerned. They knew Grumm obeyed Arain, but were not so sure how safe they were if left alone with him. The soldiers would most certainly be sleeping with one eye open tonight.

As they continued on, the daylight faded and night approached. It had been a good, hard ride that day, and Valin finally deemed it time to make camp. They stopped just outside the forest of Abadon and used the tree line for shelter. Valin dismounted his horse and began issuing orders immediately. "You two work on getting us a warm fire to dry out by, and you," he commanded, pointing at the shortest of the group, "take care of the horses. I want them ready for another long day tomorrow. The rest of you, Grumm included, secure the area. Let us not forget this is Malik's land, and I don't think he'll take kindly to us taking it from him."

They fanned off in all directions to scout around where they would sleep that night. In a relatively short time, there was a fire blazing and food being eaten around it. Grumm wiped out the rations in one sitting and was still hungry. Valin noticed he kept eying the horses every so often. He looked at the ogre square in the eyes. "Listen to me very clearly. You are by no means allowed to eat our horses or any of your comrades. Do we understand each other?"

Grumm's only response was a grunt of disappointment. He stood up and wandered off into the darkness, grumbling under his voice. The troops watched him disappear.

"Well, that's disconcerting, that man-eater is out there and we can't see him," one man commented.

Valin was already drifting off to sleep when he spoke. "He will obey . . ."

The troops took turns sleeping while two stood guard at all times. It was a long night for all but Valin and Grumm. Every noise from beyond their sight brought visions of the ogre attacking them. Occasionally, those on guard would see his massive outline in the shadows for the briefest of moments. When the dawn finally approached, the sky lightened and the sun cracked over the horizon. The once-raging fire was now just glowing embers. "Thank goodness it will not be another rainy day," replied the last guard on watch.

Valin roused for the first time all night. He stretched before standing up, and put his blankets back into the pack that his horse would soon be carrying. He looked over at his soldiers, who were getting prepared for the day ahead. They looked tired but didn't complain, as just moving on made them happy. Valin called over to the men and asked where the ogre was. "Not sure," one of them replied. "He never came back last night."

They heard heavy footsteps in the distance, closing in on their location. Grumm emerged from the forest chewing on a horse hind quarter and holding the leg like a stick. As he walked closer, Valin could see fresh wounds on his arms and legs, not to mention a short sword that was still embedded in his left thigh. Grumm stopped in front of the awestruck company as he slurped in the rest of the horse's leg, hoof, and all. The silence was palpable as the ogre crunched away like he was eating a large carrot. With little care, Grumm plucked the sword from his thigh and used it to dislodge some flesh from between his teeth. One soldier emptied his stomach without delay. Valin, on the other hand, was pleased to see the resilience of the creature.

"Well, looks like you found enough to fill that rather enormous stomach of yours," said Valin.

"Yes, Grumm's tummy is full now, so he can make it to Fenrir without starving to death," he replied as he rubbed his distended abdomen.

Valin looked at the sword that the ogre had just used to pick his teeth, it bore the insignia of the house of Malik. "Where did you encounter these men?"

"It was a long walk south," he responded while pointing in that direction. "There was another road with soldiers blocking it like they were expecting someone."

"Indeed, they were Grumm. I think they were waiting for us." Valin questioned him for a few moments longer, trying to ascertain the threat level. "How many would you say there were?"

Grumm put a hand to his chin and scratched while he recalled. "No more than fifteen I'd say, Lord Valin."

"You dispatched fifteen trained soldiers alone and walked away with little more than scratches?"

Grumm nodded his head. "Yup, the first few put up a fight, but once I started crunching on 'em they pretty much walked right into me stomach!"

"Very good, Grumm," was all Valin said, but inside he was absolutely giddy with the sheer gluttony and ferocity these ogres were capable of. *I can't wait to see a few hundred of these things laying waste on the battlefield. It will be glorious*, he thought. "Let's get a move on. We make Warwick before nightfall!"

With that command, they were off, with Grumm in the lead. The ogre could cover ground fast with his wide strides. They traveled deeper into the forest of Abadon. It was quiet in the forest, as no creature big or small dared make a sound when the ogre passed by. The road ahead was clear. The merchant that spotted them yesterday obviously went back to the port town and warned them of the creature heading this way.

Morning turned into afternoon as the group was almost through the forest. Once they reached the other side, it would only be a few hours' travel to reach the town. The clearing was directly ahead of them when Grumm suddenly stopped and sniffed the air. Just as he was about to speak, a crossbow bolt made a *thud* noise as it embedded itself in the right side of his chest.

"It's a trap!" shouted Valin as Malik's troops moved from concealment to attack. Bolts and arrows whistled this way and that, hitting Grumm throughout his body. The ogre barely flinched as he lifted his mighty hammer and rushed into the densest position of troops. With mighty swings, his hammer found its mark on the armor of many foes, making a loud, metallic crushing sound, followed by screams from the recipients. The men with Valin entered the fray.

Missiles of light shot forth from Valin's hand, hitting two enemy soldiers and blowing holes clean through their armor and their chests. They were clearly outnumbered, but the skills of fighting this small group possessed were second to none. The clang of swords hitting metal rang out throughout the forest as the battle continued. Malik's soldiers were taking the brunt of the casualties as some thirty men lay strewn about in various forms of carnage. Two of Valin's troops had succumbed to injuries, while the other three were still in the fight. Grumm was laying waste to victim after victim, but it was clear from the amount of black blood oozing from his wounds and the arrows sticking out of him, that it was only a matter of time before he fell.

A knight arrived on horseback wearing the royal dark blue-plate mail. From beneath his enclosed helmet, he shouted, "Keep up the fight, men, we have them beaten.

King Malik will reward you all handsomely for that creature's head!"

Valin knew this battle had turned and was about to issue a retreat into the forest when, in a fit of rage, Grumm charged the knight. "You want Grumm's head, come and take it!" He closed the distance to the knight quickly as he raised his giant hammer over his head to deliver a fatal blow.

Schwink!! Two massive steel-toothed jaws slammed around Grumm's legs, shattering the bones as he fell forward in a howl of pain. The ogre had not seen the trap buried just in front of the knight. "Ahhh!! You gonna die for this, puny human," he wailed as he tried to pry open the jaws on the massive trap. The royal knight dismounted his horse, and in one quick motion, drove his longsword through the back of Grumm's neck and into his brain. Grumm ceased to move and his arms slumped to the ground. The knight removed the blade with a satisfying sound. King Malik's remaining troops roared in delight that the beast was dead.

Valin knew this was his chance, as he and the remaining three soldiers were all but forgotten for the moment. With a few words and motion of his hands, Valin sent a fireball into the remaining group of soldiers collected around the dead ogre. By the time they realized it, it was too late. The fireball struck them and exploded, sending flames and bodies in all directions. The ones that were not killed instantly were on the ground, writhing in pain as the fire burned them alive. Grumm's belly blew wide open from the impact, and its contents of human and horse body parts spewed out. The knight was pinned by the sheer mass of ogre and flesh that had blown on top of him. The fluids suffocated him as they filled his helmet. Valin walked up to him as he coughed, gagged, and choked on the vile mixture flooding into his mouth and nose.

With the evilest of looks, the only word Valin spoke was, "ENJOY!"

The knight slowly and horribly drowned in the bodily fluids and entrails.

"What do we do now, Lord Valin?" questioned one of his men.

"Whatsoever do you mean? Let's continue on and get what we came for."

"Yes, Lord Valin," replied the remaining three as they gathered up the horses and tended to any wounds as quickly as they could. Within the hour, they were exiting the forest and on their way to Warwick. No further ambushes or traps encumbered them as they arrived in the port town. It was, however, extremely quiet as the residents looked on at the four cut up and bloodied men riding into town. They had seen the town's troops head off that way earlier, but these were not them.

Valin trotted his horse into the town center, where a statue of King Malik stood. He walked his horse in circles around the monument. "To the patrons of Warwick, it is I, Lord Valin," he shouted. "We come to liberate this town in the name of the goddess Arain Drake!" People slowly approached the circle in the center of town where Valin and the monument were located. Valin continued on, "King Malik's troops that were stationed here have all been relieved of duty."

An old merchant with a cane hobbled forward. "You have no business here, begone!" shouted the old man.

Valin snapped his fingers and the man's head exploded, sending bone, flesh, and brain matter into the onlookers. Women and children shrieked in terror as the rest of the body dropped to the ground.

Without so much as a second look, Valin continued. "You are all now in the service of her majesty. Are there any further questions or complaints?" The crowd of merchants, townsfolk, and sailors all fussed about, but offered no rejection.

One dock hand spoke up, "What is it you want, sir?"

Valin walked his horse to the man. In an almost melancholy voice, he replied, "I need a ship!"

CHAPTER TWENTY-ONE
LETTER FOR THE ELDERS

I t was early morning when Sebastian awoke in his small but adequate barrack. Those that served his highness, King Elrick, were given a home to call their own. The higher you progressed in the king's military, or the number of years you served, gradually granted you more lavish residences. The generals all had splendid homes around the castle itself, while they typically housed the new recruits twenty to a barrack. It all worked well as you progressed and moved into something bigger and better, and then someone of lower rank gets promoted and given your old home. Since Sebastian was still at the early stages of his service, the accommodations fit the position.

He rolled out of bed and used the chamber pot to relieve himself. *Now, that's better*, he thought, while he washed his hands in a water bowl on the small table. It was a big day for him, as this would be his first time traveling to the City of Knowledge, and the message he was to deliver was being regarded with the utmost importance. Sebastian had been up late the night before, preparing for the journey. He had gathered needed supplies from the castle storehouse and was just now finishing getting dressed. He placed the two full saddle bags outside the front door. Sebastian could see a squire heading straight for him with a letter in his hand.

"Sir Sebastian?" asked the squire.

"Yes, that is me." The squire handed Sebastian the sealed letter.

"From the king and queen, sir, for your delivery."

"Thank you. Would you go now to the stables and have them bring me my horse?"

"Right away, sir," said the squire as he ran towards the royal stables.

Sebastian placed the letter inside his tunic for safekeeping and walked back into his home. He had just enough time to devour some dried meat and bread before the squire returned with his horse. With one last swallow, breakfast was finished. He strapped on his belt and sword, and headed out of the house, closing the door behind him. Now he could see the squire wasn't alone, there were two of the king's soldiers on horseback following him.

"Here you are, sir," said the squire as he handed over the reins.

"Thank you," was all Sebastian could say before the boy moved on to his next duty. Sebastian looked at the soldiers. He could see one was a woman and a cleric, as she was wearing the traditional light chain mail armor worn by the clerics of the king's army. The other was a larger man with a sword on his hip and a round shield on his back. His armor signified him as a brute, a soldier trained for pure hand-to-hand combat.

The cleric was the first to speak. "Good day. You must be the messenger, Sebastian. King Elrick himself sent us to accompany you to the City of Knowledge. My name is Seline Evenshure and that big brute is my brother and companion, Uluck Evenshure."

Sebastian looked up at the two. "Pleasure to make your acquaintance," he said as he lashed the packs to the saddle and mounted his horse.

"Shall we head off, then?" she said in a stern but soft voice.

Sebastian nodded. "Let's go."

Uluck took the lead as they made their way through the city, heading west. He was a good-sized man, over six feet tall, with short black hair and a scar above his right eye. Seline was about the same height as Sebastian, with long, braided brown hair and blue eyes. These two looked slightly older than him and had most certainly seen battle before. He was used to traveling alone, but some protection on this journey may not be such a terrible thing, he thought. They spent most of the way through the city in awkward silence as Sebastian sized up his new companions. While he was no slouch with a sword, his guess was that either of them would have little trouble defeating him. Uluck's armor had evidence of past damage and repairs, as did his round shield.

"He's seen his share of combat," replied Seline as she rode up next to Sebastian. She had noticed him inspecting her brother. She was also sizing up this messenger, trying to gauge his abilities so that if trouble found them, she would know how much protection he would need.

Sebastian looked to his right where Seline now rode. "What about you? Have you seen much combat?"

Seline had a pretty face, which was even more so when she smiled at him with the reply. "That is why we are both here, messenger."

The rest of the morning passed quickly as they wound through the city streets and onto the main roadway heading west. Now they could pick up the pace, as the road ahead wasn't congested with townsfolk like the city. The three passed farmlands and pastures with animals grazing on the lush grasses. *It was a good day to travel*, thought Sebastian as he looked skyward, seeing a bright blue sky with the occasional cloud and bird flying overhead. They had stopped only once to water their horses at Fantail Lake. Sebastian checked his map during the brief stop. For the first day, they were making pretty good time. He had worked out the distance from Westlin to the City of

Knowledge when he finished packing for the trip the previous night, like he has always done.

Seline walked over to him and looked over his shoulder at the map. "Well, Sebastian, how many days are we looking at?"

"It looks like about four days, including this one, if my calculations are right."

"Is that so? Hmm, what do you think, Uluck?" she shouted over to her brother. "Sebastian figures three more days after today and we'll be to the city!"

"Hahaha," laughed Uluck as he chewed on some dried fish jerky. "Maybe if he grew wings and flew there," he shouted back.

Seline laughed, "You've never actually made this trip, have you?"

Sebastian shook his head. "No, we typically travel from one city to another, delivering and receiving items for the king and queen. My route is from Westlin to Shady Vale and back, which is two days, round trip."

Seline cocked her head to the side. "Well, it looks like your world is about to get a lot bigger on this journey. It will take at least seven days to reach the City of Knowledge, and that's if we have pleasant weather and no interruptions." She walked in front of Sebastian, still holding the map unfolded in his hands, placing a finger well past the upcoming town of Shady Vale.

"This right here, Sebastian, is where the king's forces thin out and some less than lawful individuals begin to show up."

He looked her in the eyes. "King Elrick would never allow thieves and bandits to roam his lands unchecked."

There was that smile again as she stepped away towards her horse. "The king and his men do their best, but it's a big land he possesses, and he doesn't have the body count to cover it all." Seline mounted her horse and looked over to Sebastian, who was putting his map away. "Don't worry, messenger, we have been back and forth to the City of Knowledge plenty of times. We'll keep you and that letter safe." With that, she turned her horse and began following Uluck westward.

Sebastian swallowed hard and mumbled, "Great, this is going to be fun." He was on his horse a moment later, following the siblings.

By the end of the day, the situation was precisely as Seline had suggested. Nothing but a few travelers, merchants, and farmers had been along their path all the way to Shady Vale. Not much else was said during that time either, as Seline and Uluck rode together some twenty feet ahead of him. The town was a decent size, with everything one would need on hand. There was the local smithy that ran the ironworks, as well as merchants of every sort, from food to gems and even an apothecary called *Up in Smoke*. A squat, fat fellow named Trimble Sint owned the place, and he had a bit of everything, from potions to spell books and everything in between. There were three taverns in town to quench one's thirst and get some food, maybe even a room for the night. The best one was the *Feral Fox*. A burly man by the name of Gilliam Crunk owned this establishment, and it was the least sleazy and dirty of the three. Then there was the *Sultry Lass* on the far edge of town. This was a place one could go to find some company for the right price.

King Elrick had a garrison of troops always stationed in Shady Vale, and along with them, housing barracks and stables. They proceeded to the quartermaster first, a woman by the name of Abigail Latear. Sebastian dealt with her frequently, as this was his route. Abigail was often mistaken for a man; her physique was roughly the same as Uluck's. She was a large, muscular woman who could beat every man in her command at arm wrestling. She wasn't a bad-looking woman, and was in her late forties, with gray hair and brown eyes. Sebastian rode ahead to her office and jumped down from his horse. Abigail was already walking from her command room to greet him. Abigail had a thing for the younger, weaker men, as she enjoyed being the dominant partner. As Sebastian turned to face her, she greeted him with a back-cracking, possibly bone-breaking hug. "So good to see you, Sebastian," she said as she practically engulfed the messenger, lifting him off his feet. Her embrace was so tight, he could barely speak.

"Hello, Abigail," he said, with the last bit of air still in his lungs.

"Oh dear, my apologies," she said as she set him back on his feet and released her grip. Seline and Uluck looked on and chuckled at the sight in front of them. "I forget me own strength sometimes when I'm happy to see someone." Abigail had her eye set on Sebastian and as of yet, could not sway the young man. He was the prize that she was determined to win!

Sebastian, now able to catch his breath, began the introductions. "Quartermaster Abigail, these are my traveling companions, Seline Evenshure and her brother Uluck."

Abigail walked in front of the two, who were still on horseback. "Good to meet you. I see you're a cleric of the king, and you look to be one of his elite brute soldiers."

"You have a keen eye, Abigail, that is correct," replied Seline.

Sebastian walked next to Abigail. "If you would be so kind, Ms. Abigail, we need a place to rest for the night before we continue on to the City of Knowledge."

She nodded her head and turned to him with a smile. "Of course, my dear, whatever you three need. We'll get your horses taken care of and your supplies topped off." She leaned in uncomfortably close to Sebastian and spoke in a soft voice, "and maybe later we can get together and discuss what's taking you all the way to that city in my private chambers." The look in her eyes was unsettling.

Sebastian knew that a woman this size could easily overpower him and do what she pleased. For her, the game was just as exciting as the prize.

With a turn, Abigail headed back to her station and commanded two of her subordinates to take care of preparations for them. Two soldiers immediately approached the horses as Seline and Uluck dismounted and grabbed their things. Taking the reins, one soldier guided the horses to the stables to be cleaned and fed. "This way," motioned the other man, and led them to their quarters for the night. It was a small home with two levels. It had the basic amenities, including a kitchen, fireplace, and two bedrooms. The soldier spoke to Sebastian before leaving. "If you can get me a list of the supplies you need, I will see that they arrive before morning. I will also have someone come by and supply you with wood for the fire."

"Thank you," replied Sebastian, and the man exited through the front door.

Seline and Uluck had already dropped their packs and headed upstairs to inspect the rooms. A short while later, two young boys, no more than thirteen, arrived with a cart full of wood. They unloaded it all and even started the fire for them. "Thank you very much," said Sebastian as he handed the boys each a copper for their services. Out the door the boys went, excited that they now had money to buy sweets with. The fire crackled as he stood there smiling at the boys running off with their empty wood cart. His stomach groaned in protest.

"Sounds like we should get some dinner, don't you think?" asked Seline from behind, startling him.

Sebastian turned to face her. "You scared the hell out of me. I didn't even hear you come downstairs."

She smiled. "That's the point, messenger. You get distracted easily and that could get you killed. It would serve you well to be more mindful of your surroundings from now on. So, where should we all dine tonight?" It surprised Sebastian at how quickly she could go from dead serious to lighthearted.

Uluck was walking down the steps at this point. "Nothing for me, I have a date with a certain *Sultry Lass*." A devilish grin was on his face as he strode past the two and headed towards the brothel.

Seline shook her head in disgust. "What a pig!" Any man that had to pay women for sex appalled her, even her own brother. "I suppose you will be off as well," she probed.

Sebastian cocked his head back and put his hands up. "Who, me? What kind of man do you take me for?"

Seline shot him a side look. "Like you've never visited a brothel?" she asked sarcastically.

He shook his head. "No, not once. The notion of paying a complete stranger to pleasure me just feels wrong."

"Hmm, well then I guess you and me will be eating without him."

"That's fine. Why don't we go to the *Feral Fox*? From my experience, it's the best place in town." Selin agreed. "Hold on a moment, I need to leave a list of supplies for the guard when he comes back." Sebastian found some parchment and a coal stick to write with. With her help, he jotted down the few items they needed more of, like dried meat and fruit. "There we are," he said as he set the coal stick down next to the note on the table. The two of them headed out towards the *Feral Fox*, which was a short distance away. The mood seemed somewhat lighter as the two walked. Sebastian was first to strike up a conversation. "So how long have you and your brother been enlisted in the king's army?"

"That has been quite some time," she replied. "We were orphaned when the plague ravaged our village, killing our parents. One of the king's clerics found us when he was trying to aid the dying villagers and he brought us back to Westlin, where we trained from early on to be his majesty's elite warriors. Over twenty years have passed since then."

Seline trailed off, as thinking back dredged up horrible memories, but some good ones as well.

Sebastian could clearly see she was holding back tears as her eyes became glassy. "Are you alright? I didn't mean to pry."

"It's all right. It's all in the past where it belongs."

As they neared the tavern, sounds of music and laughter grew louder in the streets. A sign with a fox foaming at the mouth hung above the entrance doors. Sebastian held the door for Seline, who walked in first. It was a lively place, full of all sorts of people. Soldiers, merchants, and commoners alike were all eating, drinking, and having an enjoyable time together. There were a handful of women walking back and forth, delivering the mead, wine, and whatever else was on the menu to the tables full of people. One such woman walked over to Seline. "There are still a couple of tables in the far back, miss, by the hearth."

"Thank you," replied Seline, and gestured for Sebastian to follow her.

Back through the congested tavern, they walked towards the large stone hearth. Nobody paid much attention to Sebastian, as the royal messenger was fairly frequent in this establishment, but the beautiful cleric was a different story. Many eyes followed her as the two walked to a smaller table in the back and sat down. There was a band of sorts in the opposite corner on a small stage, playing various melodies on their wooden instruments. Occasionally a bard would get up there and tell a tale of times past, or a lark might sing some songs. Tonight, though, it looked as if it would only be the usual band.

The server that met Seline at the door was now walking back to their table. She was a pleasant woman as she greeted them. "Welcome to the *Feral Fox*. Would you like wine or mead tonight, ma'am?"

"I'll have the mead."

"And you, sir?"

"I will have the same."

"For food, we have a corn, cabbage and beef stew or a chicken, carrot, and corn pie," said the server.

Both ordered the chicken pie and with that, she was off to the kitchen to fetch their food. The two sat across from each other enjoying their first chance to relax all day.

"So, messenger, I told you a bit about myself; now, what's your story?" The flickering flames of the fire in the hearth danced off of her face and made her eyes sparkle, giving her a surreal but beautiful look. The server was back as she placed the two tankards of mead on the table, then turned and disappeared back into the crowd.

"Well, I'm afraid my story isn't nearly as exciting or sad as yours," he replied, as he picked up his drink and took a big gulp. "Ahhh, that's good," he commented, setting it back onto the table in front of him. "My siblings and I were born and raised on our family's farm on the outskirts of Westlin, to the East. It was a good childhood, but pretty early on I knew it wasn't what I wanted to do for the rest of my life. So, when I was old enough, I went into Westlin City and joined his majesty's service."

The server came back again and delivered two twelve-inch=round chicken pies with a golden-brown flaky crust. "Thank you," said Sebastian, before she vanished again.

Seline pulled her chair closer to the table and leaned in, taking a deep breath. "This smells divine. I do hope it tastes as good as it smells."

Sebastian pulled his chair in as well. "Trust me, it does. This is what I usually get when I travel here."

Seline, picking up a spoon from the table, began digging in immediately. With the first mouthful, she leaned back in her chair, letting out a sound of pleasure as her eyes closed momentarily. "This is magnificent! This will definitely be on my list of stops next time I travel this way."

Sebastian smiled. "I told you it was good," he said as he took a heaping spoonful of the pie.

After a few minutes of intense enjoyment from the food, Seline sat back in her chair and slammed the entire tankard of ale. Sebastian's eyes were as big as saucers at the sight. He thought to himself, *how is such a well-carried woman able to do that?* He was impressed—that's all there was to it.

"Go on, continue with your story," she urged, now that she was full and slightly buzzed.

"Oh, right, as I was saying, I joined his majesty's service as soon as I reached the age requirement. I made it through all the required basic training and learned how to use a sword, shield, and bow proficiently. Mind you, I wasn't the best or the worst, but I could hold my own. As you are well aware, being in the army as well, the best swordsmen and women went on to be trained more intensely as brutes, like your brother. Meanwhile, others went into more specialist disciplines like marksmen, alchemist, mage and clerics like yourself."

Not to be outdone by her, Sebastian downed the rest of his tankard. Like clockwork, the barmaid was back to clean off the table and refill the mead. Sebastian watched her disappear again. *That woman is a master of her craft.* It was impressive how she was so quick and efficient in her job. He looked back at Seline, who was downing her second full tankard before slamming it back on the table. A moment passed as he looked at the empty drink and back at Seline.

"At that point, I had few options. It was either a guard, soldier, or royal messenger. Being a trustworthy person who wanted to see the world, I became a messenger, and that's what I have been doing for the last few years. Now I finally get my chance to travel and hopefully do some good for my king and this kingdom."

Seline sat there silently in her chair. The second round of drinks were hitting her now. "Thank you for sharing that, Sebastian." Her voice was softer, and she seemed a little less guarded than earlier in the day. Again, the barmaid was back, ready to fill the glasses again.

"No, thank you," he spoke up. "I think we're done for the evening. How much do we owe?" He reached into his right pants pocket, producing silver, copper, and gold coins.

"That'll be two silvers, sir," she replied, and held out her hand for payment.

"Let's see," as he picked through the coins in his palm. "Here you go, one silver, two silver, and two coppers for the excellent service as usual." He placed the coin in her palm and put the rest back in his pocket. The barmaid bowed her head and thanked him for the tip. She grabbed the empty dishes and headed back to the kitchen. Sebastian paced himself as he drank his own glass of mead. He knew they would both be drunk if he downed it as she did, and finding their way back to the house might prove challenging. Sebastian could see Seline was clearly a little more relaxed at this point, and thought it would be a terrific opportunity to find out more about his new companions. "So, Seline, how much combat have you seen in your time as a cleric?"

Her eyes looked up as she tried to think back. "I would have to say over a hundred hand-to-hand battles." Her voice was ever-so-slightly slurring from the drink.

"A hundred!" he exclaimed in awe.

Seline shrugged her shoulders, "I did what I needed to do to protect myself and my kingdom. With my magic, I have healed and protected ten times that amount." In her mind, it was a constant balancing act. She may have taken more than a hundred lives, but had saved a considerable amount more.

He realized she felt bad about killing others, but it was unavoidable to protect the weak and innocent. *That's enough for tonight,* he thought as he finished his drink and stood up from the table. "How about we head home and get some sleep? We have many days to go."

"I agree," she said as she stood up and wobbled just a bit. Sebastian walked over to her and put his arm around her waist to steady her. A faint smell of flowers caught him off-guard. She smelled good, but he kept that to himself for now.

"All right, I've got you. Let's get going."

The couple walked together down lantern lit streets and arrived at the home they were lent for the night. A note was nailed to the door from the quartermaster, Abigail. It read, "To the royal messenger, Sebastian Longfellow. I have finished with my duties for the evening and would like to request you meet me in my personal barracks for dinner and some conversation at seven o'clock tonight. Yours Truly, Abigail Latear." She placed a rather large lip print on the note. He plucked the note down, tearing it from the nail still embedded in the front door. In they went, and he closed the door behind them. The fire started earlier was settled in nicely, with bright red coals and an orange flame rising from them.

"Here we go," Sebastian said, walking Seline over to one of the chairs at the small dining table. He very gently sat her down. The small house was quiet and there were no signs that Uluck had returned. A pile of supplies on the table let him know the soldier had fulfilled his duties. Walking over to the pile of wood by the fireplace, he grabbed a few pieces and placed them onto the coals. The fire greedily flared as it engulfed them. He stood up and brushed his hands off on his breeches. A quick check in his tunic interior chest pocket confirmed the letter was safe. Walking over to Seline, he bent down, putting his arm around her, and helped her to her feet. "All right. What do you say we get you upstairs and into your bed?"

"That sounds like a good idea," Seline mumbled. Now completely intoxicated, the two walked upstairs to the first room. Her mace and armor were neatly placed against the wall on the floor.

"This must be your room."

They walked in and he pulled back the blankets of the modestly sized bed. "Here you go," he said, gently sitting her down on the bed. Next, he removed her boots and placed them next to her other gear. He saw she was wearing a belt with a dagger on the right hip. Reaching in, he undid the buckle and pulled off the weapon. "We can't have you stab yourself while you sleep now, can we?"

"No, that would look bad."

"Okay, that should do," he said, standing there pleased with himself.

Seline stood up close to him and gave him a hug. The smell of her perfume flooded his nose again, and he hugged her back. She released him a minute later, giving him a kiss on the cheek, and whispered, "thank you" as she crawled into bed.

Covering her with the blankets, he asked, "What was that for?"

Her eyes were already closed. "For being a proper gentleman," she whispered, the last word trailing off as she slipped into a peaceful sleep.

He stood back up and put his hand to his left cheek where she had kissed him. Talking to himself, he walked back downstairs. *Well, that was unexpected . . . not unwanted, but definitely unexpected.*

Let's see here, he thought, walking over to the table where the supplies were piled. He conducted a quick inventory of the items before packing them into the packs. *All set.* But looking back at the table, he saw the note he had pulled from the door. It was getting pretty late at this point. *I really hope she doesn't hold this against me,* he thought as he dropped the note into the fire. It turned to black ash seconds later. He hoped Uluck wouldn't be back till morning; as he scanned around the room, he realized there was no other place to sleep but in the second bed. Either that, or he would have a rude awakening when Uluck returned. Taking his chances, Sebastian headed for the other room and was soon fast asleep.

CHAPTER TWENTY-TWO

THE LONG ROAD

Arain Drake and her remaining forces were packing up camp and getting ready to set out for another full day of travel. Tents were packed in wagons, food was inventoried, and the horses were cared for before having their saddles and bridles put back on. Her barracks were always the last to be packed and the first to be unpacked. Arain summoned Commander Seget to her barracks for a briefing, along with three of her generals. Arain's front door was open, and one by one the men entered. "Good morning, my queen," was the first thing each man said while bowing.

The detailed map that she and Valin were previously looking at was hanging on the far wall. "Over here, gentlemen," she ordered as she stood by the map. The soldiers did as they were told.

Seget was the first to speak. "We are ready for your orders, your highness."

"Good, Seget. As you already know, Valin, Grumm, and a few men have broken off to go to the port town of Warwick." As she spoke, she pointed to the map so the men could all follow along. "Once there, Valin and company will secure a ship and sail offshore to the Fenrir Mountains."

Wilson, one of the mage generals, spoke up. "Please forgive the interruption, my queen, but I have never heard of such a place."

Stepping to the side, Arain revealed the new land mass labeled *Fenrir Mountains*. There was some confusion in the room, as this place they never heard of was clearly right in front of them. Arain smiled at the four of them, all of whom were perplexed. "You see, gentlemen, I have learned something as of recent days. You were all witness to that ogre I created, were you not?" The four nodded. "It would seem I have the power to create living and nonliving items with my sheer will. When I create a new sentient creature, I also create its place of origin." The commander and generals were in absolute awe. A few even stood with jaws agape and eyes wide.

Another general by the name of Hestis spoke. "There has never existed a being of such power."

"And yet, here one stands before you," interjected Arain with an irritated tone. Few if any that had scorned her had lived to talk about it.

"My sincerest of apologies, my queen."

"Are there any more interruptions, gentlemen?" she queried, but the look on her face warned against it. No one made the mistake of saying another word. "Good, now back to the map. Valin and company will arrive on this new landmass where there is said to live nearly two hundred ogres!" Arain let that sink in for a moment. The four men were trying to grasp the power that force would add to their ranks. "This horde is loyal to me and me alone. They will then load the ship and bring the lot of them to meet us here at the outskirts of the Kragg. Then gentlemen, we will take control of Malik and his forces."

Seget replied, "In the queen's name, it will be done."

"We will need to make it to the City of Delvin by day's end. Once there, we will claim it as my own." With the meeting concluded, Arain dismissed the commander and generals to relay the information to the troops. "Oh, and Commander Seget, I want to be under way within the next thirty minutes."

"Yes, your majesty," he replied, and off he went.

Arain walked over to her bed where Timber was lying. She sat next to him for a moment, stroking his head. The wolf closed his eyes as it enjoyed the attention. A group of soldiers stood outside the entrance to her tent. "Pardon the interruption, your highness, but all other camp structures are stowed and ready to go. May we begin with your personal quarters?"

"You may. Looks like it's time to go, Timber."

The wolf rose to his feet and stretched with a yawn wide enough to easily fit a man's head inside. The group of troops flooded into her quarters and began carefully packing its contents. Arain and Timber walked from the tent to find a woman soldier holding the reins to her prepared horse.

"Your majesty," the woman replied as she handed Arain the reins. Taking them, she quickly mounted the horse and headed out after her army, which was already lining up and beginning the long march to Devlin. It looked as if it was going to be a better day for travel, as the sky was overcast, but no rain had fallen. The column of troops followed the road as it wound around Horseshoe Lake. Arain was letting her horse lead while she focused on making her new abilities work. Seget appointed ten of her best soldiers to encircle her as she rode. They would not let their queen be ambushed again. Timber, as usual, was here and there looking for anything out of the ordinary, but was never too far from his master. Arain spent all of her attention on trying to figure out the trigger that unleashed her new gift. When she created the Morlocks and the ogre, she was feeling tremendous rage. She knew for sure that rage was a major part of it, but those levels she was at when the creation occurred were not very common. Of course, she got irritated and even angry at times, but that all-consuming hate and rage . . . her thoughts trailed off.

Smack!! She slapped at the relentless mosquitoes and biting flies that were thick around the lakeshore. The summer heat and humidity from the previous rains only exacerbated the discomfort. The assault on her areas of exposed flesh was constant. It was then that a pine wasp buried its inch long stinger into the back of her neck. Arain shrieked in pain, trying to dislodge the attacker. The surrounding men weren't sure what was happening. Her blood was boiling, as her gauntlets kept her from being able to reach the wasp that was repeatedly stabbing the nape of her neck. She yelled at the top of her lungs as flames exploded from her in all directions. The surrounding troops were all blown off their horses. Arain opened her eyes to find herself kneeling on the ground with charred remains of her horse scattered around her. Quickly, she pulled off her right gauntlet and checked to see if the insect was still there. There was nothing on her neck now. In fact, there weren't any bugs around her at all. She did, however, feel her plate armor, which was hot. The guards rushed to her side as soon as they regained their senses, but she was already on her feet.

One man handed her a cloth. "Your majesty, your nose is bleeding," he informed her. Arain took the white cloth and placed it on her face. A moment later, she pulled it away and could now see it soaked crimson red.

"Are you all right, my queen?" inquired another guard.

"I am fine, but I will need another horse," she replied, looking down at the remains of hers.

"Right away, your majesty," said the man, and then he was off to meet the approaching column that contained the extra horses and all the supplies needed for the campaign.

Arain, quite drained at the moment, made sure not to show any weakness to the men she commanded. She also had this very unusual sound in her ears, like bubbles popping. It wasn't just her hearing this, either. She followed the sound to the edge of the lake, as did the troops that were present. "What is that, my queen?" asked one of the men.

Out in the middle of the large lake, the surface roiled about like a kettle of boiling water over a raging fire. "I think we're all about to find out," she responded. Soldiers unsheathed their weapons and stood ready for whatever was approaching. The appointed guard closest to her placed a hand on her arm and suggested she move back for protection. Before she could respond, a tongue shot from the lake in front of them and snatched the man off his feet, dragging him into the water. In one fluid motion, he disappeared. The water churned about in the location the man went in, and its blue color turned bright red with blood. Everyone started backing away from the shore. All but Arain.

Slowly, a green-skinned, slime-covered humanoid being emerged from the bloody cloud in the water in front of her. This creature had similarities to a horned toad, but it was the size of a grown man. It made a clicking noise of sorts as its wide-open mouth revealed several rows of needle-like teeth. Bits of the guard's flesh were still stuck in between them. The clicking continued as it stood just feet from her. Arain cocked her head as she stared into the black eyes of the beast. It held a golden trident in its right hand. Dark-colored horns ran from its head to its tail. The larger horns were seven to eight inches long and were on its head. The closer they got to the tail, the smaller they became. A low growl came from Timber, who was now at Arain's side. The creature turned its gaze to the giant wolf.

"No," Arain commanded with such a stern tone she startled some of the troops. Timber backed down and lowered his lips to cover its teeth. The creature looked back to Arain as if waiting. After a few moments of looking into those eyes, the beast submerged back into the water. Arain turned away and walked over to her fresh horse, mounting it. "Let's move." Everyone sheathed their weapons and did as commanded. Arain looked down at Timber, "You can go boy, I will be safe." Timber understood his master was in no danger and continued his patrol.

The now nine guards encircled her. "You can go as well, I have new protection." Before the lead guard could object, row after row of those creatures emerged from the lake with tridents in hand.

"Very well, my queen," they agreed, and continued on to catch up to the rest of the troops. With a crack of the reins, Arain's horse walked. The legion of lake creatures filed in around her and followed. Lastly, the supply convoy continued on behind them. Her forces had almost doubled in size when these web-footed frog men joined the ranks. Arain couldn't help but grin as she looked around at the new troops. It was about all she could do as she noticed the creation caused immense fatigue. *I more than likely can't do that more than once until my strength returns,* she thought. It was a powerful gift, but for a time after, it exacted a heavy toll, rendering her almost useless. *This is a price I am willing to pay repeatedly* . . . She dozed in and out of sleep the rest of the day. It proved difficult to get proper sleep and rest on the back of a horse, but it was all she could get for now.

Reaching into one of her saddlebags, she produced a small cube of cheese and some dried meat. Not only did the act of creation exhaust her, it made her famished. Arain slowly ate the meal as she looked again at her frog men. The occasional slime-covered tongue snapped out at lightning quick speed to capture enormous amounts of those damned biting insects. She then noticed that since their arrival, not one of those biters even made it close to her. Arain also noticed that the one she first encountered was much larger than the rest, as were his horns. Even his trident was more ornate. *That one must be the species' king of sorts*, she thought. *I will make him a general in my army, no one except for me is KING.*

She could slowly feel her strength returning, but was all but sure it wouldn't be until the following day that she felt back to normal. Walking along, she thought back to when she was staring into that creature's eyes. She swore the two were talking, but the more she thought about it, she realized she never opened her mouth. *Was it all communicated in my mind?* she wondered. This was certainly something new, and yet another thing she needed to examine and learn about. "Am I able to communicate with all my living creations if not by mouth, then with my mind?" she whispered to herself. *I'm way too tired to think about this right now,* and with that thought, she tried to just rest.

It was just before nightfall when they arrived within sight of the City of Devlin. This city was fairly open, with farmlands on all sides. A road led out in all four directions for commerce to arrive and leave to King Malik's other cities. There was a stone wall around the entire city at least ten feet high and gates at the four entrances. Commander Seget and the bulk of the army arrived first and immediately sent out assassins and mages to scout the area.

"I want a defensive perimeter laid down by the mages and a sweep for traps so we may set up camp when the supply carts arrive," Seget, atop his horse, barked the orders that his generals passed down along the ranks. A group of black mages worked their magic, laying down the barrier that would warn them of approaching enemy forces during the night.

Shortly after, Arain arrived with the rest of the forces and the supplies. She turned and addressed the men. "Set up camp in this location. We stay here tonight and take the city in the morning." Arain located the frog soldier leader and stared into his eyes, connecting their minds. "What is your name, warrior?"

She could hear him reply, "I am head of the Krillox warriors, and my name is Glub Widegrin, your majesty. What will you have us do, my queen?"

"Glub, you will instruct the rest of the Krillox to assist with the setup of the camp as needed, and by no means are any of you to eat your comrades!"

"As you command, my queen." Glub looked away and relayed the orders through various loud clicks and gurgles. The mass of Krillox warriors soon began communicating the message to one another. They spread out and dispersed among the humans to assist them. With limited communication, the human soldiers primarily used the warriors for muscle, having them move tents to various locations for setup.

"Glub, come with me," instructed Arain, and the two walked over to where Seget was standing, surveying the city ahead. There was a definite uneasiness between the humans and the Krillox. Despite this, they were all devoted to the queen and her goal. Putting the awkwardness aside, the two races continued on working.

"Commander Seget, what can you tell me?" queried Arain as she stood beside him with Glub.

"Well, your majesty," he began to say, until he turned to her and saw the frog-like creature.

"Go on, Commander!"

"Right, sorry, your highness. The mages have set up the defensive wall and the assassins have swept the surrounding area for traps. A few mages have also gone out and are looking for magical wards or traps that may be in our path. The city looks well-protected, with stone walls on all sides and four iron portcullises, one at each of the entrances."

Arain looked out at the city. "What about enemy forces, numbers, classes?"

Seget stood there at attention. "Still gathering those estimates as we speak, my queen."

"Very good, Seget, as expected," came her reply. "What do you say we have a closer look at our opposition, Commander?" Arain turned back towards the city and waved her hand as if tracing in midair as she spoke two magical words. She closed her eyes. A small blue sphere now hung directly over the center of the town, hundreds of feet in the air. Arain moved her hand this way and that, causing the sphere to move. She had cast a sphere of scrying and was now looking directly down at the city. Arain relayed to Seget what she was seeing.

"They lined the walls with about sixty archers, fifteen on each wall. It looks quite busy in town, with people closing their homes and hiding inside. On the northeastern corner, there is a considerably sized military structure with soldiers flowing in and out repeatedly. I would estimate another hundred soldiers, possibly some cavalry mixed in. Most likely, this is the command post and barracks. To the northwest corner is a mix of mages from different disciplines. They also have six constructs . . . earth golems, from the looks of them." Arain opened her eyes, and the sphere vanished. "There you are, Commander. We attack at first light!"

"Yes, my queen. I will draw up a plan and have it to you shortly."

"By the way, Commander, this is General Glub, our newest addition to my forces."

Seget looked at the Krillox in awe and extended a hand in greeting. Glub followed the gesture and did the same in response. Seget shook his cold, slimy hand but showed no evidence of how repulsed he really was. When Arain and Glub departed, he quickly and vigorously wiped his hand on his armor, trying to remove the slime.

General Hestis approached Seget and looked on as Arain and Glub walked away. Hestis looked over to Seget and asked, "Is that what the guards were ranting about earlier, Commander?"

"Yes, Hestis, that is General Glub, a Krillox warrior."

"A what, Commander?" Hestis asked in shock.

"You heard me, General. We may as well get used to the fact that this campaign is only going to get stranger by the day."

Hestis nodded in agreement. "I think you're right, sir. I would like to inform you that the barrier is set and we have found no signs of traps or wards of any kind."

"Very good, General. Let me know when the war tent is set up so we can plan the attack at dawn."

"Will do, sir," replied Hestis as he headed off into the sea of troops.

By the time night descended, the camp was set, and guards were positioned on a rotating watch. The commander, four generals, and Arain all met in the war tent to go over the plans. A rectangular table with a map of the city was sprawled out across it. They placed designated pieces on the map to signify friendly and enemy troop locations. Seget led the briefing and laid out the sequence of the attack. Everyone agreed until the area of the six golems came up. Leaning on the table, Seget looked around at those seated. "What do we know about these things?" he questioned. "Weaknesses and strengths, preferably, we need to know how to destroy them."

However, nobody at the table had ever battled against one golem, let alone six.

Arain was the first to speak up. "We all know this would surely be a question for Valin if he were here, but in his stead, I will handle them. They are little more than dirt and sand driven by magic."

The men were not as confident. They had heard the stories of ancient wars where golems of all kinds laid waste to massive forces before finally being destroyed. They also knew that their queen was not to be underestimated.

"Very well, the constructs will be left up to you, my queen," answered Seget. Arain, through the whole briefing, was relaying the plans to Glub for him to inform the Krillox troops.

Arain was the first to leave her seat. "Good night, gentlemen. I will see you all on the battlefield tomorrow." It took every last ounce of energy to make it back to her tent and strip off her armor before she passed out on the bed with Timber by her side.

CHAPTER TWENTY-THREE

BELROSE

L ucious woke up next to the smoldering fire with Morgan beside him. He laid there, not wanting to wake her as he examined every detail of her beautiful face. Her hair draped over her cheek as she slept. She was clutching something in her curled-up hand that was lying on her chest. *Must be the pendant and the necklace I gave her last night*, he thought. Lucious continued to watch her as she lay there peacefully. All that swimming must have exhausted her, Morgan was usually pushing *him* to get up by now. Selim must have been on last watch, as Lucious noticed him walking back from the river. When Lucious looked back at Morgan, her crystal blue eyes stared back.

"Good morning," he greeted her.

She smiled wide and replied in kind, "Good morning, Lucious. How did you sleep?"

"Great, actually. I was so tired, full, and warm that I didn't wake once."

"That is good. I think today we should skip the swimming, though," she commented with a laugh.

Lucious chuckled to himself. "Yeah, no more swimming for a while. I take it you slept pretty good too?"

"Yes, and I didn't wake once."

The two of them could hear Selim and Ulandra cooking breakfast. "You two gonna get up or sleep the entire day away?" asked Selim.

Lucious sat up and stretched. "Ouch!" He grimaced in pain as his joints cracked.

Morgan, who was getting up as well, voiced concern. "Are you all right?"

"Yeah, I'm just very sore from all that exercise yesterday. I'll be fine once I get moving." Lucious flipped his blanket away to get up and then realized he had never gotten dressed. "Ahhh!" he screamed, trying to cover himself again.

Morgan, shocked at the sight, quickly turned away. A sudden flush of warmth swept over her face. *I must be blushing*, she thought.

"Umm, Morgan, would you be so kind and hand me my clothes from the line?"

"Sure."

She walked over to the line, pulled the clothes down, and passed them to Lucious. As quickly as he could manage, he dressed under the blanket. Morgan, in the meantime, had packed her gear back into her pack and was getting breakfast from the pot on the fire for Lucious and her. By the time she walked back over with the plates, Lucious was already up and fully clothed this time.

I can't believe that just happened, Lucious thought to himself while he rolled up the blanket and latched it to his pack. Morgan handed him a bowl of soup Ulandra had made with some of the leftover dried fish. "Thank you," as he took the bowl from her. As usual, the soup was wonderful, and in no time, only empty dishes remained. They were cleaned and packed away once they finished. Before they headed out, they extinguished the fire with the leftover dishwater.

The group traveled as they had been, with Selim and Ulandra out front and Morgan and Lucious a little further behind. It was another warm, sunny day for travel, with very few clouds in the light blue sky. It was, however, windier today, which helped keep them cool under the scorching sun. They only traveled a short distance before reaching a stone bridge that arched over the river. Lucious looked over at Morgan. "If we come back this way, we should fish from the bridge and maybe use some proper fishing poles."

"It would certainly be much drier."

Lucious was already thinking of the town of Belrose that they should easily reach today. "Morgan, do you think you can change into a human again?"

"I believe it shouldn't be much of a problem. Why?"

"I just think it might be best when we get into town so we don't draw any undue attention to ourselves."

"Yes, it would be wise," she concurred.

He felt ashamed at having to ask her to hide who she truly was. "I hope that someday soon the world will know of the Draconian race, and that we may coexist without prejudice."

Morgan reflected on what he was saying before she replied. "I hope that as well, Lucious, but change may not be such an easy thing for some."

Nodding, he agreed. "It is common for other races to distrust one another." Lucious grabbed her arm and gently pulled her to stop and face him. "I promise you, Morgan, I will make this world safe for all, or I will die trying."

"I know, Lucious," she answered, placing a hand on his face. "But let us hope the latter is not required." Her touch was delicate, even though her fingers were tipped by sharp nails that could probably kill him.

They continued onward, discussing their arrival in Belrose. "Do you think Selim and Ulandra could disguise themselves as well?"

"My guess is that all Draconians should be able to shift to a human form."

"Can you ask them, and if not, maybe teach them how to do it?"

"I will do what I can," she replied as she picked up her pace to catch the two in front of them. Morgan relayed the request and told the two what the plan was once reaching the town. Selim, Ulandra, and Morgan spent the rest of the morning walk perfecting the skill of transformation. Ulandra changed into a woman with fiery red hair and pale green eyes, while Selim looked like a muscular blacksmith, with short brown hair and brown eyes.

Watching this happen in front of him, Lucious thought how surreal it was. *I don't think that will ever get old, seeing them do that,* he thought. Their change was so spot on that he could find no flaw that would alert someone that anything was out of the ordinary.

Their plan was set, and each one knew what had to be done. Lucious and Morgan would work on purchasing horses along with saddles and bags, while Selim and Ulandra would procure extra supplies to fill them with. As far as Lucious had been told, there wouldn't be a town after Belrose and before the outer City of Westlin. There might be two-or three more-days' travel between the two. The small party of adventurers encountered a few merchants and farmers traveling the same road, with nothing more than a smile and nod exchanged in passing. Everything was working out well for a change, the Draconians seamlessly blended in with the humans.

It was midday by the time Belrose came into view in front of them. The four were walking much closer together now as they reached the town. A short wall was around the town for protection and at the front gate stood two guards watching for trouble as people came and went. The guards wore light mail armor with the king's crest of the gryphon on the chest plate. Each one held a long spear in one hand and a round shield in the other. The guards eyed them as they walked by, but saw nothing of concern. They were more than likely interested in the size of Selim. Few men boasted his height and muscular build. Once inside the gates, the four stopped to the side while Lucious produced his pouch of coins. "Here you go," he said as he handed Ulandra a few coppers and silvers. "We will meet you two at the north entrance when you're done." Then Morgan and Lucious were off to find the stables.

Belrose was a quaint town, used mainly as a hub between the southern cities and villages and the massive City of Westlin. Rows of stands lined the main roadway through town. Fruits, vegetables, eggs, and other consumables were on display for sale. A blacksmith hammered away on his anvil, forming what looked like horseshoes. Children laughed and played in the street while a dog or cat occasionally strolled by or slept in the sun. A few more of the king's soldiers were in town for protection. They were only present to ward off any would-be thieves more than any real threat.

The odor of manure was easy to follow, and Lucious and Morgan soon found the stables. A man in his fifties was grooming an all-black horse with a brush as he talked to the animal. Two younger men around the same age as Lucious were shoveling manure and stocking the hay. Lucious cleared his throat to get the older fellow's attention. The man continued to brush the horse as he asked, "What do you need?"

"We are looking to purchase four of your horses, along with saddles and bags, sir," conveyed Lucious.

Still brushing, the man said, "Well, that's not going to be cheap, son."

Morgan spoke up, and that caused the man to stop stroking the horse's tail. "Sir, how much will that cost us?"

She now had his full attention.

"Well, well," he said as he put down the brush on a bench and walked over to get a closer look at this beautiful young woman. "I always was a sucker for a pretty face," said the man, standing before her. Lucious felt like this stable owner had completely forgotten he was even there.

Morgan asked again, "So how much for what he asked?" clearly referring to Lucious.

"Oh, right," the stable owner replied, looking toward Lucious. "Lemme see, you're looking at a gold piece for each horse saddled with bags."

That was expensive, Lucious thought as he opened his coin pouch. Luckily for him, Ezra had placed a fair amount of money in the bag. He produced four golden coins with the king's stamp on them. "Here you are. One, two, three, and four," he said as he placed four gold pieces in the stable owner's outstretched hand. "Oh, and here," he added, producing a silver piece to go along with the gold. "We have a rather heavy fellow with us, so we need one of them to be your biggest."

The man nodded in agreement and whistled loudly. The two young men dropped what they were doing and ran up like obedient dogs. He instructed his sons on what they needed and which horses were to be sold. "Have them ready to go and deliver them to this couple."

"Yes, sir," they answered, and then they were off doing as instructed.

The man turned back to Morgan. "It will be at least an hour until everything is ready. How about I treat you to some lunch?"

His intentions were clear, but Morgan declined with not so much as a thought on the offer. "Let's go, Lucious," she commanded, and they walked away to find something to eat.

Meanwhile, Ulandra and Selim were moving from merchant to merchant, gathering what they needed. Both playfully kidded around, with the occasional exchange of an intimate touch. At one point, while Selim was bartering with a woman over some apples, a confident young fellow approached Ulandra, enchanted with her beauty. "Good day, my lady, I couldn't help but notice you from across the way."

"Oh really, kind sir, I would suggest you go back from where you came."

"I can't leave until I know the name of someone so beautiful," the man retorted with a chivalrous bow.

By now, Selim had made his purchase and had walked up behind her. The would-be suitor looked back up and saw him towering over him. Fear was all that came to mind, and he excused himself abruptly.

"Is that guy bothering you?" Ulandra turned and pulled Selim down to her level and kissed him passionately.

"No, my love, he was just apologizing for being in my way."

With a sultry smile, she turned and continued shopping. Selim didn't leave her side again while they finished their task.

Lucious and Morgan found the local tavern and stopped in for some food and drink. *The Horny Goat* was written on the sign with a carved picture of a horned goat. They walked in and sat down at a small table off to the side. It wasn't busy at this time of day. The tavern owner, an average-looking older man, walked over from behind the bar. "We have a fresh batch of spice-weed ale, or a lighter brickle berry wine. For food there's bread, cheese, and a beef stew," he told them. Lucious ordered the spice-weed ale, as did Morgan, along with the beef stew. "Coming right up," said the bartender, heading to the kitchen.

Morgan sat back in the wooden chair. "It feels good to get off our feet, does it not?"

"Yeah, it almost feels normal today . . . just the two of us sitting here, having something to eat."

"Yes, indeed. We should enjoy the pleasant times when they occur," replied Morgan.

The bartender returned, placing the two mugs on the table. They were filled to the top with the ale. With his other hand, he set down the bowls of beef stew. From his apron, he produced two metal spoons and placed one by each bowl. "There you go. Now, if you two need anything else, just walk over to the bar and give me a shout. My name is Cooth, and during the afternoon I'm the only one working."

Cooth finished his service, and then disappeared back behind the bar and into the kitchen to continue preparations for the dinner rush.

Morgan and Lucious dug into the thick, meaty stew. They had burned through breakfast hours ago and were hungry. It was delicious and reminded Lucious of the meals his father would make. The spice-weed tasted like cinnamon, with a nutty aftertaste.

"Do you like it?" asked Lucious, between swallowing and taking another mouthful.

"Yes, very much so. I have never had anything quite like this ale before."

The two of them continued to eat and drink while they waited to go back for the horses. Lucious thought now would be a suitable time to find out some more about his companions. He finished the last bite and sat back, pleased, with a full stomach. "Morgan, what can you tell me about your homeland?"

She paused and thought about it while finishing her stew. "From what I can remember, it is a beautiful green and lush place with warm weather year-round and beautiful silver-colored sandy beaches. It does, however, rain a lot, which helps the bright green moss grow everywhere. We Draconians call it the Emerald Isle."

"Wow, that sounds like a beautiful place. When we finish with the quest, I would very much like to go back there with you someday."

"I would like that very much also, Lucious."

"Do the Draconians have long lifespans, and if I may be so bold, how old are you?"

She smiled at the question. "I do not know how long we live. From what I can remember, we are all mostly young adults just entering the part of life where we start mating and reproducing. I am that age as well, about eighteen."

"That sort of makes sense," he said as he leaned forward on the table with his elbows. "A new species would need to be sexually mature in order to have a good starting point for growth."

"It seems your gifts are even more powerful than first thought, Lucious," answered Morgan.

Cooth walked back over to the table. "Would you two like anything else? A refill on the ale, maybe?"

Morgan spoke up. "Thank you, but no, we must be on our way."

"How much for the meal, Cooth?" asked Lucious.

"That will be one silver and eight coppers, please."

Lucious pulled two silvers from his pouch and placed them on the table. "Thanks, Cooth, for the excellent meal," he said, and the two of them got up to leave. They walked towards the stables to check on the progress. When they arrived, they could see the two boys strapping the last sack to one of the horses.

"Here you go, sir, and thank you for your business," announced one son.

"You're very welcome and thank you for such fine steeds," Lucious replied.

The two boys hurried off to complete their other chores.

Morgan and Lucious, with two horses each, walked to the north entrance as planned. Selim and Ulandra were there, gossiping and eating bright red apples. Lucious handed the reins of the biggest horse of the four to Selim. It was a large, silver-haired steed. Selim gave the rest of the apple to the horse, who snatched it up and crunched away happily. The women each picked their preferred horse. Morgan's was brown with white spots and Ulandra's was almost entirely white, with a big black spot around its right eye.

"That leaves you and me, buddy," Lucious said to the pure black one that the stable owner had been brushing when they arrived.

After the introductions, they placed all the supplies they purchased into the bags. It was time to get moving, they still had a few hours before nightfall. Everyone mounted their horses and out the north gate they went, leaving Belrose behind.

CHAPTER TWENTY-FOUR
FENRIR MOUNTAINS

V alin and his three subordinates were busy using the village healer to treat the wounds they had suffered in the previous battle. Then the mayor of Warwick walked in. He was a weasely looking fellow. He was small and thin, standing about five feet tall, and he wore square spectacles at the end of his long, pointy nose. His attire was that of a man in office who was hired for his smarts and not his physical prowess. "Good evening to you, Mr. Valin, sir. My name is Leo Bishop. How may I assist you?"

Valin was sitting in a chair and getting a cut on his left arm tended to, leisurely chewing on a green pear. "Mr. Bishop, where are we with the ship I requested?"

Leo was obviously nervous after the exploding head incident earlier in the town square. "I have the dock workers unloading the last bit of cargo from our largest ship as we speak."

"Good," replied Valin as he tossed the core of the pear on the floor. "Let's make sure there is plenty of food and water on board for a few hundred souls." He leaned forward towards Leo and looked him square in the eyes. "And Leo, it's Lord Valin. Let's not forget that."

Leo was visibly shaking in fear. "Yes, Lord Valin. I will notify you when the ship is ready."

"You are dismissed, Mr. Bishop, and take these soldiers with you. Their wounds have already been treated, so I would like them to oversee the progress of the ship."

Leo couldn't get out of there quickly enough. He headed to the port master to relay the orders.

The ship was a massive wood and steel work of art. Three large, round masts towered above the top deck, some sixty feet in the air. A lion with its teeth bared adorned the bow. There were multiple levels below deck. Portholes were evenly spaced around the ship for fresh air. They designated the second level for storage from mid-ship aft. Mid-ship forward was the captain and first mate's quarters, which were quite lavish, especially for being on a ship. The third deck was intended for crew quarters and storage. No one on the ship had their own room except for the captain and his first mate, so they composed these living quarters of racks from ceiling to floor, with beds stacked four high. They filled the fourth level with benches and long oars used to propel the ship if winds were not adequate alone. The fifth and final level was for food storage, as it was well below the waterline and would keep perishables cold. There was no weaponry to speak of on this ship besides spears and swords. King Malik made it a point to always have the first mate be a trained and tested battle mage for defense if the need ever arose. Naval battles were nonexistent, as there was no way to reach enemy waters. The fog only allowed ships to travel one hundred yards from shore at the most. Between King Malik and King Elrick's provinces were extremely shallow, rocky reefs that only a small fishing boat could navigate without sinking.

Valin was all patched up and proceeded to the docks to have a look. When he arrived, he could see the Fenrir Mountains far in the distance, rising from where the fog once was. He stood there, exhilarated at the thought of seeing the army of ogres he was to enlist soon. One of his soldiers approached. "Lord Valin, all the cargo is unloaded and they are beginning to load the provisions."

"Very good," Valin spoke without taking his gaze off of the distant mountain range. "Send the captain to me, along with his first mate."

"Yes, Lord Valin." The soldier wasted no time locating them.

A gray-haired older man approached with a tall blond-haired woman in red mage's garb and a long wooden staff in one hand. "My lord," spoke the captain, "my name is Kander Faulk, and this is my first mate, Talia Fin." Both of them bowed with the introduction. "How may we be of service?"

"Captain, do you see those mountains out there?"

"Yes, my lord, the fog parted a day or so ago and they appeared."

"As soon as the ship is loaded, that will be our first destination," Valin informed the captain.

"Very well, sir, is there anything else?"

"Yes, there is, actually. We will use this ship to transport a powerful force to attack your former king. Will there be a problem fulfilling this duty?"

Kander looked to Talia for a moment before facing Valin again. He had heard of what happened in the town square, and figured he liked his head where it was. "No problem, Lord Valin."

Stepping past Kander, Valin stood in front of Talia. He locked eyes with her as if sizing up her abilities. Her hazel eyes met his gaze. "There will be no problem, my lord."

"Good, very good. You may proceed with your duties," instructed Valin. Talia and Kander took their leave.

Talia did not fear this black mage like Kander did, but she knew he wielded considerable power. She was one of the gifted, as well as being able to use magic with ease, requiring just her words and hand gestures to cast spells. Her demeanor was more curious. Things were changing in the world, as evidenced by the new landmass, and she was borderline excited to see what else was going to change in the future. *This Valin fellow is connected to it all,* she thought to herself as the two of them returned to the ship.

Within an hour's time, the crew was all aboard, and they released the boat from the pier. They kept the sails stowed, as the wind was blowing in the wrong direction for westward travel. One by one, the long wooden oars protruded from both sides of the ship. With coordinated pulls on the oars by the many men below deck, the ship started to glide through the water. Captain Kander stood on the fly-bridge, as did Talia, Valin, his soldiers and a handful of deckhands. One deckhand was manning the large, steel spoke wheel used to steer. Kander barked orders to his crew as the ship sped along into uncharted waters. "I want all eyes on the sea, men! Not once have I ever struck the bottom, or lost a ship, and today will not be the first time."

All along the bow and forward sections were deckhands leaning over the sides looking for shallow water or rocky outcroppings. Today the sea was smooth as glass, and the large vessel effortlessly glided through the water. The only disturbance was from the water cresting off the bow as the ship split through it.

The air on the sea was crisp and clean, thought Valin as he inhaled deeply. He hadn't been on the water since he was a child. It was a time long ago, when he wasn't a powerful mage, but just a little boy who enjoyed fishing out on the lake with his father. It was a happier time, and for a moment, Valin's hard demeanor lowered. He could see it as clear as the deck he was standing on. They were a happy, loving family until one day when he was being punished for hurting the neighbor's child in a game of roughhouse. Valin, in a tantrum, released a magical wave of energy that killed his father. "I didn't mean to," he spoke under his breath, and his eyes began to water. The sadness he felt was quickly replaced with hatred towards his family who cast him out for being a freak. People who used magic were usually feared and misunderstood. He could still feel so much pain mixed with equal amounts of rage in his heart. He begged and pleaded to be forgiven, but instead he was shunned and told to go to the City of Knowledge, where his kind belonged. Before his father was even buried, Valin was gone. After that incident, his mother soon lost touch with reality. Her one true love had been murdered by her son. Her descent into heartbreak and eventual madness caused her to take her own life within the year. Valin was mistreated and abused, as he was picked up by slave traders to be sold. It was common then for orphans and the homeless to be taken and sold for whatever their new owners desired. Some were for labor and others used for more sexual purposes. It took some time as the slave caravan traveled from city to city, selling its wares, before Valin could recreate the power he wielded that fateful day. When he had his chance, Valin used the same energy that killed his father to implode one of the slaver's skulls so he could escape. After that, he reached the fabled city, where he spent the rest of his childhood training.

Valin snapped back to the present as Talia approached. "Lord Valin," she greeted him, "we should arrive at the island within the hour. The captain is taking it slow until we get a gauge on the depth ahead."

Valin turned to her. "I leave the matter of seamanship to you and the captain, my dear," was all he said before moving to the captain's quarters to have a meal before their arrival.

As the ship rowed ever closer, the sheer size of the island took shape. Tall, snow-covered mountains encircled most of the perimeter of the island, and the beach was covered with black volcanic sand. In the bowl of the mountain range, there were lush green trees and grass on smaller hills. Seagulls could be heard now as they scoured the shallows and tide pools for anything edible. The ship progressed closer and closer. Now structures could be seen on the beaches up against the tree line. They were large tents made from the resources on the island. About a hundred yards from shore, the call came out from one deckhand on the bow. "Bottom in view, captain!"

Quickly, Kander gave the signal for an all stop and then yelled, "Drop the anchors!" Within seconds, two hatches opened on the bow of the ship and two large anchors attached by two-foot links were released with a crash into the water below. The masses of steel raced each other to reach the ocean floor. "Lower the larders," Kander shouted as he handed off command duties to Talia.

Walking briskly, Kander went to give Valin the update. Just at that moment, he could see Valin exiting the captain's chambers. "Lord Valin, we are anchored and the shore boats are in the water awaiting your command to go ashore."

The excitement on the ship was palpable, with the black mage being the most elated of all. On the top deck, Valin relayed his orders to the crew that would be heading ashore. "Captain, I need you to stay on the ship while myself and Talia head to shore. I will lead the first boat and all others will come when I give the order. By no means is anyone to speak but me, and do not wander off. The indigenous creatures enjoy human flesh." The oarsmen and the boat lead all swallowed heavily as they looked at one another. Being eaten alive was not on any of the crews' wish list today.

The ten smaller boats were manned and set off for the beach ahead. Valin could clearly see creatures resembling the deceased Grumm wandering about. The structures they could see from the ship were indeed homes, and a carved statue of a figure twice the size of an ogre stood with what looked like a sword and shield in hand. *It is strange*, he thought, *unless this monument is to a great ogre leader of some sort.* The sound of wood on sand resonated as the boat pushed up onto the shore.

Wasting no time, Valin jumped off onto the fine black sand and began walking towards the monument. In front of him, he could see no less than ten Grumm-sized ogres walking toward him, garbed in animal skins, and carrying large sized weapons. The men on the first boat pulled it farther on shore so the tide wouldn't pull it back out. They were petrified at the sight in front of them and were praying silently to make it out of there alive. Valin reached the monument and inspected it with awe. Someone exquisitely chiseled the detail into what must have once been an enormous rock on the beach. He recognized who this was a depiction of and smiled a wide, evil smile.

By now, the group of ogres had encircled Valin as he continued examining the sculpture. He paid them no attention while he did so. The biggest ogre of the group wore a headpiece similar to a crown. The fact that this little creature in black ignored his presence enraged him. With a crude stone hammer some ten feet long, the chieftain swung it down onto Valin.

*Boom!! Crack!! T*he hammer exploded, sending shards of stone flying in all directions. The force of the explosion sent everyone around Valin flying. The ogres were stunned, and some were even unconscious. Valin, done with his examination of the statue, walked over to the chieftain, who was lying flat on his back, sunken into the sand. He stood up on the massive ogre's chest and looked down at the still dazed chieftain.

"I am Lord Valin, and you and your ogre brethren are to assemble for war immediately!"

"I take orders from no man, human," barked back the chieftain.

"The orders are not mine alone, they were given to me by the goddess, Arain Drake." The ogre could see he was pointing at the statue. The chieftain's look immediately turned from one of defiance to obedience. Valin stepped off his chest and with arms raised, addressed the amassing group of ogres. "Arain Drake has sent me on a mission to gather her devotees and bring them to her so that this land can be cleansed and rebuilt in her image!"

The throngs of ogres spoke amongst themselves for a moment until, one after one, they knelt to their goddess. The sight was unreal. He looked out over the mass of those pledging their lives to the will of Arain. He looked back at the boats waiting just offshore and gave them the signal to land on the beach.

Still down on one knee, the head ogre spoke. "I am Chieftain Adlin Bonecrusher. What does the goddess will of me?"

"Rise, Bonecrusher, and call forth every able-bodied ogre on this island. Spread the word that their creator calls them to battle. Prepare yourselves and load onto the boats with haste."

Valin stood there, watching as the crowd dispersed to do as he commanded. Adlin stayed behind for a moment to speak with him. "My lord, the other clans are in the forests and up on the mountains. It will take some time to assemble them all. We will use the signal horns and send out messengers immediately."

Valin looked up at Adlin. "Do what is needed and be quick about it. And one more thing, Adlin. Make sure all those that are to travel know that their human comrades are not to be eaten!"

"Yes, my lord," said Adlin, and with that he commanded certain ogres to head out and others to get on the horns. Within minutes, the first boatload of ogres was on their way to the ship. Because of their size and weight, the small larder boats could carry only four or five ogres at a time. The men labored as they rowed the boats back. Boat after boat landed on the beach before heading back to the ship to unload. Soon the loud wails of the signal horns could be heard echoing through the mountains. Ogres lined up as more appeared from the forest, replacing the ones that had already departed. Valin watched on as the process continued throughout the day and into the night. During the night, they replaced the human men rowing the boats with one ogre, as exhaustion began to set in.

Captain Kander made the call to have his crew get some rest while the loading continued. Kander barked orders to the few men that were still working to distribute the massive reserves of food and drink that they were carrying. Kander stood there on the top deck, where the ogres were amassing. The sight before him was disturbing in every sense of the word. His location gave him an upfront and personal view of these creatures. They were the ugliest things he had ever seen, and the smell was even worse. The enormous ship began to lower deeper and deeper into the water as the deck filled with them.

Talia had come back with the last group and was assisting with instructing the ogres where to go. "This is unbelievable," Talia remarked as she walked over to the captain. "Bet you never imagined this in your wildest dreams."

Kander stared out into the crowd. "My dreams? No, more like nightmares!"

"Indeed, captain, I would not wish to meet these creatures in battle."

"Talia, why don't you try to get some rest. I will oversee the rest of the loading."

"Very well, captain, I will retire." Talia had turned and begun heading for the stairs down to her room when a fight broke out between two ogres. The others on deck cheered on at the entertainment. *I guess I better handle this before they destroy the ship*, she thought. With haste, Talia approached to find one ogre smashing another ogre's head into the center ship mast. Splinters of wood were breaking off from the mighty impacts. As she reached them, she uttered the words, "Allum! Sacrum!" while she pointed her staff at the aggressor.

In mid-swing, an ogre was encased in a solid block of ice. The cheering crowd stopped and looked at the ogre frozen before them. Talia proceeded to the center of the crowd. "I will not tolerate this behavior on my ship! Do I make myself clear?" Her tone and focus left no doubt that she was serious.

Clap, clap, clap, rang out from behind her. She turned to find Valin standing there, smiling, and clapping at the performance.

"Well done, my dear. It's good to see you handle yourself well." Valin stopped clapping and put his staff back into his right hand as he walked up to the frozen ogre. "I think it's important to have order as well, Talia, but I like to know for certain that my point has sunk in. Illunum."

His final word incinerated the two combatants where they were, leaving only two piles of ash within a pool of water. With no further discussion, Valin walked over to the captain. "I have been told we will be here a few more hours, Kander. Once everyone is aboard, I want to be on our way to the city of Kragg." Without waiting for a response, Valin headed off below deck to rest in the captain's quarters. "What an amazing day" were the last words Kander heard before the black mage was gone.

Talia was still standing there, looking down at the piles of ash as the breeze gently blew them away like they never existed. *Never in my life have I seen such a cold and calculated person as that man,* she thought. *No thought, no care, no emotion, just total, and utter conviction in his deeds. I will certainly be more cautious around him.* Talia, seeing the commotion now finished, went back to her room for some much-needed sleep.

The remaining few hours of night went by, and Adlin Bonecrusher was the last ogre to board the ship. The larder boats were hoisted up and stored for the journey. Captain

Kander gave the order to wake the men and pull the anchors. As dawn approached, the ship, with its new cargo, turned about and headed toward the city of Kragg. The wind had picked up overnight, and it was now at their backs.

"Hoist the sails!" bellowed the captain as the deckhands scurried through the crowd of ogres to reach the ropes and pulleys used for the job. Up and up, they went as they hoisted the three dark blue rectangular sails into place. The fabric of the sails made a sound as they filled with the wind, like the noise one hears when shaking out laundry before hanging it out to dry. The ship lunged forward with newfound speed. Oars were now stowed, and the ports were closed. Kander knew from his years of sailing these waters that the three-day trip to the Kragg would be little more than a day if the wind continued at this rate. *The sooner the better,* he thought, as he wanted to be rid of these creatures as soon as possible.

CHAPTER TWENTY-FIVE
THE SWEEP OF DEVLIN

T he night hours were beginning to wane, giving way to morning. Arain Drake's soldiers were busy preparing for the assault on the city of Devlin. Arain and Commander Seget had just finished a final morning briefing before he rushed off to relay the information to his generals. The men and women, both human and Krillox, were all excited for the coming battle. Glub had his commands from the queen, and the Krillox knew their part.

Arain strolled from her tent, carefree with Timber beside her. "Can you feel that, boy?" she asked him. Arain often had conversations with her closest friend and ally, even though they were pretty much one-sided. "The smell of the crisp morning air and the sweet stench of complete and utter victory! The first of King Malik's cities is about to fall!"

A fresh dew was forming on the fields of grass between them and the city. It gave the ground a shimmering look as the sun crested the horizon. From what she had seen the day before, the forces protecting the city were insignificant. News of her army's approach may have made it to King Malik, but not in time to send out his massive armies to intervene. In row after row, her soldiers fell into their designated formations as the generals rode their horses, giving words of encouragement to them. Commander Seget, General Glum, and Arain all stood in the forefront. With Arain's lead, the army marched forward, toward the city's southern gates. As she had described the previous day, there were archers lining the walls, but this time there were foot soldiers and earth golems there as well. Still, her army of black and green approached. On they went, till they were just outside of the archer's range. Arain raised a hand, and the advance stopped. She alone approached the gate with Timber. The archers on the walls notched arrows and waited for the command to fire. The commander in charge of the defense of Delvin shouted out, "Who dares to threaten his majesty's city?"

Arain stopped advancing halfway between her forces and the city. She was well within the range of all the archers on the south wall. "It is I, the goddess Arain Drake, here to purge this land of all who stand in my way. This will be your only chance to surrender and kneel to your new ruler, or be cleared away like mud from my boot!"

The troops, along with the commander on the wall, laughed wholeheartedly. A moment passed as the commander thought about what craziness this woman was spouting. "Fire," was his response, and they unleashed a rain of arrows at the two of them. Arain Drake smiled widely and their fate was sealed. The arrows slammed into an invisible wall, ricocheting in every direction. A small ball of blue shot forth from an outstretched finger and exploded over the city. A dark blue haze floated in the air above. The soldiers looked skyward, wondering what it was. As the city commander looked back to mock her, his head caved in and his neck snapped with such force his body was flung clear off the wall and landed on the ground in front of her. With a satisfying thud, the man lay lifeless, hemorrhaging blood everywhere. The golems atop the walls began laying waste to the troops. Bodies flew in all directions as the constructs turned on their comrades. Arain began laughing loudly when the gates to the city swung wide open. She turned and gave the signal for the Krillox to advance. The guttural noises that came from the frog men were eerie, and they began bounding towards the walls, closing the distance amazingly fast. When they reached the walls in a wave, they sprang over the barriers and landed in the courtyard below.

Arain gave a nod to Seget, signaling their advancement through the open gates. The battle was short and precise, with the enemy's spirits broken quickly. Once the Krillox engaged the troops on the ground, a bloodbath ensued. Pink-colored tongues snapped out left and right, pulling whatever they stuck to back to the gaping jaws that awaited. Screams of horror rang out as they ripped off body parts with ease. What paltry forces remained threw down their weapons and surrendered. Arain and Timber strolled into the courtyard without a care. The ground was stained red from the carnage. Seget sent out the command to gather all the townspeople and whatever remaining soldiers they found. They were to be brought to the courtyard at once.

Stepping over a pile of entrails, Arain reached the throng of Krillox that surrounded the prisoners. They parted on her arrival to allow her access to them. Fifty or sixty soldiers were on their knees before her. Some were archers, while the others were foot soldiers. Three of the six mages knelt in the back. The other three had been killed. Arain saw them and relayed her approval for a job well done.

"Come forth, my faithful, and be rejoined with us," she commanded. The rest of the prisoners were confused. Slowly walking back and forth, she let them in on the secret. "My father, Lord Valin, in preparation for this day over eighteen years ago, had placed saboteurs throughout the lands in every town, village, and city. So, when the time came, they could wreak havoc from within." The six golems lumbered into the courtyard and waited for their next command. "You thought they would be your saviors, but instead they brought your doom."

One soldier in the front row was shaking as he asked a question. "Wha-what are you going to do with us?"

"Me?" she responded, almost offended. "I won't be doing anything to you. To show me your worth, I will spare the twenty souls out of the lot that kill the others. Unless you prefer, I let my Krillox warriors continue feeding?"

The petrified soldiers looked at the gaping maws surrounding them. Bits of flesh and the occasional piece of armor graced row upon row of teeth. Without needing further incentive, the soldiers brutally began slaughtering one another. One by one, the bodies dropped until only twenty soldiers remained. Blood-covered and injured, they knelt before her and pledged their lives to the goddess. Arain looked across the courtyard at Seget, who was still on his horse. "They're all yours, commander!"

A nod to the waiting frog men signaled the go ahead to consume the mortally wounded that did not make the cut. Arain looked entertained as she strode over to the gathering of townsfolk.

"Citizens of Devlin, welcome to your future! King Malik has forsaken you and left all of you for dead. I am not here to kill you, I am here to liberate you into my kingdom. If there are any among you who do not wish to be in my kingdom, please see my green-skinned friends to my right." Arain stepped aside with an outstretched arm pointed towards the feasting Krillox. The sights and sounds were horrific. It was no surprise that all the townsfolk bowed a head and bent a knee. She surveyed her subjects. "Good. Now who will watch over this city for me while I am gone?" Arain walked over to an older woman with hair that was beginning to gray. "Rise. What is your name, my dear?"

"Bella Munet, my queen," she responded in a quivering voice.

"You will take care of my city, Bella, will you not?"

"Yes, my queen, I will do as you command."

Arain leaned in close. "I know you will, my dear," she said as she shot a side glance at the carnage. She stepped back and addressed the crowd. "Bella must approve everything that happens in this town. Her authority is absolute! After I liberate the capital, I will send troops to fortify the city. Until then, clean this place up and show me you deserve the town I allow you to dwell in." Arain signaled Seget, who trotted over on his mount. "We're done here. Let us be underway quickly."

"Yes, my queen, right away." The commander was off shouting orders to the troops and generals. Before midday, they were on the march again, leaving Devlin far behind.

CHAPTER TWENTY-SIX
TIME FOR PRACTICE

The next few days, Lucious, Morgan, Selim, and Ulandra traveled without incident or problem. They were enjoying the speed and the lack of sore feet, thanks to the horses. Lucious and Morgan had spent a lot of time talking mostly about Lucious' earliest memories, the childhood he knew growing up with Ezra, and learning how to wield magic. Morgan had no recollection of a childhood, as she did not have one. Lucious had a few nagging questions to ask and now seemed like a suitable time.

"So, Morgan, do you have someone back in your village?" Lucious asked.

She looked over at him, not quite sure what he was referring to.

Lucious gestured up to Selim and Ulandra. "Someone like Selim, perhaps?"

"You mean a mate?"

"Um, well, yes, a mate," he replied as he stumbled on his own tongue. He had almost no experience interacting with the opposite sex since most of his time was spent learning magic and tending the farm.

Morgan was quiet for a few minutes before she shook her head. "No, I do not believe there is anybody paired to me back in Ruuk."

"Is that the name of your village?" he asked. This was the first time he had heard that name.

"Ruuk is the name of both the landmass and village where all Draconians live."

"I'm sure it's a lovely place. Well, I guess I better spend some time on figuring out this power. It's not going to be much help if I don't learn my abilities."

"I will leave you be then, Lucious," she said, and began to ride up to the others.

"No, Morgan," he called to her. "I would like you to be with me while I practice."

Sworn to obey her creator, she agreed to stay by his side while he worked. Truth be told, she didn't want to ever leave his side, for the two had begun developing a connection.

Lucious recalled the state he was in for the first creation. With his eyes closed, his mind searched the memory, looking for clues to solve this riddle. *What was I feeling at that precise moment the Morlocks were killing me?* Reliving the hellish situation was horrible. *It hurt so bad as those claws ripped into my back,* he thought. *I screamed in pain and tears were flowing down my face uncontrollably. I felt so helpless and futile as I attempted to get up, but I didn't have the strength to help myself. I remember screaming "help me," and then it all goes black.* With a jolt, Lucious opened his eyes to feel the wetness streaming down his cheeks. Tears flowed without end as he felt a knot in his stomach and a burning around his head.

Morgan pulled her horse close and set a hand on his shoulder. "Lucious, are you all right?" she asked, monitoring his condition. His nose was running, but the tears stopped falling and his heartbeat slowed to a more normal rhythm. Morgan was concerned and caressed his head. His hair moved to reveal the glowing ring of glyphs that were burned into his flesh. Her head cocked back in surprise and she ran a finger over the marks. "Lucious, have these marks always done that?"

"Those were burned into my skin when the powers were first awakened."

"But do they usually glow?"

"What?"

He reached a hand to his forehead and felt the runes extremely hot to the touch. The glow gradually faded before Morgan's eyes.

"They stopped," she said as she retracted her hand.

Lucious quickly wiped his eyes and nose. *I must look like a scared child,* he thought.

Morgan, with a tender look, could tell he felt lost. In the most caring tone, she comforted him. "It will all be okay, Lucious, I am here for you."

Taking a deep breath, Lucious raised his head and stared at her. "Thank you, Morgan, I am grateful for a friend like you." Lucious felt tired but calm now as they continued on. Morgan called for setting up camp earlier that evening when there was at least another full hour of riding until the sun reached the horizon. She did it for Lucious, knowing full well he was done for the day, but his pride wouldn't let him show it.

That night was quieter than the rest. Lucious went right to sleep, not even eating dinner. Morgan, ever watchful, was at his side with her arm around him. Gently, she brushed his hair with her hand. The other two Draconians walked over to her and sat down, concerned as well.

"Is he okay?" asked Selim, trying to whisper as best as he could.

Morgan smiled back at him. "He'll be fine. These gifts he has are powerful, but to use them is hard on the body, that's all."

"Ulandra and I will split the watch, you stay with him."

Morgan nodded. "Thank you."

It was amazing how such an intimidating creature could be so kind. Ulandra figured she had better get to sleep, for she knew how quick her half of the watch would come. Morgan stayed awake for a while, but eventually succumbed to exhaustion and drifted off into a deep slumber.

Lucious was dreaming about everything the past week had brought. It was like watching a movie of his life, and every move played out in front of him. He could even see the things he wasn't present for, like the last moments between Ezra and the Morlocks as the house exploded into flame. Now he was over the village of Ruuk, a bustling settlement of hundreds of Draconians going about their daily business. It was a beautiful place, with leafy palm trees and arid sandy beaches surrounded by the clear blue ocean. After a quick flash, Lucious was standing and watching from a distance as strangers peppered his sister with arrows and she died, only to be resurrected to create the abomination she referred to as an ogre. A moment later, he stood by a lake as hideous frog-like creatures began marching from its depths. Lucious then felt a hand on his shoulder and a familiar voice in his ear. "I'm coming for you, brother!"

Lucious' eyes opened wide, and he was thankful to be back with his friends. Looking around, he could see the campfire smoldering with wisps of smoke rising from the coals. His head laid on Morgan's lap, while her hand rested on his head. Her smell filled the air, and it comforted him. As much as Lucious wanted this moment to last, he knew he must make haste and reach King Elrick to inform him of what was coming. He gently sat up, trying to not wake Morgan.

"How are you feeling, Lucious?" Looking up with a smile on his face, he could see she was already awake.

"I'm feeling much better, thanks to you."

"I'm glad I could help." The smile quickly faded, replaced with a look of concern.

"I have seen my sister, and it is not good." Getting up, Lucious lent a hand to Morgan, assisting her up as well.

"Thanks," she replied, as her legs were a little stiff from not moving from that sitting position all night.

Lucious and Morgan went to sit next to the others, and he began sharing what he had seen. "Arain is quickly growing stronger. As you know, she has the same gift as I do, but is using it to amass an army of horrific creatures. Morlocks, ogres, and now bipedal toad-like creatures she created just yesterday, are all at her command. When she overthrows King Malik and heads this way to claim Westlin, there will be no stopping her."

The news hit the group hard, with concern mirrored on everyone's face.

Morgan's demeanor changed instantly, and she took charge of the situation. "We need to pick up the pace, and now!" She pointed to Selim and Ulandra. "You two get the horses ready to go. Lucious and I will get the camp packed up. I want to be on the move in ten minutes."

There were no objections as they all went to work. Five minutes later, they were heading out, eating a cold breakfast while they rode. Morgan was now leading with the others in the rear. The pace was brisk, with minimal stops only to rest the horses. They had no warm meals until they made camp. That only happened when the sun had set, and the moons were creeping up in the sky to take its place.

Lucious pulled out a map he had purchased from a merchant in Belrose and looked it over as he ate. Morgan was reading it as well since she was close to his side. They agreed on their approximate location by referencing a giant willow tree that was drawn in as a landmark. Lucious informed the others. "Looks like we made up about a half day from where we should have stopped. If we keep this pace, we should arrive in three days."

Morgan agreed. "Good, we have to get ahead of Arain Drake. Selim and Ulandra, I'll take the last watch. Good night, everyone," she said as she rolled out her blanket and settled in for the night.

Lucious marveled as he watched her. *So determined and focused. A born leader. I need to do my part as well,* he thought as he felt the weight of his sister's abilities and the lack of his burdening him. Determined, Lucious walked away to sit alone and practice. For hours, he tried to create something, anything. His magic flowed with ease, but it was not actualizing what he was trying to accomplish. His frustration built as he looked over to Morgan and Ulandra sleeping peacefully. *I can't let them down.* Placing everything else aside, Lucious continued on.

Selim returned from one last perimeter check before waking Ulandra. "Has he even slept?" he whispered to her as he laid down.

"No, he's been over there working things out."

With a kiss, Ulandra told her mate to get some sleep. Without disturbing Lucious, she strapped on her weapons and headed out to patrol. Throughout the night, she checked back at the camp and Lucious was still hard at work. When Ulandra returned to wake Morgan, she could see Lucious slumped over and asleep. With a shake on her shoulder, Morgan's eyes opened. "It's time to get up for your turn. Nothing to report except for some deer and a couple of owls." Ulandra headed off to bed and snuggled up to Selim.

Morgan stretched and quickly panicked, as Lucious was not next to her. Her shining blue eyes fixed on the slumped figure. Morgan stood up and took her blanket over to Lucious to wrap around him. She placed a tender kiss on his forehead and whispered, "Sleep well, my king." Lucious never stirred and continued his slumber. Morgan equipped herself and followed the perimeter laid out by the others. She came across the small group of deer while the owls hooted occasionally. The moons were getting low in the sky, signaling to Morgan it was time to get moving. It would be light soon. "Time to get going, Lucious," she said, giving him a little nudge.

"I did it," he replied through a sleepy daze.

"What?" she asked.

He opened the blanket to reveal a small, fluffy fawn-like creature snuggled up sleeping in his arms. Its hair was white and black, forming intricate patterns. It picked up its little head to show its two ears protruding out to the side. A cute little snout with an ivory and brown horn about five inches long protruded from the bridge of his nose. Two big brown eyes opened sleepily to meet Morgan's. Her heart melted at that moment, and she reached in to pick up the creature. It was about the size of a puppy, and it yawned wide. Lucious stood and began folding the blanket. "I call it an Arabis."

Morgan was instantly in love, and she held the Arabis to her chest, cuddling it. "It's so beautiful, Lucious," she cried, tears welled up in her eyes.

"Why are you crying?"

"I'm just so happy for you, that's all."

The Arabis was making a purring sound as Morgan continued holding it.

Lucious handed her his blanket. "I got blood on yours, so take mine."

"Are you injured?"

"No, I think it's from the act of creation. The strain on the body is immense and a bloody nose seems to go with the territory."

Selim and Ulandra finished their preparations and walked over to see what all the commotion was. Morgan handed the Arabis to Ulandra. The creature had the same effect on them as well.

"It's amazing, Lucious," remarked Selim, stroking its soft hair with a massive hand. Meanwhile, Morgan packed her things and readied for the day's journey. Ulandra gently set the Arabis on the ground and watched it playfully bound around. Lucious watched how quick and agile his creation was.

Morgan was ready and mounted her horse. "Let's get moving," she urged the others. With great ease, the Arabis leapt into her lap. "You are quite the jumper, little one."

Turning her horse to the trail, she again took the lead. By now, the sky was beginning to lighten as the rest of the group followed.

CHAPTER TWENTY-SEVEN
NOT DEAD YET

A thin, older man with short wheat-colored hair and scruffy beard lay in bed, asleep. Bandages were wrapped around his head and various other locations throughout his body. A short, younger woman entered the room with a bowl full of water and a washcloth. Placing the bowl by the bedside table, she began washing him. She infused the water with special plants and herbs to promote healing. When the healer finished, she took the washing supplies out of the room with her. The room now smelled like lemon-grass from the mixture. The man lay there, not moving. His chest rising and falling was the only sign that this was not a corpse. Slowly, his eyelids twitched as he roused. His eyes opened for the first time since being found outside that burning house three days ago.

"Ugh," he let out a groan. *I'm so sore and my head is pounding. What happened to me?* he thought to himself. It took some effort, but he managed to sit up. His stiff joints cracked from the lack of use. He put his right hand to his head to assess the damage. Feeling multiple bumps, he figured he must have taken quite a good blow to the head. He peeled the bandage from his left forearm to reveal some minor burns and cuts. Throwing the blanket off him, he could see much of the same. "My head is so fuzzy," he whispered as he tried to think back to what had landed him here.

"Welcome back to the living," a woman's voice came from across the room. Through the doorway came the healer who had been taking care of him. "Take it easy now, you've taken one heck of a beating."

"What happened to me?" he asked, still not able to remember.

"Your house exploded, shooting you a respectful distance away. The Wumblums found you when they came over to house sit. Huh," she chuckled, "guess that won't be an issue now."

The man shot her an ice-cold glance. *Knock, knock, knock.* The sound came from the front door. "Excuse me, I'll be back momentarily," the woman said, and off she went to see who it was.

The man could overhear that it was another woman, and by the greeting, they seemed to be good friends.

"Well, hello, Edna. It's good to see you, my dear!"

"You look well, Doris, how have you been?"

They chatted for a few minutes before Doris walked back into the room. "I will be out front for a few minutes. The Thwis merchants are here from Belrose with my supplies." Doris left the room, leaving the man alone.

Belrose, he thought, *that name seems familiar somehow.* It was nagging at his brain, but he just couldn't grasp what it was.

A short while had passed as Doris and Edna made multiple trips from the supply cart to her home. The two exchanged their goodbyes and best wishes and the front door closed. "Sorry about that. Edna is quite the chatterbox, if I must say. She was going on and on about the most adorable couple they ran into on their way here. I believe she said their names were Morgan and Lucious Drake."

It was as if time stopped as she spoke the names. Like a dam bursting, releasing a flood of water, his memories came rushing back. Doris was still yammering away, but Ezra was lost in thought, not hearing a single word she said after that. She stopped mid-sentence. "Are you alright?"

Ezra nodded. "Yes, I think I am now."

With unexpected agility, Ezra was up out of bed and getting dressed.

"You need to take it easy, there."

He noticed his sword sheathed and leaning against the wall in the corner. He walked over and strapped it back on. "I am grateful for your aid, Doris, but I must be going."

Before she could object further, Ezra was out the door and heading after the Thwis merchants.

"Where'd they go?" he whispered to himself. "Ahh, there you are." He spotted the wagon at the street's end. As fast as his injured body would carry him, Ezra rushed after them. He reached the wagon, breathing deeply from the exertion. The little old man, Hensey, was sitting in the driver's seat with the horse's reins draped over his lap.

"Excuse me, kind sir. I was told that on your trip from Belrose you had met a couple by the name Drake?"

With a nod, the old man agreed. "Why yes, a lovely, young couple. And that girl, Morgan, what a sight to behold! Reminds me of Edna and I when we were newly married."

Ezra was unsure who this woman was, but that would need to get figured out later.

"When you saw this couple, did they look injured or hurt?"

"No, not that I recall. They both seemed in good health. The young man even bought some supplies from us for his trip."

An ounce of relief washed over Ezra. Lucious had made it out alive and was heading north.

"Thank you for your assistance, sir. I must be going."

Ezra left the supply cart behind and headed to what used to be his home to see if there was anything left, he could use. As Ezra approached, he could see charred pieces of wood lying about a suitable distance away from the structure. Very little remained, and what was there was burned beyond recognition. Ezra began sifting through the debris, looking for something.

"Where is it?" he wondered, searching feverishly. "Aha, there you are!"

It was a small metallic chest laying on its side in the ash. Ezra flipped the box upright with a grunt. He had forgotten how heavy this thing was. There was no keyhole, and for that matter, no indication the chest even opened. Ezra placed his hand on the top and spoke the word, "Eliste!" The box clicked and the lid cracked open. Inside were a stack of tomes, a scepter, three small leather bags, and some magical trinkets. Ezra grabbed a triangle talisman hanging from a silver chain and placed it around his neck. Next, he grabbed the scepter, two bags of coins, and a red-bound book.

"That'll do," he mumbled as he closed the lid. With the same click, the chest locked, and the seam where the lid was vanished. He placed the scepter in a loop on his belt and headed back to town to purchase everything he would need to follow his son.

By midday, Ezra headed out, pushing the horse at a breakneck speed to make up some lost ground. Just before nightfall, he came upon the corpses of the Morlocks that had attacked Lucious. He also found scraps of his son's clothes in a dried pool of blood. Ezra had no choice but to stop and let his horse rest for the night. It would also give him time to look over the sight of the battle in the morning. He could use some rest as well. Every movement caused pain, he was far from fully healed. *I better not push too hard or else when I reach Lucious, I will be of little help*, he thought.

Ezra setup his makeshift camp and ate a cold meal before he relaxed and fell asleep soon after.

CHAPTER TWENTY-EIGHT
MOUNTAIN PASS

S ebastian was sleeping like a baby and dreaming of warm sunny days where the wind was gently blowing, caressing his face. Sitting there in front of him was Seline, wearing a beautiful summer dress. The two were having a picnic without a care in the world. *I'm so happy*, he thought to himself as he took a bite of the sandwich, she had made him. "This is divine, Seline. You are a fantastic cook."

Seline smiled with affection and moved closer to him. Sitting at his side, she gently blew on his neck and in his ear. It was very arousing, to say the least. It gave him goosebumps, but he liked it. Seline seductively got to her knees at his side and began licking his ear with her warm, moist tongue. Sebastian let out a groan of pleasure. "That's nice, just like that."

Things were going great until she plunged her tongue deep into his ear. *Ahh!!* he woke with a jolt to find Uluck inches away with his tongue out, laughing.

"Hahahahahah!" he bellowed. Tears were rolling down his cheeks and he couldn't catch his breath.

Thoroughly grossed out, Sebastian wiped the saliva from his left ear. The perfect dream had turned into a complete nightmare. Angry, he jumped out of bed and began getting dressed. "You're one sick son of a bitch, ya know that, Uluck?"

The brute was still wailing away to the point where he almost passed out from lack of air. Down the stairs went Sebastian, eager to get away from his molester. Seline was already awake and at the table eating some breakfast she had made.

"Your brother is disturbed!"

She smiled and got up to make him a plate. "I'm sorry, I should have warned you. My brother is quite the prankster when the opportunity presents itself. Here, have a seat and eat." Seline set down the plate with eggs, potatoes, and some type of meat.

Sebastian sat down. "Anyway, thanks for the breakfast."

"Don't mention it. While you were sleeping, Abigail stopped by to make sure we had everything we needed."

He swallowed a mouthful. "Yeah, Abigail has a heart of gold under that massive chest." The two shared a chuckle at the remark.

"If you want, next time we're here, I can have her go upstairs to wake you."

"No, that's all right. I wouldn't have gotten out of there with just a wet ear and a bruised ego."

Seline got up from the table and cleaned the dishes before putting them away in the cupboard. "I packed the rest of the supplies that were on the table. They also brought the horses and tied them out front."

Sebastian downed the last few bites and took care of his dishes. Uluck came down the stairs, exhausted from laughing so hard.

"Sorry about that, son, I just had to do it!"

"Forget about it, Uluck, I can take a joke."

"That's good, cause life is too hard as it is not to laugh now and then."

Outside they went, closing the door behind them. Seline was already on her horse and ready to go. She headed out, leading the way to the west gate. Uluck and Sebastian were soon to follow.

Sebastian was in the middle of the three as they continued on the path. With his map unfolded, he plotted where they were and what they were going to encounter that day. It was hilly terrain, with bright green grass and the occasional tree and bush. In front of them were the Vesper Mountains that they would have to pass through to reach the town of Tellium. From what he had heard, it was mainly a mining town where they processed ore dug from under the mountains to make gold, silver, and copper ingots. The finished ingots were then sent by guarded caravan to the castle where it would be placed into the royal vault.

Within a few hours, the trio had reached the base of the Vesper Mountains, where they gave the horses a rest and ate some food themselves. The terrain had gradually changed from the grassy hill to more of a tundra with moss-covered rocky outcroppings. As they sat and ate, they discussed the road ahead. Seline did most of the talking, as Uluck was still working off his hangover. "Now as of late, there have been reports coming in of a group of thieves hiding in the mountains and stealing from multiple travelers at sword point. King Elrick's soldiers have been routinely scouring the area, but have not yet been able to pinpoint their hideout. It is imperative, Sebastian, that we all keep an eye out for anything out of the ordinary on the road ahead. That letter is top priority!"

He kind of got the feeling that the letter was more important than his well-being. "I will let you know if I see anything, Seline," said Sebastian.

"Good, now get up, Uluck. It's time to move on," said Seline, and they headed up the mountain.

The higher they traveled, the colder and more isolated their environment became. The road they traveled was much nicer than Sebastian expected, since it was the supply line for the kingdom's money. The gray and white stone of the mountain rose from the trail on both sides. All three scanned the rocky crags for any would-be ambushes. As they reached the highest part of the trail, Sebastian looked back and stared off into the distance, where he could still see the massive spires of the Westlin Castle. It was freezing at this point, and the wind had picked up, making it feel worse. The warm, moist air from the horses' nostrils lingered in the air with every exhale. Eager to start the descent, Seline pushed the group onward. The road wound this way and that as they traversed the peak. Small pockets of snow lay scattered about in low spots. Sebastian thought to himself how bad it would be to get stuck up here if a storm rolled in, which happened from time to time. He hoped that at least it was too cold up here for people to be waiting to ambush them. As they crested the peak, they could see the town of Tellium far below. Sebastian breathed a sigh of relief at the sight. *Maybe we won't have any problems after all*, he thought.

Seline had slowed and pulled her horse beside him. "Just up ahead is where the last robbery took place." She raised her hand and rode her horse in a circle around them while chanting a spell. When she finished, she led the way forward. "Let's be quiet and move quickly." The descent began as they followed the crooked trail down the mountain. When they passed the site, Seline pointed out a couple broken arrows lying on the ground, which caught Sebastian's attention. His stomach tensed as his nervousness rose. "I sure hope whatever spell she cast was a good one," he muttered to himself.

As they came around a blind corner, two persons dressed in gray clothing stood in the road with bows drawn. Off to the right, something moved, causing Sebastian to snap his head in that direction. It looked like the rocks were MOVING!

"Uluck, look," Sebastian said, pointing to the rocks. As they drew closer, he saw that wasn't the rocks moving, it was more people garbed in the same gray clothing allowing them to seamlessly blend into their surroundings. There were six of them, plus the two in front. All had arrows notched and were ready to fire. Sebastian was shaking with the rush of adrenaline and asked, "What do we do?"

Seline pulled her war mace from her side and Uluck unsheathed his sword. "When I say go, we ride out of here as fast as we can." Sebastian pulled his sword, hoping he wouldn't need to use it.

"Nobody has to die here," came a man's voice from one of the six to their right. "Lay down your weapons and give us everything you've got, then we'll let you walk out of here alive. Resist and we will kill you!"

Seline spoke for the group. "I have a better option. Why don't we just charge through you and kill everyone in our way?" Before waiting for a reply, she spurred her mount forward into the two ahead.

The arrows flew straight and true, but were deflected. Before the men could reload, Seline was on them with mace raised. In one fluid motion, she crushed the would-be attacker's skulls, leaving their bodies to lifelessly slump to the ground in their own blood. Sebastian was right behind her, as was Uluck. More arrows came their way, but all seemed to miss at the last moment. Sebastian held onto the reins as tightly as he could, the group escaped and quickly left the thieves behind. Pushing their horses hard, the three raced down the side of the Vesper. Seline only slowed down when the trail opened to rolling grasslands again. They went down to a slow walk as the horses heaved heavily for their breath.

"Good boy, good boy," Seline reassured her steed as she gently patted his neck. She looked back. "Is everyone all right?"

Both men replied with a nod.

"Yeah, all good, thanks to that spell and your amazing use of that mace," said Sebastian.

"Good. It's just a simple missile deflection spell, but it has saved us more times than I can count. Thankfully, they weren't using any enchanted weapons, or that would have ended differently, I'm afraid."

This was the first-time thieves had ever attacked Sebastian while performing his duties, and he was still a little shaken. Seline, seeing this, made the call that they would spend the night in Tellium. They continued on to the town ahead with Seline in the lead.

CHAPTER TWENTY-NINE
LAYING THE TRAP

O ri, the black-garbed leader of King Malik's assassin guild, walked into the dining hall where King Malik was sitting and having his dinner. As usual, Malik preferred to eat alone, so there were only a pair of guards and a servant present. Ori stopped at the head of the long, dark red rectangular table.

"King Malik, I have information to report from Spymaster Gallena." Malik set down his fork and motioned her forward. Ori did as commanded and knelt next to the king. "My lord, Arain Drake has sacked Delvin and is now heading towards the Stamrane Forest. Her forces should reach the forest in two days' time."

Malik's fist slammed onto the table, rattling everything on it. "How dare she!"

"There is more, my lord."

Malik's jaw clenched in anger. "Go on."

"I have also been informed that Valin, with a handful of men and a giant creature, have eliminated your troops in Warwick, effectively taking control of the port city." Ori could see his face turning red with rage at the news. "Lastly, my lord, a few hundred toad-like creatures have joined her ranks."

With a swipe of his arm, Malik cleared the table, sending everything flying across the room. It all hit the floor with a loud crash. Malik stood from his chair and looked down at Ori. "Listen to me very clearly, general. Arain Drake and her army of monsters do not leave the Stamrane Forest alive. Use whatever resources you need, but do not return until they are destroyed! Do you understand, Ori?"

"Yes, my lord. Eliminate them or die trying!"

"Dismissed, general."

Ori stood and left the dining hall with great haste. Malik stormed from the dining hall, leaving the servant girl to clean up his mess. Ori's first stop was to visit General Corwin. She found the mage in his library, searching for any mention of Arain Drake or stories relating to a goddess who would be born to rule this world. Corwin was sitting at an ornately carved wooden desk piled high with papers and books. Magic gargoyle sconces lit the room brightly. Ori walked right up to him without a sound. "Hello, Corwin."

He jumped back in his chair, startled. "Dammit, Ori, haven't I told you a hundred times not to do that?"

She was smiling under her black mask. "You should be more alert, Corwin. You never know who might try to sneak up and slit your throat, getting your precious books all bloody."

His fright quickly turned to anger. "Watch yourself, Ori, cause next time, I might have a surprise waiting for you."

She leaned in close. "I can't wait."

"What is it you want, assassin?"

"His majesty, King Malik, has tasked me with the disposal of Arain Drake and her armies. What I need from you are mages with exceptional fire skills."

Corwin smiled and let out a chuckle as he sat back in his chair. "Planning on having a little roast, are we?"

"Something like that."

"Well, you're in luck, then. I stationed some of my best fire mages to the south, in Angor City."

"That is fortunate," said Ori. "Have you been able to find anything new about our would-be attacker?"

Corwin shook his head. "No, my search has uncovered little, I'm afraid."

"I'll let you continue on, then. I need to talk with Vermillion before I leave." Ori turned and headed out of the library.

"Good hunting, Ori," Corwin called out, but she was already gone.

Vermillion was just finishing up with a handful of new archers at the shooting range when he saw Ori heading his way. "Good work today," he told them. "Everyone get some rest and be back here in the morning for your next lesson."

The recruits went about cleaning up the range and maintaining their bows. Ori reached Vermillion a few moments later.

"Good evening, Ori, to what do I owe this visit?"

"I need you and one hundred of your best to accompany me and some of my assassins to Angor. There, we'll pick up the rest of our forces and ambush Arain Drake before she leaves the Stamrane Forest."

"Is this an approved sortie?" asked Vermillion.

"King Malik himself has tasked me to eliminate the approaching threat by any means necessary."

"Very well then, when do we leave?"

"Assemble in the courtyard and be ready to go in one hour."

"Very well, I will see you then," said Vermillion before heading off to gather his sharpshooters. Ori continued on and gathered her assassins along with something special from the alchemist, Pogo.

The group was on their way to Angor within the hour. They rode through the night and into the next day, pushing themselves and their horses to exhaustion. Ori knew that Arain Drake's army should be entering the Stamrane Forest in two days' time. It would take a day, maybe more, to navigate the forest and come out the other side. The trip to the City of Angor from Kragg was two days, and from Angor to the forest exit was another. It was going to be close if they were to reach them in time, but she must. Her life depended on it.

As they pressed on, they gave only enough time to rest and feed the horses so they wouldn't die before they reached the city. Day turned into night as the hours blurred into one another. Two horses went down during the night, finally succumbing to the strain. Their riders were battered and bruised from falling with their mounts. Ori ordered them to return to Kragg on foot when they were able.

On and on she pushed until, on the second day, they reached Angor City. The city was bustling as news of the approaching army had already reached them and preparations were being made to defend it. Angor was easily twice the size of Delvin, with thirty-foot stone walls and watchtowers. The military presence was substantial, with at least two thousand troops of all disciplines stationed there. Large iron gates barred the entrance and exit of the city. Weary and worn, the group entered the city.

Ori faced her troops. "Excellent work to you all. Now take your horses to the stables and get some food and rest while you can."

Ori and Vermillion headed to the captain's office to inform them of the king's orders. Both of them dismounted and handed over their tired horses to be tended to before heading inside. Their legs were sore from the intense journey, but there was no time to take care of themselves. The two came to a desk where a woman soldier was sitting, filling out some form of paperwork. "General Ori and General Vermillion reporting in with urgent orders from his majesty, King Malik."

The woman stopped what she was doing when she looked up to see the king's generals before her. She sprang from her chair. "Follow me, please."

They went down a hallway to a wooden door with the engraved nameplate *Captain Thadius Vane* on it. The woman rapped on the door three times before a man's voice from inside called back. She swung the door open and proceeded to introduce the two generals. The secretary then excused herself, closing the door behind her.

Sitting there at a beautifully crafted alder desk was an older man with long gray hair and a white beard. Thadius stood and shook the hand of both generals. "Welcome to the City of Angor, generals. My name, as you might have guessed from the nameplate on the door, is Thadius Vane. How may we assist you?"

Ori did the talking. "King Malik has sent us to destroy the army approaching from the south. King Malik has also given me full operational command on this mission. We will need a thousand of your best foot soldiers and all of your mages and archers. Arain Drake's forces should be entering the Stamrane Forest as we speak. We will advance to the northern exit of the forest and set up an ambush. She will not make it out of there alive. Myself and General Vermillion are going to prepare. We leave in six hours, have everyone ready and waiting by that time."

"Yes, general. I will make it happen."

Ori and Vermillion headed off to eat and get some sleep, while Thadius barked orders to his subordinates, relaying the general's expectations. Soldiers donned armor and weapons. Archers tightened bowstrings and packed quivers full of arrows. Mages gathered potions and memorized spells. Supplies were packed, and they pulled fresh horses from the stables.

By the time Ori woke and exited her room, everyone was ready as she had ordered. Vermillion wiped his eyes, clearing the sleep away. The troops they had brought were now present and ready to continue on.

"Onward to Stamrane Forest," she commanded, and the mass of troops marched four rows wide out of the city, heading south.

The crisp cadence of armored soldiers echoed through the air. Before long, Angor disappeared in the distance and they could see the faint outline of a massive forest ahead. As they rode, Ori and Vermillion discussed the plans for ambushing the approaching army. Troop formations and positions were all laid out using the map she brought from the castle.

"The forest ahead is very dense from what I remember, Vermillion, so excellent cover and concealment will work in our favor."

"Agreed, Ori. Placing archers high in the trees will offer protection and the high ground advantage as well."

"My assassins will lay traps and thin out her forces as much as possible before they reach the bulk of our forces. We'll try to concentrate on their mages and officers first."

The excitement was building as the day progressed and they eventually reached the tree line. Ori and Vermillion laid out the plans to their second and third in commands, who in turn tasked the troops with specific orders that pertained to each group's class. Ori and her assassins headed into the forest first, going in the farthest to set up a variety of traps for the unsuspecting enemy. She gathered her assassins and explained the objective. "We are to infiltrate the enemy ranks and assassinate as many as possible without raising too much attention. Kill with extreme prejudice!"

Like shadows in the night, they dispersed and disappeared without a sound to wait for their prey.

Vermillion placed the archers in optimal locations, giving them clear lines of sight and good concealment. He then placed the mages to cover a large area from where they could rain down fire. The foot soldiers were the last line of defense and were placed just outside the tree line so that they might mop up anyone or anything that managed to get through. The trap was set, and everyone waited silently for Arain Drake to arrive.

CHAPTER THIRTY
DANGEROUS CREATURES

*T*he travel this day was much more upbeat, thought Lucious as he peered about at his companions. The Arabis, or the fact that he used his power, seemed to have a positive effect on everyone. Morgan was still leading the group at an accelerated pace, but nobody seemed to mind. Lucious thought about how fast he needed to reach King Elrick. He only hoped the king was going to be as receptive as Ezra believed he would be. Worrying about that, though, would have to wait. Using his power and being up most of the night had Lucious feeling exhausted. Hopefully tonight he could focus on getting some good sleep.

For the first time today, Morgan stopped and called for a break. It was a beautiful area with conifers and a fairly large-sized lake. Waterfowl were floating about, squawking their disapproval of the horses drinking at the shore of their home. The Arabis was bounding about the shore between the horses. Witnessing the carefree nature of this creature put a smile on everyone's face. Morgan, in typical fashion, was already pulling rations from the packs to make up plates for lunch. Ulandra helped her, while Selim headed out to survey the immediate area for potential trouble.

With their thirst quenched, the horses walked about feeding on the vegetation nearby. The little Arabis must have assumed he was a horse and began following everything they did. Selim returned and sat down just as Morgan was handing out lunch.

"This is nice, having lunch with my friends in such a beautiful place," remarked Lucious. The others agreed with his statement.

The cold meal was surprisingly satisfying, as was being off of the horses. As they were enjoying themselves, they didn't notice when one horse and the Arabis had wandered out of sight over a grassy hill to their left. That was, until the shrill screams rang out as if an animal were being butchered alive. Plates of half-eaten food fell on the ground and the four of them bolted towards the hill with weapons drawn. Lucious ran as fast as he could, but Morgan and the others left him with ease. As Lucious reached the top of the hill, he could see a group of hunters had the frightened Arabis in hand. Morgan, Selim, and Ulandra were on them in seconds. The ten or so hunters were bewitched by what stood before them. In all the commotion, the Draconians never shape-shifted and were now in front of the first humans, besides Lucious, to see them in their natural form.

Morgan addressed the man holding the Arabis. "Release him now, or you will pay with your life!"

Quickly, the hunter pulled a worn dagger and placed it to the creature's throat as it whimpered for release. "You freaks stay back or I will cut its head clean off!"

The hunters, not sure what to do, backed up their friend.

"Now drop your weapons and get on your knees," the man ordered.

By now, Lucious had reached the confrontation. "Everyone, please put your weapons away," he pleaded. "This doesn't have to end in bloodshed. Just release our animal and we will be on our way."

The man holding the Arabis shook his head. "No, I don't think so. I'm not sure what this creature is, but I'm sure it'll fetch a lot of gold when we sell it."

Lucious could see Morgan was ready to strike and motioned for her to stand down. Lucious pulled the coin purse from his tunic and shook it, making the coins inside rattle like a sleigh bell. "I have gold and it's all yours if you just give me back my friend there, and let us leave without a fight," he pleaded.

The man cocked his head to the side as he sized up Lucious. He put his dagger back in the sheath on his belt.

"All right, hand me that sack of coins and I'll hand over whatever this thing is."

"Fair enough," Lucious responded.

Morgan voiced her objections. "Stay back, my king. These men cannot be trusted!"

"It will be all right, Morgan. I think these men are reasonable," he reassured her, and with that he began walking towards the Arabis. "It's gonna be all right, little fella," he reassured the Arabis. Lucious made it within arm's reach, holding out the coin purse, when the man hit him full force in the jaw, sending him crashing to the ground. One of the other hunters quickly scooped up the small pouch as the Draconians attacked. Before they could reach the men, a deafening crack with a blinding light knocked them all off their feet. Lucious looked up with his jaw throbbing and blood coursing down his lip to see the Arabis standing defiantly in a large ball of electricity. Arcs were flying this way and that, striking the hunters as they squirmed on the ground in agony.

"Arabis, stop," he commanded. The little horned creature turned to face him, and the glow faded as the bolts stopped. As if nothing happened, the Arabis pranced over to Lucious and nudged his face with the occasional lick. Still slightly dazed, he patted the creature. "Thanks, little one, for the help."

By now Morgan had reached Lucious, assisting him up.

"Are you alright?" as she probed his face with her hand.

"I'm fine," he replied as he grasped her hand in his. "How are the hunters?"

Selim and Ulandra were over the hunters, looking to put down any further attacks, but they would have none. All ten men were dead, the steam from cooked internal organs rose from their mouths. The smell was horrible, like charred flesh that had been left cooking too long. Lucious felt a wave of sickness wash over him.

"My creation killed those men? I'm responsible for the grief their families must now endure!" Tears ran down his cheeks.

Morgan was quick to console him as she wrapped her arms around him. "It's not your fault, Lucious. You gave those men a choice to prevent any harm, but they chose greed over their lives. They would have killed that Arabis, or worse, sold it to be someone's trophy. They could have possibly killed us as well, or even sold us as slaves!" He knew she spoke the truth, but it did little to ease the guilt he felt for their deaths. Morgan released her embrace but stayed inches from his face. "You know as well as I do that by the time everything is settled, there will be more life lost than either of us could imagine. I'm sorry it's sad, Lucious, but it's the truth we are faced with, I'm afraid."

He wiped away his tears. "I know, but it doesn't mean I have to like it."

Lucious separated from Morgan and walked over to the corpses. "We at least need to give these men a proper burial. Will you guys please help me?"

"We will," answered Selim as he put aside his weapon and began piling up the bodies. Morgan helped while Ulandra and Lucious began digging in the soft, loamy soil. It took the rest of the day to bury the ten men, and by the time they finished, it was beginning to get dark.

Lucious stood before his friends, dirty and tired. "I know we should rest here, but it doesn't feel right knowing that a grave is just on the other side of that hill. Would it be all right if we rode on farther so that the dead may rest undisturbed?"

With no objections, the group headed onward, guided by a pair of magic floating orbs cast by Lucious. They traveled on for a few hours before agreeing to stop. That night was quieter yet, as they ate dinner in silence. The crackling of the fire was the only noise to be heard.

Lucious turned in early, as he feared this night would be less than restful. The Draconians took turns as usual, walking the perimeter while the others slept. Even the Arabis was sound asleep next to Lucious, the immense expenditure of energy earlier must have surely tired the little fellow out. The faces of those men haunted him that night, causing him to wake frequently. It was a relief when Morgan knelt down to wake him, as it signaled no further nightmares for now. As before, the camp was cleared quickly, and they ate breakfast on horseback while watching the sunrise. Selim was back to leading the group with his spouse by his side so Morgan could stay close to Lucious.

It was a laborious ride that day for Lucious. Between the lack of sleep and the guilt for the dead men, he was in a constant daze. A few times, Morgan had tried to strike up a conversation, but every response from him was just a simple yes or no. Eventually, she figured, he would talk when he was ready and it would be best to let him be.

The events of the previous day kept replaying in his head. *What could I have done differently?* Lucious thought. *If I would have watched my creation, maybe those hunters would have passed on by without even noticing us. Who knows, I guess. One thing I do realize is that these creations Arain and I are making are all extremely dangerous.* Lucious looked to his left and saw the happy little Arabis bounding through the tall grass without a care. *One would never look at such a creature and think it possessed so much power.*

It was afternoon by the time Morgan called for a break. "Let's give the horses a rest, and this time we'll rotate a watch so we don't have a repeat of yesterday."

Ulandra was the first to sweep the area and stay with the horses and Arabis while they grazed on the luscious green grass. She looked down at the creature. "No trouble today, little one." As if the Arabis knew what she was saying, it looked up at her, chewing a mouthful of grass.

The other three sat down and shared some fruit and dried pork strips. Lucious pulled out his map and surveyed their distance to Westlin. "Looks like we should make it to the outskirts of the city by nightfall, if we don't run into any trouble."

Selim swallowed the last of his apple and threw the remains over to the horses. "Good, I can't wait to sleep inside, in a nice, warm bed."

Morgan nodded in agreement. "Yes, a hot meal, bath, and a soft bed sounds wonderful."

Lucious looked at Morgan. "Indeed, cause tomorrow we have to convince a king to fight with us against my sister." Morgan smiled at the thought of a king having to convince another king. Lucious just hoped that the stories he had heard of King Elrick were true, and that he was a kind and just man who put the lives of his subjects first.

Selim, now finished, walked over to relieve Ulandra. "Go get something to eat, my dear, I will watch things." Ulandra gave him a kiss and returned to the others. She quickly grabbed an orange and ate it, peel, and all.

Lucious watched her. "You do know you're supposed to peel those, right?"

She was already into some of the dried meat as she responded. "It takes too much time to skin these things when they taste just fine whole."

"I can't argue with that, I guess," he replied, taking a large drink of water from his water bladder.

The group sat for a while longer before continuing on. Morgan was again by Lucious' side as they rode.

"Morgan, we need to figure out a way to hide the Arabis when we arrive in Westlin. Any suggestions?"

"Hmm. It draws unwanted attention, that's for sure. We could use one of the horse packs to keep it concealed."

"Yeah, I thought of that as well. But if it gets scared, we could have another incident."

Morgan agreed that would not be good, especially in a crowded capital city. "What if we changed the color of its fur so it looked more like a baby horse?"

Lucious pictured the Arabis dyed brown. "That would work at a distance, but the horn gives it away closer up."

The two tossed ideas back and forth as they traveled on. Nothing they came up with completely solved the problem. The Arabis just stood out too much.

Selim shouted back, "You two better figure it out soon."

As they looked ahead, they saw the castle with its sprawling city in the distance. The sight was magnificent to behold.

Lucious turned to Morgan, who had already shape-shifted. "Always one step ahead, aren't you?"

She shot him a smile and quickly suggested the others shift as well. The Arabis, for the time being, was asleep in his lap and concealed with his cloak.

"Selim, Ulandra. You two ride ahead and secure a place to stay on the outskirts of the city, and Lucious and I will hold back and await your return."

Lucious produced the coin purse, and the sight of it made his sore jaw ache with the memory. He quickly handed all three of them coins, thinking if something ever separated them, they would at least be able to buy food and shelter. The two turned about and galloped off towards the city.

Morgan was already scanning the area for a place to lie low while they waited. "There," she said, pointing to a patch of shrubs and some small trees near a wandering creek. Off they rode through the grass a short distance from the road. The trees offered a pleasant shade as the sun was descending in the sky. The stifling heat of the day was soon replaced with a cooler breeze from the north. Morgan dismounted her horse and Lucious gently handed her the sleeping Arabis. She cradled and stroked its soft fur as it made that same purring noise again.

Lucious took the horses and dropped their packs so they could rest for a bit. He walked over to Morgan, who was still cradling the creature while she sat on a stump. As he watched her, it was easy to imagine how she would be as a mother holding her child. The words *fiercely protective* and *kind* came to mind. Setting up one of the packs as a makeshift seat, he sat across from her. "I'm sorry I was so distant today, and I hope you know how much I appreciate you being there, Morgan. I just needed to work through yesterday."

She looked up with those enchanting blue eyes. "I understand, and there's no need to apologize ever." The Arabis stirred, and she quickly rocked with it. "Shhh, little one, no need to wake." Her voice and movement must have comforted it, for it stopped moving. "What do you think we should name it, Lucious?"

"I don't know. I hadn't even thought about it until now."

"Well, we can't keep calling it Arabis. You probably created many more than just one, I'm guessing." He hadn't really thought of that either, but knew she was probably right. They tried many names, but none seemed appropriate.

"How about Stormy?" Lucious suggested.

"That's a perfect name, Lucious, for he's truly like a little storm!"

CHAPTER THIRTY-ONE

SPRINGING THE TRAP

The report came from one of Arain's soldiers. "We should be through the Stamrane Forest by the end of the day, your majesty."

"Good, I'm growing tired of this restrictive place. I can't wait to sack the City of Angor!" She rode with Glub Widegrin walking next to her. Arain continued to try and figure out how she was communicating with the Krillox leader. Was it her ability, or something that they possessed? It was going to be imperative for the upcoming battles to issue commands quickly. She continued recalling the few instances where they had communicated. Was it when she spoke to herself? Was it the eye contact that made it work? "Glub," she called, causing him to turn his head and look at her. Arain's gaze met his black, soulless eyes.

"Yes, my queen," echoed Glub's raspy voice in her head.

"How are we communicating?" she asked.

"I'm not sure. We Krillox do not talk to each other this way."

"Then it must be me who is making the connection. It has to be part of the creation process, so that if I make a species that doesn't speak in the human tongue, I can talk to them."

"That would be an amazing gift, my queen," praised Glub. Arain looked away, as did the Krillox, and they continued the march.

Arain continued toying with the new ability and found she could communicate with all the Krillox within a twenty-foot diameter of her without needing to make eye contact. It was easier looking at their eyes for sure, but not necessary. She was satisfied at how quickly she was figuring herself out. *I wonder if my brother is learning as quickly?* Arain pondered that question for a short time. *It matters not, I suppose. He will die just the same.*

The day dragged on, the dense forest felt like it would never end. It dulled one's senses for noticing anything out of the ordinary. Ori and her assassins systematically eliminated a soldier here and another there. The sizable gaps in the formation were the safest place to take out their prey. Careful not to alert the rest of the army, daggers were used to slit throats from behind while a hand was used to muffle any screams. Snares were used to cinch around necks and crush the windpipe. Some were lured off the path by strange noises in the brush, only to have a trap sprung, killing them instantly.

Ori stood behind a tall spruce and eyed Arain Drake approaching, surrounded by the large toad warriors. The narrow path Arain traveled negated her growing armies' numbers, and with it, the advantage. One of Ori's assassins stood next to her. Ori had already laid out the plan with her troops ahead of time. They would kill Arain's guards and drag her into the forest, where she would be bound and decapitated. Across the way, Ori could see the others were in position. Arain drew into range and the signal was given to attack just as Timber pounced on the person next to Ori. The wolf snarled and thrashed about, killing the assassin in its powerful jaws.

Arain and the Krillox guard quickly readied for an attack. Four of the Krillox were dispatched immediately, falling in pools of green blood. The attackers were precise and extremely fast as they thinned out the guards. Glub caught one of them with his sticky tongue as they tried to flee. Like a whip, he snapped the small, black-clad person back into his open maw. With a bone-snapping crunch, the assassin died. Glub continued fighting on as he chewed away on his prey. Arain was just as fast, if not faster than her attackers. She had already caught one assassin dropping from the trees above and cut the woman in half, right up the middle.

Arain could now see flashes of light and hear loud explosions from up the trail towards the front of her army. "We need to get out of the confines of this forest now before they wipe us out!" she hollered, dodging a dagger attack from behind. Fire shot forth from Arain's free hand and engulfed a person who crumbled to the ground in screams of agony. Off to her side, she could see Timber facing off against another one of them. His muzzle was stained red as blood from his recent kill, and blood still dripped from his mouth. The wolf's dagger-like teeth shone as he readied himself for another attack. He leaped forward and disappeared into the dense foliage with the assassin.

By now, the advantage of surprise was gone, and the remaining few attackers had fled or were slain. Only a few Krillox warriors, including Glub, were alive, but each one had a multitude of injuries. The trailing forces were now catching up to Arain as she looked back down the trail. At that moment, a spiked whip snapped around her neck and dug in, ripping her from atop her horse. Pain and the feeling of being strangled flooded her mind as she slammed into the ground and was dragged off into the brush. Frantically, she pulled at her neck to try and release the whip, but it was too tight. The fighting was now getting further away as they continued dragging her by the throat on her back. Blood was gurgling in her throat from the trauma. Suddenly, her attackers stopped, and the whip went limp. Arain looked up and saw the two assassins above her, but before they could finish their work, Timber emerged from the forest and sent the two distracted attackers to the ground. With unbridled fury, Timber latched around the first one's neck and ripped the person's throat out in a bloody, dripping mass of flesh. The person twitched in his final death throes. As the second one tried to scurry backwards to escape, Timber pounced on them and clamped those massive jaws around the woman's head. Her skull was crushed from the enormous amount of force the large wolf produced. Eyeballs popped from her sockets as the snaps of bones breaking could clearly be heard.

Arain could finally loosen the whip around her neck, and she coughed out the blood that was choking her. Coughing and gasping for air, she lay on her back. Timber finished with his prey and rushed over to her, licking her face. He was obviously happy that his master was still alive. Arain smiled up at her protector and reached out her hand to pet his head. *Yelp!* Timber let out a scream of pain and collapsed. A long silver arrow was sticking out of the wolf's quivering chest. Whines of pain rang out as Timber tried to get back to his feet, only to collapse again.

"No, no, no!" Arain screamed, tears welling up in her eyes. A second arrow hit Arain in the ribs but caused minor damage as her armor stopped it. Quickly, she scurried to her feet, scanning the trees in the area where the arrow came from.

Ori was a little way off, about ten feet up on a large tree branch with her bow drawn. Another silver arrow came hurtling towards Arain. But now she was healing and almost fully recovered. With a forward motion of her hand, a lightning bolt shot forth at Ori, incinerating the incoming projectile and striking the tree branch she was standing on. With ease, Ori jumped just in time to evade the lightning with no injury. Arain was charging forward, trying to close the distance, when one of the fire mages lobbed a fireball that landed and exploded between the two, sending both of them flying in opposite directions. Arain landed in a patch of soft ferns that helped in reducing the impact with the ground. Shaking her head from side to side, she cleared the daze and scrambled back to her feet. As she looked around, she could see the trees and forest floor were catching fire from the mage's attacks. The needles of the pine trees crackled and went up in flames quickly. Her attacker was nowhere in sight. "I hope her own troops incinerated her," snarled Arain as she looked about for her injured friend.

There he was, barely breathing, lying where he last fell. Arain ran as fast as she could to his side and dropped to her knees. "Easy, Timber, easy," she said as she tried to comfort him. With a quick pull, she removed the arrow and threw it aside. Timber's breaths were slow and shallow now, he was bleeding out, causing his fur to turn crimson. Arain cried as she held the wolf's head in her lap, placing a hand over the wound.

"You're gonna be all right, boy, you're gonna be all right," she reassured him, knowing that the wound was fatal. "Thank you for saving my life," she whispered as she gently kissed his muzzle. With one last exhale, the wolf stopped breathing and Timber died in her arms. "Nooo!!" Arain screamed aloud. The pain she felt in her heart was unbearable.

By that time, the forest fire was spreading, and her troops were frantically searching for their queen. The smoke was thick as Arain sat there, with Timber lying motionless in her lap. She sobbed at the loss of her beloved companion. The pain in her heart changed quickly to rage as she caught just a glimpse of Ori hobbling away, injured from the earlier blast. The smoke swallowed her up a moment later. Seeing the assassin escaping made Arain's blood boil as she rose to her feet. The band of runes around her head glowed brightly. Blood gushed from her nose, running off her chin and onto her armor. Arain shouted at the top of her lungs. "You will pay for what you have done, assassin!" An enormous surge of power burst from her body and exploded outward in all directions. Arain collapsed under the strain and fell to the ground next to Timber's lifeless corpse.

CHAPTER THIRTY-TWO

CLOSE QUARTERS

The seas were smooth and calm as the ship glided along towards Kragg. Gulls squawked as they floated on the air currents above the ship, looking for anything to eat. The skies were clear, and the sun beat down on the ogres strewn about the deck. Each of the different factions had already separated themselves into groups. Very rarely were all the ogres on Fenrir together in one spot, yet here they were close together on a ship.

Kander was watching his passengers closely, looking for any signs of problems. *This reminds me of a powder keg just waiting for a match*, he thought. *Hopefully, the show of power Valin displayed earlier will help keep these beasts in check. If not, these things could destroy my ship, and quickly at that.*

As the morning went on the wind died down a bit, slowing their speed, but they were still traveling faster than by oar. A steady stream of food and drink were delivered from below deck to the ogres. There wasn't much to do on the massive ship, so letting them eat kept them full and tired. Kander just hoped they had enough to get them to Kragg.

Adlin Bonecrusher was walking from clan to clan, checking in with the leaders and making sure everyone behaved themselves. Adlin was the biggest and fiercest ogre, which garnered a certain amount of respect from the others. He wasn't just given his rank as head chieftain, it was earned through vicious, bloody battles with competing ogres. Usually, the duels ended with one of the combatants dropping dead.

Valin emerged from the doorway leading down to the captain's quarters and onto the main deck. The stench of the sunbaked ogres assaulted him. "Whew, I must say that is foul!" Proceeding on, Valin walked up to the helm, where Kander was manning the large wheel used to steer the ship.

"My lord, I hope you found my quarters satisfactory?"

"Yes, quite satisfactory," replied the black mage. "Have there been any more problems while I was asleep?"

"No issues to report, Lord Valin. The constant flow of food and drink is keeping them satiated for the moment."

"Good, because I don't want to lose too many of them to discipline."

Kander could see the evil smirk on the mage's face. It was obvious that Valin enjoyed disciplining others. Without another word, Valin headed down from the helm to find Adlin. The giant ogre was easy to spot, and Valin headed in his direction. The group of ogres became somewhat skittish when they saw Valin approach. Adlin walked over to meet the mage, bending down on one knee. "Lord Valin, how may I serve you?"

"Adlin, I want you to separate the ogres into groups based on skills. I would also like a tally on how many have weapons and how many do not. We need to be battle ready by the time we meet up with the goddess, Arain Drake."

"Yes, Lord Valin, I will begin immediately," replied Adlin before standing and heading over to begin his inquiries. One by one, each ogre was questioned and sent to stand in distinct groups on the deck.

It was going to take some time for Adlin to get through all the ogres, so Valin turned his attention to Talia, who had just entered to take over for the captain. Kander updated Talia on their current course before heading off to get some sleep. Talia and Kander had sailed this route hundreds of times over the years, and either of them could safely navigate the ship with little effort. Talia barked a command here and there to have the crew make adjustments to the sails.

"You're quite the captain," remarked Valin as he reached Talia.

"Thank you, my lord. How may I assist you?" Her tone made it clear that the response was more required than meant.

Valin stood beside her, looking out across the mass of ogres. "Magnificent creatures, aren't they, Talia?"

Taking a moment to choose her words carefully before responding, she finally said, "They are interesting, sir. I'm sure they will aid you greatly in the battle ahead."

"Indeed, they will, my dear. These beasts were made for war!" The thought of this many ogres fighting Malik's troops gave him goosebumps of excitement. Valin stood there silently for a few moments as the battle played out in his head.

Not sure if she should disturb him, Talia stood quietly at the helm. *It is uncomfortable standing so close to such an evil man,* thought Talia, as she hoped he would find something or someone else to distract him. "My lord, are you alright?"

"Yes, quite all right in fact, Talia." Valin turned to face the red-robed mage. "How many days do you figure it will take to reach Kragg?"

"If the weather continues to be favorable, then about two days, Lord Valin."

"Good, that should put us right on schedule to meet up with her majesty."

Curiosity was nudging at Talia to find out more about this woman he spoke of. "Beg your pardon, my lord, but what is her majesty planning to accomplish by attacking King Malik?"

"Oh, my dear, Malik is just a stepping stone for her ultimate goal of ruling this world and beyond! You see, Arain Drake is a god with immense powers that she hasn't even fully discovered yet. I was shown the future over eighteen years ago, and in that vision, she conquered everything and everyone. There isn't a being on this world that can stop her." Valin had written off her brother Lucious as being any kind of threat.

Adlin approached the helm. "My lord, I have done as you have asked. I have counted all the weapons and separated ogres by skill into groups for your inspection."

"Very good, Adlin. Show me what we have."

The ogre chief led Valin to the first group of ogres. "My lord, this group has all of our best warriors that are skilled in hand-to-hand combat. Most of them have their weapons of choice and are ready to fight immediately."

Valin nodded his head in approval. "What's next, Adlin?"

"Right this way, my lord," he said as the two walked a short way to a much smaller group of about seven ogres. "This group is all of our mages. Some have staffs, but most are without a weapon."

Valin stepped up to a bluish-skinned ogre, examining it. "Fascinating, some of your kind can actually use magic. Does the skin color have something to do with this ability?"

"I do not know, my lord, but only the ones born like this can wield magic."

"I will come back to see the extent of their magical ability later. Let us continue on, Adlin."

"Yes, my lord. Over here we have our berserker alchemists. This lot are skilled at making potions and in particular, ones that make an ogre insane with rage. Until the potion wears off, these ogres are practically unstoppable. As far as weapons, they all wield spiked gauntlets on both hands."

Valin was elated to hear this information. "We will put this lot to good use."

"Last over here, we have the rarest of all ogre-kind, the void!"

There, before Valin, stood four ogres with skin as black as night. They were larger than the other ogres, and all of them had purple eyes. "Interesting, what is their skill?" asked Valin as he took a better look at the odd-looking group.

"We named them the void, my lord, because no elemental or magical attack can hurt them."

"Is that so? I have never encountered any living thing I could not destroy." Curious to put them to the test, Valin shot forth a cone of red fire from his hand, hitting the four of them. They all stood there, not bothered by the flesh-melting flames. Valin stopped his attack and reached out to touch the skin of the closest one. The black flesh wasn't even hot. The natural defenses of these few impressed the mage.

"They each wield a large double-sided axe, my lord."

"Very good, Adlin. I want you to make sure that those without a weapon make one by the time we go ashore. Use the supplies for repairing the ship to make those weapons."

Adlin bowed his head. "As you wish, Lord Valin."

The chieftain left and went to secure the resources from the crew. Valin spent the rest of the day testing the voids' resilience and the magical capabilities of the ogre mages. They did not disappoint him with the results.

CHAPTER THIRTY-THREE
TELLIUM

The three travelers reached the eastern gate just as the sun disappeared beyond the horizon. Before them lay the well-fortified city of Tellium. Guards lined the tall stone walls and the only two entrances into the city. "Halt!" shouted one guard before walking over to question the group. "What business do you have in Tellium?"

Seline did all the talking for them. "We are emissaries sent by King Elrick himself, to deliver a most urgent letter to the Coven of Elders. We seek a room and some food this night."

The guard examined the three and could easily tell from the crests on their armor and clothing that they were indeed in the service of the king. "Very well. You may stay for the night, but be warned that we tolerate no mischief here."

Seline nodded. "Understood. I will make sure to keep these boys in line. Oh, and one other thing. We just came over the Vesper, where a group of some rather unsavory fellows attacked us. We managed to escape unscathed, but from what I have heard, others have not been as lucky."

The guard spit on the ground in disgust. "Those bastards have been a real pain in the ass of late. I will let the commander know immediately." The guard turned about and headed into the city to report the incident. Seline prodded her horse forward and into the city they went.

Tellium was a bustling place, with its round-the-clock mining and smelting. They geared the entire city towards extracting the precious metals beneath the Vesper Mountains. A massive portal in the center of the city flowed constantly, with miners entering and exiting the mines. Steel tracks exited the opening like tongues from a giant mouth. Carts full of ore were magically pushed along the tracks to the smelting furnaces. The empty carts raced back into the portal to be filled with their next load. It was a sight to behold, and Sebastian sat there, taking everything in. "Seline, this place is amazing!"

She smiled as she looked over at Sebastian. The look of wonder on his face reminded her of the first time she passed through this place. "Yes, it is quite an interesting place," Seline replied. "Uluck, why don't you head off and get us setup with rooms at the Miners Inn, and I'll stay with Sebastian."

With nothing more than a grunt, Uluck turned and headed into the residential area of the city.

"Would you like to get a closer look at the mine portal?" asked Seline.

Sebastian didn't hesitate. "Absolutely."

The two rode at a slow walk up to the giant hole in the ground. Sebastian looked down the mineshaft, amazed at how its lit interior went on as far as he could see. Miners and the magic driven carts shuttled in and out of the shaft on a regular cycle. "How long do you figure the mine system is?" he asked.

"I do not know. This is as far as we're allowed to go without an escort. I would guess it's as long and varied as the road from Westlin to here."

"That's incredible. Someday we'll have to see the depths it reaches for ourselves."

Seline agreed. "I will take you up on that offer when the time comes. Let's head to the inn now and get these horses taken care of." She turned away and began heading in the same direction Uluck went. Sebastian didn't want to leave yet, but figured it was best to listen to her.

The sounds of the workers faded as they traveled down the city streets and away from the mine. Within minutes, they arrived at the large establishment. A big wooden sign with a pickaxe crossed with a shovel and the words *Miners Inn* hung above the entrance. They could see Uluck out front, removing the saddle and bags from his horse. There was a long iron railing for tying the horses to and a water and feed trough about every five feet. Quickly, the two of them dismounted and began doing the same as Uluck. Sebastian looked up and down the long railing, counting over thirty horses tied up for the night. "Looks like quite a few people are staying here tonight."

Seline removed her saddle and placed it over the railing for storage. "Yes, it's pretty common to see this many people, if not more, lodged here on any given night. Crossing the Vesper in the dark would be unwise, so travelers usually stay here until daytime."

Sebastian thought back to the trip over the Vesper and imagined how terrible it would be traveling that at night. *No thanks. I wouldn't want to be up there in the dark either,* he thought to himself. They finished tending to their steeds and headed into the inn with packs over their shoulders.

Inside, the main hall was brightly lit, with taxidermy animals adorning the walls. Some displays were just horns fastened to wooden planks, while others showed whole animals in various poses. Predator and prey alike were displayed. A slender, well-dressed man stood behind a long, ornately carved counter. *This must be the innkeeper,* thought Sebastian. The gentleman only smiled and wished them a restful night as the group walked by. Uluck led them to their rooms: numbers thirteen, fourteen, and fifteen. Each of them picked one and went inside to unload their gear and to get washed up. There would be no late night tonight, as all of them felt exhausted from the hard day's travel. The three of them went to the tavern side of the inn and sat down for a well-deserved meal. The tavern, like the rest of the inn, was in beautiful shape. Everything was clean, bright, and welcoming.

"I'm guessing this place makes quite a bit of money," remarked Sebastian as he scanned the area. Tables were filled with patrons and miners alike. Servers were bringing food and spirits at an almost continual pace. Two large fireplaces heated the tavern to the perfect temperature and helped illuminate the room.

The three of them placed their orders with the burly woman that came to their table. The server was off quickly and returned with a tray of food. She placed one plate in front of each of them, along with a goblet of wine. She then went off to the next hungry group. They had all gotten the day's special which was deer steak, mashed potatoes, gravy, and a small personal-sized loaf of bread. Barely a word was spoken as they consumed the dinner. Uluck let out a belch as he finished and leaned back in his chair, satisfied. Seline shot him a displeased look. "Do you not possess any manners at all, brother?"

"Ahh, a good belch after a fine meal is my way of telling the cook that the food was delicious." He finished his goblet of wine and excused himself from the table. "I'll see you two in the morning." With that, he headed to his room.

Sebastian leaned forward in his chair towards Seline. "No brothel for him tonight?"

Seline took a drink to wash down the last of the meal. "Uluck knows how important it is that we make it to the City of Knowledge as soon as possible. He has never failed any task given to him and to be ready for the hard ride ahead, he knows it best to get as much rest as possible.

Remember, Sebastian, the farther we get from the capital, the more dangerous our journey becomes. Today was just a sample of what we may face before reaching our ultimate destination."

"I understand, Seline. Whatever it takes, this letter will make it to the council!"

The two finished their wine, paid the bill, and headed off to their rooms to get some sleep.

CHAPTER THIRTY-FOUR
THE MEETING OF KINGS

T he daylight was beginning to wane by the time
Ulandra had returned to Morgan and Lucious. "As
soon as everyone's ready, I can take you to the place we'll
be staying at."

Lucious and Morgan gathered what little they had
unpacked and climbed back onto their horses. Stormy was
riding with Morgan this time, as the group headed towards
the southern gates. She had placed a blanket over the
Arabis and was gently stroking its fur to keep it relaxed and
quiet.

Lucious was wide-eyed as he soaked in the sheer size of
the city and castle in front of him. "What a magnificent
sight to behold."

"Yes, it truly is magnificent," replied Morgan.

The gray stone walls stood some thirty feet high, with
watch towers every fifty feet or so. Large magical pillars
emitted a bright white glow that illuminated the entire
wall. They stationed soldiers atop it on an ever-vigilant
lookout for any sort of threat. Directly in front of them
was a drawbridge over the deep blue moat below, and a
large iron spiked gate was ahead. This truly was a highly
defensible stronghold.

People were still entering and exiting through the
southern gate as two rows of guards looked for anything

out of place. Lucious felt his stomach begin to knot as his horse stepped onto the drawbridge. He prayed that Stormy remained quiet and that the guards would offer them no resistance. Looking over at Ulandra and Morgan, he marveled at their ability to look completely relaxed and calm. They proceeded past guard after guard and were just going under the iron gate. Lucious let out a sigh of relief as they passed the last guard with no problems. *Finally, some part of this journey is going as planned,* he thought to himself.

One densely packed street after another sprawled out before them. Homes and businesses were lined up as far as one could see. Ulandra led them to the left, down a street called Oslo's Way. It looked more like a residential area, with houses lining both sides of the street. The noise from the busier main streets faded as they reached the end of the street. Before them sat a quaint little inn called *The Weary Traveler*. It was a charming, single-level establishment that at some point had probably been just a couple of houses joined together. Lanterns flickered from atop iron hooks, illuminating the place. A heavenly smell of something cooking wafted from the open front door. Selim's horse was already tied to a hitching post out front, with a bale of hay and a bucket of water. The giant horse was happily chewing away at the hay. It looked like Selim had already removed the saddle and bags and was walking out the front door to greet them. "You three can tie your horses up here and then I will take you to your rooms." Lucious looked around to see if anyone was nearby so he could let Stormy down to stretch his legs. It appeared like most people had turned in for the night, as most of the homes were dark and quiet.

"All right, Stormy, we need to make sure nobody sees you, okay?" Lucious held the Arabis and looked into its eyes as he spoke. "I'm not sure if you understand me, but there's only one way to find out." He gently set Stormy down. The little Arabis meandered over to Selim's horse and stood on his hind legs to reach the hay bale.

Morgan jumped down from her horse and placed her hand on Lucious' shoulder. "You keep an eye on Stormy and we will take care of the horses."

With a nod, Lucious walked over to where Stormy was and who appeared to be in an eating contest with the horse. He couldn't help but smile at the sight of the fearless creature. Looking over at the inn, he could see an older man and woman through one of the windows. It looked like they were preparing a table for dinner from what he could make out. Looking down, he saw Stormy sitting there staring back at him while chewing away. "Are you getting full yet, little one?" The Arabis just sat there, content.

Morgan, Selim, and Ulandra had made a handful of trips inside with the bags and gear.

"Ahhh," sighed Lucious as the cooler night air was a welcome relief from the sweltering sun. *It's a shame that this beautiful night must be overshadowed by the worries of the future to come.* With that thought, the image of his sister formed in his mind and he stood there in a daze as he mentally examined her. Morgan walked back out front to get him and Stormy, only to find Lucious staring off into nowhere. She snapped her fingers in front of his face and pulled him out of his head.

"Oh, sorry about that. I was just enjoying the night air when I started thinking about Arain. I must have zoned out momentarily," explained Lucious.

Morgan knelt down and picked up a rather satisfied Stormy. "Let's get you two into your room now." She handed Stormy to Lucious and he hid him under his cloak. Off they headed for the entrance, and with every step the smell of the food inside grew stronger. Lucious' mouth watered in anticipation. "They are just now putting out dinner, so I had Selim and Ulandra go ahead and eat so they could watch Stormy for us." As always, Morgan had everything efficiently planned.

Upon crossing the threshold, they entered a warm and inviting little dining room with three tables and a fireplace. To one side of the room was a counter where the innkeeper conducted business, and to the back was an open doorway which looked like it led to a kitchen. At one table was Selim and Ulandra, enjoying a tasty-looking meal with two tankards of drink.

"This way," guided Morgan, and they walked out of the dining room and down a hallway to the right. The inn only had four rooms, and Selim had rented two of them.

"Good, it looks like the other rooms are empty for now," remarked Lucious.

Morgan agreed it was good fortune that they didn't have anyone else besides the innkeepers to contend with. "Here we go, room number four is our room," Morgan announced as she opened the door and went inside.

Lucious was taken aback for a moment when he realized she would be sharing a room with him. He followed her inside and closed the door behind.

"Here you go," he said, setting Stormy down on the dark brown wooden floor.

The room was a decent size. A small wood-burning stove was against the north wall and gave the room a nice, cozy feel. There was a small green couch facing the stove and a large bed extending out from the southern wall. Two brass lanterns were lit and provided ample light for the space. There was a copper wash basin on top of a wooden vanity in the corner, which also displayed a rectangular mirror.

"This is a very nice place, don't you think?" asked Morgan as she sat down on the bed. Stormy, who was inspecting the room, jumped up beside her. "See, even Stormy likes it," she remarked as she gave the Arabis scratches.

"Yes, it is a very inviting little place." Lucious, having had little interaction with the opposite sex, felt awkward looking at the beautiful girl sitting in front of him. "You can have the bed and I will take the couch, if that's all right with you?" he asked, trying to be chivalrous.

"Nonsense, Lucious. You by all rights deserve the more comfortable sleeping arrangements." Morgan seemed almost offended by the thought that he would be forced to sleep on the couch.

"I insist, Morgan, you and Stormy enjoy the bed." He could see she was about to object, but gave her no time as he removed his cloak and sat down in front of the stove. "Hey, this couch is actually pretty nice," he said while he gently pushed down on the cushions. The thought of her king sleeping there appalled Morgan, but she knew he wasn't going to give into her request.

"There's hot water in the basin over there, along with some washcloths and some citrus soap. Lucious, why don't you get cleaned up, and I will take Stormy to the other room. I took the liberty of getting washed up while you were out front with the horses and Stormy." Morgan picked up the Arabis and stood up from the bed to leave.

Lucious, still sitting on the couch, turned his head to face her. "You don't need to leave, Morgan. I would like it if you would just stay and relax." He smiled at her, "It's not like you haven't seen it all before, anyway."

Instantly her cheeks flushed red. "Very well, I will sit on the couch, so at least you have some privacy." She set Stormy down and walked over to take a seat. Lucious stood up and stepped over to the basin while taking off his shirt and placing it on the vanity top. Morgan could see him from the corner of her eye and couldn't help but slightly turn her head to get a better look. *This human is truly fascinating*, she thought, as her eyes traced out what little remained of the scars across his back. His body is frail by Draconian standards, but the power inside him is immense. She continued to observe as Lucious lathered up one of the washcloths in the hot water with the soap and began the chore of washing the grime of the day away. Stormy had hopped up on the vanity and was sitting next to the copper basin, watching his every move. Its little nose twitched as it sniffed the air, trying to figure out where the good-smelling fruit was.

"Would you like to get a bath, little one?" queried Lucious. Stormy cocked its head as if trying to understand what he was saying. Lucious just smiled and continued on. Morgan sat there watching the two of them. It made her happy being able to be there alone with them. Lucious was trying to reach around to clean off his back when he felt the warm, gentle touch of Morgan's hand on his shoulder.

"Let me," she offered with an outstretched hand. This was exciting and scary all at the same time. Here he was, alone (well, almost alone) with this beautiful young woman who was touching his half-naked body. He gladly handed her the washcloth, and with the gentlest of touches, she began to clean his back.

This feels so good, he thought, standing there, and enjoying every moment. Morgan took her time and made sure to do a thorough job.

Knock! Knock! Knock! The sound on the bedroom door shattered the serene moment. It was Ulandra, letting them know they were finished with dinner and the two of them could go eat when they were ready. Morgan set the washcloth down next to Lucious' shirt and headed over to the door. Lucious, somewhat deflated, finished up and got dressed with the clean change of clothes in his pack. He rolled up his pungent, dirty linens and headed to the door as well. Selim and Ulandra came in to take over babysitting duties, and Morgan and Lucious headed back to the dining hall.

The table where their companions had eaten was cleaned, and fresh servings were already waiting. A woman who he could only guess was the innkeeper's wife came over and took his ball of soiled clothing. "Let me take care of that, dear, and they'll be back to you in the morning," she told him. Then off she headed, going behind the counter and through the door to get the clothes soaking with the rest of the others.

The food looked as delicious as it smelled. The two sat down and enjoyed a nice, relaxing dinner together. The food did not disappoint. It was lamb shanks and mashed potatoes smothered in savory brown gravy. They said very little until the plates were emptied. The innkeeper appeared from the kitchen area to remove the plates and refill the mead. "Is there anything else I can get the two of you?" he asked, before returning to the kitchen. Morgan and Lucious were pleasantly full and had barely enough room for the drinks.

Lucious looked across the table with a serious expression on his face. "Morgan, I need you to promise me that no matter what happens tomorrow, you and Ulandra will not reveal your true selves to the king. I fear they would hurt you. It's just human nature to kill what they do not understand."

Morgan could tell he was adamant about his request. She leaned forward, placing her elbows on the table. "As you wish, Lucious. We will remain as you see us now."

"One other thing. I want there to be no bloodshed if the king doesn't react the way we hope he will."

Morgan looked down at the table and was silent. "There will be no bloodshed, I promise." She stood up from the table, displeased with his requests. "It's getting late. We should get some rest." Morgan turned away and headed back to the room.

I know she's not happy, but I can't let harm come to any of them. It's my obligation to protect them, Lucious thought. He finished his drink and headed off to get some sleep. When he walked down the hallway, he could see Selim and Ulandra leaving and heading to their own room.

"Good night, Lucious," greeted the two.

"Good night," he replied in kind. Lucious opened the door to be greeted by an excited Stormy. "Well, hello there! I missed you, too," he said as he bent down and gave the creature a quick scratch behind the ears.

"Good night, Lucious," was all Morgan said before crawling into bed under her blankets.

"Good night, Morgan." Lucious walked over to the wood stove and put another piece of wood on the fire. The small iron door squeaked as he moved it. "That should do for the night."

He kicked off his boots and laid down on the couch, pulling the pillow under his head. Stormy jumped up at his feet and snuggled in for the night. Morgan blew out the lantern and the room grew dark. The only light was from the small window in the wood stove door. Lucious laid there for some time, just watching the flames lick the glass as they consumed the wood. Thoughts of all the different ways tomorrow might go danced in his head and kept him from sleep. Hours had passed, and still he struggled with his thoughts.

Morgan could see from the bed that he was still awake. "Lucious," she called out.

"Sorry, did I wake you? I just can't seem to fall asleep."

"Come to bed, Lucious." The invitation made his heart race.

"Are you sure?"

"Yes, come to bed."

Lucious quietly got up and did as he was instructed. Morgan pulled the covers back on the opposite side of the bed, inviting him in. Not sure with what was happening, he crawled in next to her and she covered him up. He had his back to her, not sure what to do. Morgan was not so shy as she gently pressed up against him, wrapping her arm around his waist. The warmth of her body was soothing and her scent was intoxicating. He could feel her warm breath gently hitting the back of his neck. It was pure bliss, and before long his eyelids felt heavy and he drifted off to sleep.

Morning came with the pitter-patter of rain hitting the roof. Lucious awoke in the same position he had fallen asleep in, except he could feel Morgan's tail wrapped over his legs. She must have shifted in her sleep. He could feel the soft scales of her hand on his abdomen. *I wish we could stay like this all day*, he thought. He would be so comfortable and safe with a young woman he was growing close to. The moment, however, did not last long as Stormy jumped up and began showering him with kisses. "All right, all right . . . thank you, Stormy." It hadn't crossed his mind until now, but the Arabis probably needed to go outside and relieve itself. As much as he hated it, he had to get up. Morgan barely moved and only checked once to make sure all was well. "Go back to sleep. I think Stormy needs to go out. I'll be right back." Lucious threw on his cloak and haphazardly covered the Arabis. When he opened the door, it shocked him to see a little girl placing the clean clothes outside the rooms on the floor.

"Hiya, my name's Emily. Mom said to deliver these clothes to rooms three and four as part of my chores."

"Haha, hi Emily. My name is Lucious. It's nice to meet you, and thank you very much for the delivery service."

She looked up at him with big blue eyes. "You're welcome, Mr. Lucious."

She was about to turn and walk away when Stormy sneezed from under the cloak. Lucious' heart stopped, he hoped she didn't notice the sound. The look on her face said otherwise.

"Whatcha got under there, mister? A cat?"

He was caught and couldn't lie his way out of this one. Lucious bent down on one knee and pulled back his cloak to reveal Stormy.

Emily inhaled deeply with delight. "It's so cute! Can I pet it?"

"Sure, you can, Emily, but I need you to keep this little fellow a secret. Can you do that for me?"

"Sure thing, Mr. Lucious. I promise I won't tell anyone."

Lucious could see the excitement was killing her, so he gently handed Stormy over. The Arabis looked huge in her small arms. Emily hugged and snuggled the creature lovingly. "What kind of animal is this, Mr. Lucious?"

After debating whether or not he should lie to the child, he decided to be honest. "It's called an Arabis, Emily."

"I love it, Mr. Lucious," she gushed, squeezing it tightly. That was all it took, and Stormy couldn't hold it any longer. He urinated a stream that nearly hit Lucious and landed on the floor. "Ooopsy, it looks like Mr. Stormy had an accident! Don't worry, I'll clean it up." Emily handed Stormy to Lucious and headed off to get a towel.

Lucious stared face to face with the Arabis and shook his head. "Really? You couldn't hold it for just a few minutes more?" Stormy's nose twitched slightly as he stared back at him. "Well, at least we know for sure you're a boy now!"

Emily rounded the corner and ran down the hall with the towel in hand. Without hesitation, she went straight to work, soaking up the puddle. "There we go, all clean. I have to go do my chores, Mr. Lucious, but maybe later I can play with him?" Her tolerant, accepting little self caused Lucious to smile. He wished everyone could be like her.

"Sure thing, Emily, but not until later, when I get back from some errands I must attend to."

"All right, Mr. Lucious. I will see you later." With one last nose-to-nose rub, Emily turned about and headed off to do her chores.

Lucious hadn't noticed until he stood up that Morgan was watching from a slightly cracked open door this whole time. She opened it and the two exchanged a smile. "That is one great kid, Morgan. I think she'll do some good in this world someday. It seemed ages ago that I was that young without a care in the world." Lucious stepped back into the room. "Well, I guess it's time to get ready and head to the castle."

"Indeed, it is. You go ahead and prepare, and I'll get us some breakfast." Morgan was back to her human form as she headed to the dining hall.

Lucious picked up the clean clothes and closed the door. Stormy was bounding around the room. He was on the bed, then on to the couch, and then over to the vanity. Lucious gave him a disapproving glance, and he stopped and sat on the bed. "Listen, Stormy. I have to go out for a while today and I don't know when I'll be back. I need you be on your best behavior for Selim while we're gone, all right?" By the look on his little face, Lucious could swear that the Arabis understood.

Morgan entered the room with a tray of breakfast foods. Selim and Ulandra followed her into the room and sat on the bed next to Stormy.

"Well, let us eat and go over the plan for today."

Morgan handed out the plates of food, and the meal was quickly devoured. Morgan pretty much took charge and passed on the specific orders Lucious had given the night before. Selim was to watch Stormy while the three of them went to the castle.

One by one, Selim hugged each of them and wished them good luck. His embrace was not as gentle as Morgan's, and his scales were not nearly as soft. His massive arms engulfed Lucious, and at that moment gave him an idea of the power Selim possessed.

"I'm glad you're on my side," he remarked as the Draconian released his embrace. Lucious was the last to leave, taking one last look at Selim and Stormy on the bed before closing the door.

Before leaving, Morgan dropped off the breakfast dishes with the innkeeper's wife. "I hope you don't mind, but it was rather nasty last night, so we moved the horses and saddles into the stable," the woman informed Morgan.

Morgan thanked the woman for her kindness and the three of them headed outside. The rain was slowing to a light mist as they walked over to another house that was turned into a stable.

"Huh, I didn't even notice that when we arrived last night," said Ulandra. The other two shook their heads, they had not noticed it either. Sure enough, as they walked through the large doorway, they could see all four horses warm and dry, enjoying some barley. They quickly readied the horses, and then the three of them headed off to the castle. The city was bustling, as one would imagine, with merchants and shops lining the main streets. Suppliers, farmers, commoners, and even guards carried about their business like any normal day. *I shudder to think what an invading army would do to this place,* thought Lucious. They progressed slowly down the busy streets towards the castle. Lucious noticed that every so often they would come to another stone wall similar to the one that surrounded the entire city. At each wall, there was a major gateway and a portcullis. Just like the main entrance, a fair number of guards were stationed there. The pattern repeated itself the closer they got to the castle. *That must be one of the city's defenses,* pondered Lucious.

"It looks like rings of a tree all the way to the core," he commented. "Quite genius, wouldn't you say, ladies?"

"Indeed, it is," replied Ulandra. "This would make for a highly defensible capitol."

It was almost noon when they finally reached the courtyard of the castle. This magnificent structure sprawled before them in all directions. They couldn't help but stop for a moment and marvel at its beauty.

"What is your business here today?" A group of guards was standing there waiting for an answer.

Morgan was ever ready. "Oh, sorry, we have never been here before and were just taking in the view. We have come seeking an audience with King Elrick, sir."

The head guard ran through a list of questions he posed to all who wished to see the king. "You will need to surrender all weapons until your business is concluded with the king. You will follow all instructions given to you by his majesty's court magistrate or be removed from the premises for failure to comply. All animals must be checked into the holding stables located to your left. You will be given an allotment of time to speak with the king and no more unless his majesty requests it. Failure to follow these instructions as I have given them will result in removal and or up to imprisonment in his majesty's dungeon. Do you all agree to these instructions as I have explained them?"

The three of them all acknowledged with a yes.

"Good, now please dismount your horses and sign this day's ledger with your first and last names. Do any of you have weapons on your person?"

No, was the unanimous answer.

"We will pat each one of you down to confirm this."

One by one, they were checked for hidden weapons.

"They are clean, sir," the guard doing the search informed their questioner.

"Good. You may now head over to the holding stable and hand over your horses. Agnus here will be your escort until you are finished with your business."

A slender female guard stepped forward. "My name is Agnus, would you please follow me?"

She took them to the stable so they could sign in their three horses. Agnus then led them out of the courtyard and into the main entrance to the castle. They went through the elegant foyer and into a large, open doorway to the throne room. It was a shame they were being ushered through so quickly, as one could spend days examining every marvelous thing in these chambers. Once in the throne room, they could see a handful of people from all walks of life lined up waiting for their turn to speak with the king. Agnus led them to the back of the line.

"Wait here until the magistrate calls you," she told them. "I will bring you back to the stable when you are finished." Agnus walked off a ways and stood in another line next to a row of guards.

Morgan looked at her companions. "Those must be all the escorts for the people in front of us. Good idea, I suppose, in case someone gets out of hand."

There were quite a few people waiting in front of them, which made for a painfully long wait. Person after person presented their issue or request to the king as he sat upon his throne, taking the time to genuinely listen. Not everyone that left when their time was up was happy, but Lucious understood that trying to please everyone would be impossible.

On and on the line moved until it was their turn to speak with the king. The knot in his stomach cinched even tighter. The magistrate motioned them forward. "You will have roughly ten minutes to discuss your concern with his majesty. Be polite and respectful at all times. Do you understand?"

"We understand," replied Lucious.

"Very good, you may now step forward but do not go further than just before the first step." The magistrate stepped aside, letting them approach the king.

Elrick was an imposing sight sitting on his throne. He exuded an unquestionable air of authority. With a simple bow of the head, they presented themselves.

"Good day, my king. I am Lucious Drake, and these are my companions, Morgan and Ulandra." He gestured to each woman with his hand.

"Well met everyone, what is it that brings you to this meeting today?" replied Elrick.

Lucious swallowed the lump in his throat and looked over at Morgan for a moment. "Your highness, what I am about to tell you will seem like the ravings of a madman, but I assure you I am telling the truth."

Elrick shifted in his chair and leaned forward as if to hear him better.

"My king, I am here today to ask for your aid and the aid of all of your military to fight a growing threat!"

Elrick listened intently as he realized this encounter wasn't the typical everyday complaint about thieves or neighborly disputes.

"On the western shores, there is an army amassing that threatens to consume the entire known world."

The king looked over at his magistrate and motioned him to come over. Elrick whispered to the man, who in turn apologized to the remaining patrons while having the guards quickly escort them from the room. The mood changed quickly as the king stood from his throne and walked down to stand before them. Guards encircled the four of them. Morgan and Ulandra immediately went on the defense to protect Lucious, but he quickly gave them a gesture to stand down. The king stood there in front of Lucious with his hands clasped behind his back.

"Continue," Elrick said.

"My twin sister, Arain Drake, leads this army and will stop at nothing to make all the world grovel at her feet."

Elrick's lip furrowed in an almost frown. "Hmm, that does indeed sound like a serious problem. Is there anything else about your sister I should know?"

"Well, yes, your majesty. She has powers the likes of which this world has never seen."

Elrick thought back to the letter, which told of something remarkably similar. "How am I to know that you are not in league with this so-called woman? Maybe she sent you here to gain my trust so you could infiltrate and sabotage from within?"

"My lord, I would never."

"Silence!" Elrick's demeanor had changed as the situation became much more complicated. "I suppose you already know that this woman has sacked the coastal town of Warwick and the City of Devlin?"

Morgan gasped and put her hand to her mouth upon hearing this news. Lucious hung his head, shaking it from side to side. "Then she is well on her way, and that means we have no time to waste!" Elrick motioned to his guards to detain the three.

"What is the meaning of this, your majesty?!" shouted Lucious as they were all placed in shackles.

Elrick leaned closer to Lucious. "I know not what your motives truly are, and whether you be friend or foe. So, for the time being, you will be detained. I will deliberate with my council and see if we can make sense of this matter." He turned to his guards. "Take them away and make sure no harm comes to them, for now."

Morgan and Ulandra resisted with all of their being to honor Lucious' command as the guards rushed them off to the lower levels of the castle where the dungeons were located. The majestic, awe-inspiring castle twisted to a thing of horror as they descended the winding stone steps. Gone were the bright, beautifully adorned halls. The air grew cooler the farther they went down, and it smelled of mold and decay. They reached the bottom of the stairs and it opened up to a large, torch lit level with rows of cells. There were various other rooms whose purpose Lucious did not wish to find out. From the looks of it, only a few of the cells had occupants.

The lead guard opened one of the cells. "Here we are, your new home for the time being," one of the guards stated. Lucious, Morgan, and Ulandra filed in to find a couple of less than comfortable-looking beds, a latrine bucket, and a water bucket. One of the other guards removed the shackles and locked the barred door behind him. There the three of them stood, surveying their accommodations. The only light in the room was from the single barred window some ten feet off the floor. Other than that, the torches lining the dungeon cast a faint glow through the bars on the door. It was eerily silent, and none but the two dungeon keepers on their rounds made noise.

Lucious walked over and sat down on the nearest bed. "This is not how I imagined things turning out today. What a fool I was to think we could just stroll in here and the king would side with our cause without issue." His head hung low with defeat.

CHAPTER THIRTY-FIVE
THE POWER OF ANGER

Arain was surrounded by blackness as she floated in nothingness.

"Wait, what is that over there?" she said out loud, pointing to a light. At first, it was just a small spot in the darkness, but it was growing larger every second. Within moments, the darkness completely faded, and she was outside the City of Westlin. She could see Lucious and three others enjoying a night at some inn. Time flashed forward and now she stood beside a large bed where her brother and a beautiful woman lay holding him.

"This must be someone he desires. How touching. I will make sure she dies before him!"

The woman suddenly changed into a lizard-like humanoid.

"What is that?" Arain whispered in disgust. "So, brother, I see your powers are growing as well."

Instantly she catapulted from that moment and was now inside a massive room with many cells. Arain panned around, examining her new location. *This looks to be some sort of dungeon I would guess, but the lack of screaming from people being tortured leads me to believe I am in Westlin Castle.* There were footsteps of people approaching, and soon guards appeared, escorting Lucious and two women bound in shackles. Arain smiled as wide as she ever had at the sight. They put the captives into one of the cells. The guards unshackled them and headed back up a long flight of stone steps. Eagerly walking over to the cell door, she peeked through the bars to see Lucious sitting there looking totally defeated. She couldn't help but laugh at the sight.

The next moment her eyes opened, she was being carried through smoke and charred trees. Arain faded in and out of consciousness, seeing only snapshots of what was happening around her. A large, muscular creature carried her with ease. Thick gray fur covered its body and large clawed hands cupped her securely. Arain looked up to get a glimpse at the creature's face, but she was drained, and passed out again. This time there were no visions of her brother, just quiet and darkness.

Arain slowly opened her eyes. Looking around, she soon realized that she was in bed inside her tent. A familiar face peeked inside. "There you are, boy, come here." Timber raced over and jumped onto the bed, nearly smothering her. Licks of affection rained down on her face. "I'm happy to see you too, boy. I had this horrible dream you had died, and I would never see you again." Arain embraced the wolf, hugging him tightly. She immediately could tell that something was different. Her wolf was even bigger now, and much more muscular than before.

"Permission to enter your highness?" came a voice from the entrance.

Timber immediately became irritated at the intrusion and bared his teeth, growling in the man's direction.

"It's fine, boy, nobody is going to hurt me."

The wolf laid down by her side, facing the entrance.

"You may enter."

Commander Seget slowly entered the tent. "It's great to see you well, my queen. It has been a rather turbulent few days since the attack."

Arain pulled herself to a sitting position while one hand stroked Timber's neck. "Then it wasn't a dream. We were in fact ambushed while trying to leave Stamrane Forest?"

Seget bowed his head. "Yes, my queen, we were ambushed and suffered quite a few losses in the restricted confines of the forest. It was a well-laid trap, and the forest burned all around us. Then, from out of nowhere, this wave of energy burst forth in all directions, leveling trees as far as one could see. We rallied, and our would-be attackers were all but slain, except for a handful that retreated to Angor. We regrouped and set up camp two days ago to treat the wounded and repair our supply wagons. You were carried out of the forest and placed where you lie now to recover. Timber has guarded the entrance to your tent since that time, not letting anyone in to tend to you. It is only when one of the men saw the wolf no longer at the doorway that they called me to check your condition. It pleases me greatly to see you awake and healed."

Arain thought back to what she had seen while unconscious. "Seget, you said I was carried out of the forest?"

"Yes, my queen, that is correct."

"Carried out by whom?"

Seget's eyes nervously shifted to Timber. "By a terrifying creature that resembled your wolf."

Arain looked down at Timber, who looked back at her. "You really died in my arms, didn't you?" Timber laid his head down on the bed. Arain turned her attention back to Seget. "What happened to this wolf-like creature?"

Seget shook his head. "I do not know, my queen. It held you until your quarters were set up, and then it disappeared inside with you. Shortly after, Timber emerged and sat in the entranceway. If I were to hazard a guess, I would say that thing was Timber, your grace."

Arain puzzled it over in her head, but there were too many gaps in her memory. It was entirely possible that this is yet another power she had unlocked. The thought of having more abilities was thrilling.

"Your highness, we were able to imprison three of the attackers for interrogation. What would you have me do with them my queen?"

"Bring them here. I wish to question them myself!"

"As you wish, my queen." Seget turned and headed for the entrance.

Just outside the tent, Arain could hear him shouting orders to bring the prisoners in immediately.

"Ahh, I guess I better get dressed before our company arrives." Arain climbed out of the warm soft bed and walked over to her dresser, from which she pulled a fresh change of clothes. Once dressed, she proceeded to don her armor and weapons. By the time she finished, Seget was requesting to re-enter with the prisoners. "You may enter!" she shouted while buckling on her belt.

Arain turned around to see Seget enter, along with three wounded men and a small group of guards. She walked across the room and stood in front of the three bound men. Without a word, Arain examined them all, paying particularly close attention to their clothing.

"What are your names?"

The prisoners stood silent in defiance.

"Come now, it's a simple question with a simple answer."

Still, there was nothing but silence.

"Hmm, I take it you all would like to be tortured then as you do not wish to talk?"

Two of the men held their ground, but the third man's resolve shattered like little pieces of glass. "I beg you, please spare my life and I will tell you whatever I know." The man's voice was trembling with fear and tears rolled down his cheeks. "My name is William, this is Phillip, and the one on the end is Vermillion."

"Shut your mouth, you pathetic excuse for a man," snapped Vermillion. Rage welled up in him as he glared at William.

"See, now that wasn't so hard, was it? Thank you, William. What rank do each of you hold in Malik's pitiful army?"

Again, William spewed forth the information. "All three of us are archers."

Arain could easily tell from the difference in clothing that all three were not just lowly archers. The first two dressed almost identically, but the third wore much higher-quality clothes, which signified him as the holder of a much higher rank.

"So, what you're saying is Vermillion is an officer?"

Without thinking, William started to say yes, but stopped mid-word. Arain walked up to William and put a hand on the side of his face. He knew he made a fatal mistake and gave away his only leverage.

"You've been a great help, William, I will let you go. Release him, he can leave."

The guard behind William removed his shackles and pointed towards the entrance. It was too good to be true, but maybe, just maybe, he had saved himself. Without looking back, he ran out of the tent as fast as he could.

"Your highness, are you really going to let him go?" asked Seget, somewhat puzzled.

Arain gave him an evil glance that removed all doubt that no such thing would happen. Seconds later, a loud pop could be heard from outside the tent. A headless body laid there in the grass, twitching violently. Arain walked over to stand in front of Vermillion. Arain was uncomfortably close to his face when she asked, "Who was the woman assassin that attacked me and killed my wolf?"

"You will learn nothing from me, witch!"

"Hahahaha! Witch? Oh no, I'm afraid I am much more than that!" With a flick of her hand, Vermillion's right arm snapped, sending the pointy bone through his flesh for all to see.

"Ahhhhhhh!!"

The screams echoed throughout the camp.

Arain gradually walked back and sat on the side of the bed next to Timber.

"The woman's name?"

Vermillion was in agony, but managed to compose himself and remain defiant. He didn't speak a word this time, but instead spit at her in disgust. It made it far enough to land on the toe of one of her boots. Seget immediately sent a crushing blow across Vermillion's jaw, knocking him to his knees.

"Pick him up!" Arain ordered. Two guards hoisted him up. Arain stroked Timber's head for a moment. "He's all yours, boy!"

Timber, not hesitating, got down off the bed and slowly approached Vermillion. *Crunch, crack, snap!* With each step, Timber's body contorted and changed. Seget and the guard's eyes were wide with fright at the sight before them. The wolf grew tenfold, and by the time it reached Vermillion, he stood on two legs like a man and towered above the broken archer. He had rippling muscles, clawed hands, and a muzzle full of long, white teeth. Arain sat there, enjoying the spectacle before her. With lightning quick speed, Timber snatched Vermillion from the guards and lifted him in the air. The razor-sharp teeth found their mark as Timber latched onto the area between Vermillion's neck and shoulder. With a rip, a mouthful of flesh and bone was removed, sending a crimson spray in all directions. The guards and even Seget were doused. Timber dropped Vermillion, who slumped onto the floor in a lifeless heap. His blood pooled around him. The wolf swallowed the chunk he had removed. The blood glistened off his fur as it dripped onto the floor. Timber's chest heaved with deep, powerful breaths. The last prisoner stood there coated in red. He shook violently as he went into shock.

Arain was now standing next to the bed clapping. "Wonderful, absolutely wonderful!" Timber looked back at her proudly.

Snap, crunch, crack! The sounds came again. Everyone looked to where the sound was coming from. It was Vermillion's lifeless corpse. It was moving and changing. Seget and the guards backed away a few steps and drew their weapons, not sure what to expect. The creature stood facing Timber and looked to be an almost exact replication. The only noticeable difference was in size. Timber was bigger in every way, like the alpha of a wolf pack. Arain approached Vermillion, circling him, and inspecting this new species.

"How utterly fascinating you two are," she commented. She turned to face the blood-soaked prisoner. "I wish to see this again!" Timber began walking forward. "Not this one, I wish to see if those that are turned can do the same to others. Vermillion, kill him!" Without hesitation, Vermillion jumped onto the comatose soldier, knocking him to the ground. A savage bite to the throat removed the windpipe, along with the jugular artery. Blood pulsed from the gaping wound in all directions as the man gurgling in his own fluids convulsing on the ground. Moments later, he lay there dead from the loss of blood. Vermillion stood up and backed away. Warm blood dripped from his muzzle. Just as before, a few minutes passed and then the dead soldier reanimated into another wolf-like creature. Seget and the guards shot a glance at each other before sheathing their weapons. Nobody said it, but it terrified the lot of them that they would be next.

"Commander, you and your men may take leave now and have a few servants sent over to clean up this tent." The troops bowed their heads before exiting the room.

"Timber, would you be so kind and change back to yourself?"

The hulking beast stepped away and began the transformation. Arain watched intently as Timber contorted and writhed on the ground. That same cracking of bones was clearly audible. It took very little time before Timber was back to himself, and soon he jumped back onto the bed and laid down facing her. She could never have imagined such a complex creature could exist. Vermillion and Phillip stood there silently, waiting to be commanded.

"Now, you two. Change back to your human forms." It took them a little longer as it was their first time, but soon enough there stood a half-dressed and completely healed Vermillion and Phillip. Arain sat back down next to Timber. "Tell me, how do you feel?"

"I feel incredible," answered Vermillion.

"I as well," said Phillip.

"What do you remember from you wolf-like state?"

Again, Vermillion spoke up. "I remember feeling strong and powerful, like nothing could stop me. My senses were heightened tenfold, and I hungered to hunt."

"It was the same for me," said Phillip.

The next question was the most important one. "Who do you serve?"

Both men bent the knee. "We serve you, my queen!"

"You may rise. It's good to see your loyalties have changed."

"My apologies, my queen, for how I acted earlier. Since being blessed with this gift, I see now there is only one true master and that is you, Queen Arain Drake," pledged Vermillion. She smiled with pleasure at hearing those words.

"Go and speak with the guard outside my barracks and have them get you clothing, armor, and weapons."

"Right away, your highness," they said, and out they went to do as their queen commanded.

Arain looked down at Timber. "I have a very special task for you three tomorrow!"

Chapter Thirty-Six
BEING HEARD

Water dripped from the ceiling landing in a puddle on the floor in the corner of their cell. It made an eerie noise as the sound echoed off the walls. The sound of a girl's laugh came from the cell door, causing Lucious to rush over and look through the bars. Nobody was there, and he wondered if he was starting to hear things.

"What is it, Lucious?" asked Morgan.

Lucious turned from the door to face her. "Didn't you just hear a girl laugh just now?"

"No, I only hear the water dripping." Walking forward, she put her hands on his shoulders. "Are you all right, Lucious?"

"I'm fine, it must just be my imagination playing tricks on me." He went back over to sit on the bed. "Thanks for asking, though."

Morgan and Ulandra were searching every inch of their cell for a weakness or a way to escape. Morgan jumped up and latched onto the bars of the window with ease. She grunted under the strain as she tried to pry the bars loose, but it was no use. Just as quickly as she jumped up, she was back on the ground.

"No luck with the bars, they built this cell extremely well."

The two Draconian women sat down.

"It looks like breaking out isn't going to be easy, if at all possible," voiced Ulandra.

It frustrated Morgan, who was sitting next to Lucious. "I wish you would have let us at least break through the guards when we had a chance. We could have escaped and laid low while we figured this out!"

"I'm sorry you two, this is all my fault. I thought the king would be more receptive to what I had to tell him." Lucious let out a sigh. "It seems I have much to learn."

Morgan's irritation quickly turned to remorse for being so hard on him. Morgan jumped off the bed. "Why don't we use a spell to unlock the door, or maybe just blow it off its hinges?"

Lucious looked down at the floor again and shook his head. "No, that won't work. My guess is they embedded anti-magic wards when this place was built, just to stop those exact things."

"You guess, but you're not absolutely sure."

He looked up and could see she was silently asking for his approval to try. "Go ahead then, give it a try, but nothing too . . ."

BOOM!! rattled the cell before he could finish suggesting not to use too powerful of a spell. Morgan had launched an ice spike spell at the door and it exploded on contact, knocking her back on her butt. The door stood there without so much as a scratch. Lucious still had ringing in his ears when he rushed over to help Morgan to her feet.

"Are you alright? Are you injured anywhere?" he asked as he quickly ran his hands over her body, looking for wounds.

It's adorable how concerned he is for my well-being, she thought. "I'm fine, Lucious, thank you for helping me up."

He just now realized that he had his hands on places he probably shouldn't have. "Oh, thank goodness. Ulandra, are you alright?" Lucious asked.

At that moment, Ulandra burst out laughing. "Hahahaha!! You should have seen the look on your face, Morgan, when that ice spike hit the wards."

Morgan was not amused. "I'm glad I could give you some entertainment, sister!"

Clink, clank, clink, clank came the sound of the keys jostling on the guard's belt. A burly looking fellow peered through the bars at them. "I wouldn't advise doing anything like that again if you know what's good for you. The first attempt is just a nasty little explosion, as you have just witnessed. The second attempt will cause some actual wounds and the third, well . . ." the guard trailed off. "There hasn't ever been anyone to try it a third time." The guard, now done with his orientation, wandered off to check on the other residents.

The three of them sat back down on the two cots. Each one was thinking of scenarios to escape. "What if we charge the guards when they bring us food at mealtime?" blurted out Morgan.

Lucious pointed to the cell door. "No, that won't work either. See that rectangular spot on the door? They will probably slide the food through there to prevent having to open the door."

Morgan laid back, putting her head against the cold stone wall. They sat there in silence for some time. It must have been getting close to nightfall, as the light from the window overhead had all but vanished. Morgan and Ulandra were still and quiet.

If I didn't know any better, I would say those two are sleeping, thought Lucious. *I got us into this mess and I need to figure a way to get us out. This cell, as we have found out, blocks magic, but I wonder if it can stop my other powers?* He laid down beside Morgan and placed his arm around her. The cot wasn't very comfortable, and it smelled of mildew, but her smell and warmth made it seem not so bad. For some time, Lucious laid there awake, working out the details of how they were going to get out of this and convince the king to aid them. The constant dripping of the water onto the floor wasn't so eerie anymore, as the rhythm it created lulled Lucious to sleep.

For at least a few hours, he dreamed like any other normal person. He had happy visions of he and Morgan swimming in a cool blue lake on a hot summer's day. But soon it changed as he was being pulled away and sucked under the surface. He now stood in front of a large red tent with golden trim. There were other tents and armed soldiers scattered about. Two men emerged from the red tent, wearing only the remains of tattered trousers. They walked over to one guard to discuss something, and then they were off. Lucious slowly walked towards the tent and stepped through the entrance. There was blood splattered in every direction and a pool of blood was coagulating on the floor.

"What horrific act transpired here?"

As he turned to his left, he saw his sister by a bed with an enormous wolf laying on it. Both of them stared directly at him as if they could see him. *That's impossible,* he thought, *this is just another one of those dreams.*

Arain stood up from the bed without breaking eye contact. She was wearing an evil smile when she said, "Timber, would you show my brother your new trick?" The wolf jumped down onto the floor.

"You can see me? How is that possible?"

He slowly backed up as the wolf drew closer. With every step, the wolf changed into something much worse. Lucious backed into the wall of the tent as Timber stood towering above him, fully transformed. Its massive jaws were wide open as it roared louder than anything he had ever heard. In that instant, Lucious jolted awake, slamming face first onto the floor of the cell. The noise startled Morgan and Ulandra, who jumped from their beds ready to fight. They soon realized that the noise they heard was only Lucious. He slowly pushed himself up off the floor with Morgan's help.

"What happened? Are you alright?" asked Morgan.

Lucious just stood there with concern mirrored on his face. "No, I am not all right, not at all. None of us will be if we don't get out of here now!" Lucious walked over to the cell door with determination, clenching his fist and closing his eyes. The runes in a ring around his head lit up fast this time, bathing the room in a bright, golden light. Lucious opened his eyes and turned his balled fist towards the door and opened his hand. In a flash, the runes stopped glowing and Lucious dropped to one knee. He steadied himself and breathed deeply. The blood dripped from his nose and puddled on the stone floor.

Morgan and Ulandra raced over to his aid. "Let's get you over to the bed to sit down." Morgan tore a piece of her sleeve off and began cleaning the blood from his face.

Ulandra stood there looking down on him. "What were you trying to do? You heard what the guard said, the second time magic is used it will cause injuries!"

Lucious raised his head and looked at her. "I wasn't using magic." The sound came from the door, drawing the two women's attention.

Morgan stared at the door. "What did you do, then?"

The cell door creaked as it slowly swung open. Standing there were two short and sleek bipedal furry creatures. "That's what I did."

As soon as the pair stepped closer, Morgan could immediately see the resemblance. They looked like two four-foot-tall weasels, like the one that stole food from Lucious' pack. But these two were walking on two legs and wearing clothes. One of them twirled a ring with several keys on it around one of its fingers. What happened next was even more shocking. The one on the left spoke.

"Well, what are we waiting around for? The guard is bound and gagged and the door to your tiny prison is open."

Morgan and Ulandra stood there with their mouths wide open in shock at what had just happened. Lucious, on wobbly legs, stood up from the cot. Morgan was instantly by his side to help him.

"Take it easy, Lucious, let me help you." Lucious put his arm around her shoulders while Morgan held him tightly at the waist. "All right, let's get out of here quickly and quietly, if you would be so kind," Morgan requested of the creatures.

It was markedly lighter now as the morning sun's rays crept through the overhead windows in the cells. They started heading towards the stairs when Lucious stopped them. "Wait, we're not done here. I need to get back to the meeting hall we were at yesterday." Morgan began to object, but Lucious cut her off. "Listen, we can't afford to waste any more time. I must get the king's aid today!"

She wasn't happy with his request, but knew he needed to see this through. "All right, let's get back to the meeting room."

The five of them went up the long flight of stairs and back into the lowermost level of the castle. The two weasel creatures sniffed at the air and flipped their pointy ears this way and that, listening for anyone nearby.

"This way," pointed Ulandra. Morgan continued helping Lucious. They weaved their way through corridors and rooms, staying undetected. "We're almost there," Ulandra said as she peered around the corner and saw the open doors to the meeting hall.

Lucious assured Morgan he was capable of walking on his own as he stepped over to the two furry fellows. "All right you two, we're going to need a diversion so we can get past those guards. Do you think you can handle that?"

The two excitedly looked at each other, shaking their heads up and down quickly.

"Yes, master, we would love to remove the guards for you. Are you ready now, master?"

A nod was all it took, and the two darted off past the guards. Like clockwork, the ones at the door disappeared in pursuit of them.

Lucious looked back at the women. "Let's go."

Silently, they crossed the hallway and entered the room. King Elrick, a woman, and a handful of guards were the only ones there, preparing for the day's duties. The three of them headed straight for the group of people. The guards noticed them first and began rushing over to subdue the intruders. Elrick and the woman turned to see what the commotion was. Morgan and Ulandra prepared for a fight as the guards closed in, but Lucious had other plans.

The crown of runes blazed around Lucious' head as he thrust his right arm forward. A monstrous screech echoed through the meeting hall as a beautiful golden gryphon stood between Lucious and the guards. Everyone stopped and stared at what just happened. The magnificent beast stood there defiantly, looking at the armed soldiers in front of it. Its yellow hooked beak was at least three feet long and could easily pierce plate mail. The head and neck were covered in white feathers, and its body and tail were covered in golden fur. Both of the beast's front feet had talons similar to that of an eagle, and its body behind its wings resembled a lion. With another high-pitched screech, it spread its massive wings, which spanned some thirty feet across. The guards backed up towards the king and his visitor with weapons drawn. Lucious collapsed to his knees with blood running from his nose and mouth. Morgan and Ulandra grabbed him before he could fall face-first onto the floor. He was breathing heavily when he looked up at Morgan. In a tone little more than a whisper he spoke, "Help me over to the king quickly."

The two of them hoisted him up and shouldered him past the gryphon. With concern, the creature angled its head to see if he was all right. As the three drew closer to the ring of guards and the king, the gryphon followed.

"STOP!" the woman yelled. "Lower your weapons," she commanded as she walked out from behind her protectors. King Elrick wasn't quick enough to stop his head-strong wife before she reached Lucious and the two women helping him. With his last fleeting moments of consciousness, Lucious looked into the eyes of this woman.

"Please, we need the king's help."

The bloodied young man before her went limp, and his head dropped heavily to his chest. Ulandra and Morgan carried his weight easily.

"Please, is there somewhere safe he can rest?" pleaded Morgan.

"Follow me," replied the woman, heading off to a door near the back of the hall. His two Draconian friends carried him behind her.

King Elrick watched as they headed out of the hall. "You four go with them and protect the queen," he ordered. "You three seal the hall and nobody gets in here!"

The four guards ran off and disappeared through the same door as the others. Three others went and closed all the doors leading into the hall. He ordered the last guard to tell his magistrate that the king was sick and would see no one today.

It was just Elrick and the gryphon staring at one another in the great hall. The atmosphere in the room was much more relaxed now, so the massive creature sat down and collapsed its wings.

"I can't believe my royal crest is sitting here alive right in front of me," Elrick said. Elrick looked over to one of the many banners hanging down from the walls. Each one had the picture of a gryphon rearing up on its hind legs in a fighting stance. His eyes focused back on the living one standing before him. Slowly and cautiously, Elrick stepped closer to the creature. It seemed almost docile now that its master was safe. Elrick proceeded closer and closer, while the gryphon watched with curiosity as it cocked its head this way and that. Elrick was only ten paces away when the beast let out a high-pitched screech. The king put his hands out in front of him.

"Okay, okay, I get it. You don't want me any closer." Content, Elrick stood there marveling at the beast for quite some time.

CHAPTER THIRTY-SEVEN
CATCHING UP

E zra lay in a deep sleep, dreaming of those vicious Morlocks and the last time he saw his son. His mind flashed back to the night the two of them first met, and then on to various memories of Lucious growing up through the years. When Ezra woke, it was already morning. Rays of sunlight flooded through the trees and onto the forest floor below. "Uhh," he groaned as he tried to sit up. It had been some time since he had slept on the ground and his body let him know it was not okay to do so. Ezra looked over to see his horse right where he had tied it up. His second attempt to get up was a success, but a painful one. There was a crack here and a pop there as he stretched out. "Time to get a better look at this area before I get moving." He inspected the scene of the fight for clues. He knelt down and picked up a piece of cloth stuck in the dried blood. "I'm pretty sure this is from Lucious' shirt he wore that night."

There were paw prints throughout the area from the Morlocks, but there were also very strange humanoid-like foot prints from three different sizes of clawed feet. Lucious wasn't here, and that's all that really mattered, he supposed. Ezra dropped the piece of cloth back onto the ground and readied his horse. In a relatively short time, he was off, headed towards Belrose.

The pace was a little slower today, but still fast enough to keep his horse at a gallop. Minimal breaks were taken again, and they were mainly for his steed. Ezra only encountered two travelers on the road to Belrose. He stopped just long enough to ask if they had seen his son before continuing onward. By day's end, he could see the town in the distance. Ezra eased back on the reigns and brought the horse to a walk. He reached down to stroke its neck and offer praise. "Thank you for all your hard work today." The horse whinnied as if saying you're welcome.

Soon, they reached the southern entrance and headed into the town. Ezra had been to Belrose many times and knew his way around even in the waning light. "Let's see, the first order of business is to get you taken care of," he said to his horse before heading off to the stables. The owner was a friend of his by the name of Cliff Samson. Ezra dismounted his horse and walked into the torch lit stable house. Cliff's brother, Ben, was working tonight, tending to the horses, and at this moment he was mucking out one of the stalls.

"Hello Ben," Ezra called. The burly older man turned around to see who was calling him.

"Ezra, you old dog. How the heck are you?" Ben set down his pitchfork and wiped his hands on his pants before extending one of them out to shake hands. "It's good to see you, Ezra." Ben's grip was like a vice as the two of them shook and exchanged hellos.

"You as well, my old friend." Ben let go and Ezra tried to get blood flowing back to his hand by flexing it. "I see you still have that gentle grip," laughed Ezra.

"Ahh, you know me, never was the delicate type."

"Indeed. How has everyone been lately, Ben?"

"Everybody is doing well, I reckon. Me, Ellen, and our two girls are good. Cliff, Sonya, and the boys are fine as well."

"That is excellent news. I will be staying in town tonight and would like to have my horse given the royal treatment before heading out in the morning. Would that be possible?"

The big man scoffed. "For you, no problem. I have to finish a few more things and then I can take care of her."

"Great, then I shall leave her in your hands and I'm off to get some dinner and a bed." Ezra removed his bags and said his goodbyes before heading over to the *Horny Goat* tavern for the night. It was calm and quiet in Belrose tonight, and for a moment it let the mage almost feel relaxed. Walking in the tavern's door was a little louder, as the day's work was over for most of the townsfolk and now was the time to have a drink and unwind. Ezra moved to the small table he sat at whenever he visited.

Cooth noticed him and headed over to greet him. "Welcome back, Ezra. It's been a while since I've seen you."

"Thanks, Cooth, it has been some time."

"What can I get for you tonight?"

"I'll leave it up to you, Cooth. I just want something hot to eat and a glass of whatever wine you have. Oh, and I will also need a room for the night if you have any available?"

"That won't be a problem, we still have a few open. I will send over your order shortly."

Cooth headed back behind the bar and gave one of the serving girls the order. A goblet was placed on the bar and a dark orange-colored liquid poured in. In no time, the server was at his table dropping off the food and drink.

"Here you go, and this is the key to your room, you're in number three." She placed the iron key on the table beside the goblet of wine. Then off she went to serve the other guests.

Ezra dug in, as this was his first proper meal of the day besides dried meat strips. He devoured everything in half the time it took to get it. Grabbing the key, he headed out of the tavern area and down the hall to where the rooms were located. The *Horny Goat* had around twenty rooms for rent, but numbers one through five were the nicest. He went inside to clean himself up before bed. He cast barrier spells on the window and door, just in case any nasty things wanted to visit him during the night.

"This is so much nicer than sleeping on the ground outside," he said as he stretched out on the plush bed. Thoughts of Lucious filled his head as he laid there. *I sure hope that he is well and has reached King Elrick by now.* That was the last thing he thought before sleep took him.

Whether it was because of his healing wounds or the exhausting pace he was traveling at, Ezra slept through the night without waking once. The knocking on the door barely woke him.

"This is your seven o'clock wake up you had requested, sir," came a young girl's voice from the other side of the door.

"Thank you, I'm awake."

He could hear her footsteps as the girl walked away. Ezra stepped out of bed and stretched. He was still a bit sore, but definitely getting better. He grabbed his clothes and got dressed. Ezra grabbed his packs and left the room. He headed to the tavern area where a small sack of food was waiting for him.

"Good morning, Ezra. I do hope you had a pleasant stay?"

"Indeed, it was, Cooth. By the way, don't you ever sleep yourself?"

"From time to time, but running this high-class establishment requires constant tending to, I'm afraid. Let's see, the room, food, and drink will be ten silver and five copper."

Ezra handed over the coins and bid Cooth a good day before heading off to the stable.

The town was stirring as people were getting their day started. The smell of fresh bread floated on the air, coming from the bakers. Merchants were setting out their wares for the potential passerby to purchase. Ezra arrived at the stable to find his horse being brushed out and saddled by his friend, Cliff. The two men exchanged a friendly handshake.

"Good to see you, Ezra."

"And you as well, Cliff."

"She's all ready to go. Ben gave her a good rubdown last night, along with a thorough cleaning, and he even fixed a loose horseshoe."

"I did ask for the royal treatment, and it seems you delivered as usual." Ezra noticed that besides his horse, there were only three others in the stable. "Looks like you're running low on your horse stock!"

Cliff looked back at the three he had left. "Yeah, business has been good lately. Just the other day a young man and woman came to town and bought four horses with saddles and bags on the spot!"

Ezra immediately stopped strapping on the horse bags. "You say a young man and woman?"

"Yes, the woman was quite a beauty!"

"Did you happen to notice where they were headed?"

"I can't be certain, but I think they went north last time I saw them."

"How much do I owe you?"

"Ahh, let's call it six silvers, my friend."

"Here you go," replied Ezra as he handed a gold coin over to Cliff before strapping the bags onto the horse.

"This is too much, I could sell you a whole horse for this!"

Ezra mounted his horse and looked down at the stable owner. "The information you just gave me is worth it. Take care, Cliff." With that, Ezra headed off to the north gate and back onto the road.

"That's my boy, Lucious. I knew those things wouldn't kill you so easily," Ezra whispered to himself. A sense of relief eased over him. But who was this woman he was traveling with? Could it be someone he met on the road? And why were they pretending to be married? It seemed like one question was answered and many more took its place. *I must find him before he gets too far ahead of me,* he thought. Ezra traveled long and hard that day and even into the night. When his horse needed a break, he walked alongside her until they were both too exhausted to carry on. Only then did they stop for some rest.

CHAPTER THIRTY-EIGHT
REVENGE

O ri and the only survivors of her attack force retreated to Angor to regroup. Less than thirty souls returned from the sizable force that had just left two days ago. Of the ones that had returned, almost all of them had injuries to some degree. The portcullis opened upon their arrival and quickly closed once they were safely inside. The soldiers stationed in Angor looked on in disbelief. Not only had two of King Malik's generals been defeated, but the invading forces captured one of them. The healers quickly went to work on the wounded, while the few uninjured began preparing for the upcoming attack.

Ori headed directly to the station of Captain Thadius Vane. Skipping all formalities, Ori burst through the door and into his office. Thadius looked up at her, very displeased with the intrusion, but knew his place. Ori was ragged-looking, with sections of her assassin's garb torn and burned. The look in her eyes, though, was still as cold and calculating as ever. Ori stood in front of his desk, looking down at him. "Thadius, I need you to send me your fastest messenger so I may give him a report to take to the king. We can expect an attack on Angor within the next couple of days. I want all able-bodied persons armed and ready to defend this city! Send out whatever mages we have left to place warning glyphs in a thousand-yard perimeter around the city."

Thadius couldn't get in so much as a word as Ori rattled off command after command. Feverishly, he wrote down everything on a parchment pad atop his desk.

"Next, we need to stock up on fresh water and food from the surrounding farms in case of a long siege. I will leave the watch and guard rotations up to you, Thadius. I am headed to my room now. Have that messenger sent over as soon as possible."

"Yes, General, I will see to it personally."

Ori turned and exited his office as quickly as she had entered. Thadius called for his secretary, who rushed in as fast as she could.

"Yes, sir, what is it?"

He quickly wrote down instructions and handed them to her. Without another word, she was dismissed and walked out of the office. She read the note, which had a squire's name written on it. The squire was to be brought to Master Ori's barracks immediately. She headed off to the barracks to find him.

Thadius himself headed over to convene with his lieutenants. He handed each one orders and urged them to make haste. "Those orders were just given to me by the king's Master of Assassins, Ori, so do not deviate from them, understand?"

The lieutenants all nodded before being dismissed to carry on with their duties. Thadius went back to his office to begin working out strategies for defending Angor.

Ori had just reached her barracks and was removing her armaments. "Ahh," she moaned, wincing in pain as she exposed various burns and cuts on her body. Sitting at a small table against the far wall of her room, she opened a bottle containing a milky green fluid. Carefully, she placed a few drops onto a clean cloth and used it to blot her wounds. "Mmmm," escaped her mouth as she bit her lower lip from the stinging salve that she used to clean each area. When she finished, she stood up and dressed in some new clothes. It was only now in the solitude of her room that she let her guard down and wept. "I have failed you, Vermillion, as I have failed my king." Nobody had ever seen her vulnerable side, and if they did, they probably didn't live long enough to say anything about it. With a deep breath and exhale, the tears stopped and the softer side of her once again was locked away.

There was a knock on her door, followed by the secretary's voice from outside. "Forgive the interruption, Master Ori, but I have brought the messenger you had requested."

"You may enter."

The door swung open and a young man, barely twenty, walked inside. "General Ori, my name is Talo Grey and I am at your service." Ori walked back to the table to write out the letter that he would deliver to King Malik. Talo stood there silent and at attention. He had never met someone so high up in the king's military, and it made him quite nervous.

A few minutes later, Ori turned from the table with the letter in hand. It was sealed and marked for the king only. "Come here, Talo."

"Yes, ma'am," he said as he quickly strode across the room to stand before her. Ori stepped up to Talo and gave him a deep, passionate kiss. When finished, she handed him the letter.

"You must deliver this to the king as fast as you can, Talo. Your life depends on it."

Talo stood there, a little confused. "You have just ingested a nasty little poison I like to use, and in about three days' time you die an agonizing death if you do not reach the castle and get the antidote."

Talo's eyes grew wide at this revelation.

"I suggest you get going, you wouldn't want to waste any time!"

The evilest of smiles crossed her face as Talo turned and bolted to reach his horse. *Death truly is the best motivator,* thought Ori, before lying down on her bed for some much-needed rest.

Talo grabbed only what he needed and rode north at a breakneck speed.

———————◦———————

It was almost a day and a half, with no sign of the invading forces of Arain Drake. Thadius had been sending out scouting parties on a regular interval to watch for anything out of the ordinary. Suddenly, an ear-piercing whistle rang out in the distance as one of the warning traps was triggered. A bright red orb shot into the sky and exploded, leaving a crackling red cloud that slowly dissipated. Ori and Thadius stood atop the southern wall, looking off in the warning's direction. A lone figure on horseback pulling a cart approached on the main road.

"Guards, prepare for battle," shouted Thadius from up high. Ori stood there motionless, with a slight breeze making her black garb flutter at the ends. The figure continued to advance on the city gate.

Ori stood there in disbelief as she recognized who this person was. "It can't be."

"Isn't that General Vermillion, ma'am?"

"It would appear to be."

"What on Tauro is that on the cart?" Thadius asked.

"I believe that is Arain Drake's pet!" Ori turned and headed down the steps leading to the ground level. "Open the gate!" she commanded. The portcullis creaked and groaned as the hoist mechanism lifted its immense weight.

Vermillion stopped and waved at his friend. "Hello, Ori. It's good to see you made it out of there in one piece."

Clank. The catch locked the iron gate into place. Ori strode out to meet her friend, all while keeping one hand on her dagger. Something felt off, but she couldn't place it. She circled Vermillion and the bound wolf.

"Looks like you brought back a trophy for King Malik?"

"That I did indeed! After that explosion, I headed into the forest to search for you, and that's when I came across this thing lying there. I thought it was dead at first, but it still lives. Myself and three others bound it and dragged it out, but sadly we were attacked by Arain's forces and they killed the others. I managed to escape, though, and figured it best to retreat to Angor."

Ori finished circling and stopped in front of Vermillion. Timber lay there with eyes closed, breathing shallow breaths. The arrow that Ori had shot in its side was removed, leaving only the blood covered wound.

"Is everything all right, my friend?" asked Vermillion, still sitting on his horse.

"Everything's fine. It's good to see you alive and well," she informed him, but she was not completely convinced it was. "Come, I'm sure you're tired and hungry, let's get inside. Guards have this creature taken to one of the holding cells until we can deliver it to King Malik," ordered Ori.

Vermillion hopped down from his horse and embraced her with a hug. A group of soldiers took the horse with the cart still attached and headed into the city to the prison. The two generals headed inside as the portcullis lowered back into place. Thadius was waiting to welcome Vermillion back. "Welcome, general, it's good to see you again."

Ori stopped at Thadius. "Go on, Vermillion, I will catch up with you later. I need to go over some defensive plans with Thadius."

Vermillion nodded, "All right then, I'll be off to my room to get cleaned up. Maybe we can meet back up for dinner in a little while." With that, Vermillion headed off.

Ori's eyes followed him as he walked out of earshot. Without turning to face Thadius, Ori whispered, "I want you to have him watched closely, captain. I find it a little too convenient that Vermillion made it out of there without so much as a scratch."

"Yes, general." Thadius headed off to fulfill his orders.

Ori stood there for a moment before making her way back to the top of the wall, where she continued scanning the horizon to the south for the remaining hour of daylight. Torches were being lit throughout the city and along the walls. The torchlight cast a shimmering flicker to everything its light touched. Ori ordered all mages to conserve their magic in case of an attack, so no light orbs were used. Ori knew this was not the best option, but it was necessary if the mages were to be at one hundred percent fighting capacity. *I suppose I better find Vermillion and have a proper debriefing with him*, thought Ori. She headed through the city and stopped by to speak with the soldiers that were watching him. Ori could spot the two men with ease, but she was a master assassin after all, so hopefully they were good enough not to alert Vermillion to their presence. With absolute silence, Ori worked her way to their flank and drew a dagger. *Slit, slit.* Both men grabbed their necks and turned around, startled. A small trail of blood ran down each of their necks through clenched fingers.

"You scared us half to death! Did you really have to cut us?"

"Just be lucky that's all I did," answered Ori in her usual cold tone. "That's just a little reminder to always watch your back. Where is Vermillion now?"

One of the men pointed to a small cottage some fifty feet down the street.

"Has he done anything unusual since he arrived earlier today?" she asked.

"No, ma'am. He stopped and picked up some food at the tavern and went straight to his room. He has been there ever since."

Ori looked over at the small cottage, noticing the lights were out. "How long has it been dark in there?"

"Not long, maybe thirty minutes."

"How can you be sure he's still in there and hasn't just slipped out the back?"

"Thadius placed us at the front and two others at the rear of the cottage. Every so often, one of us walks to the next street over to verify with the others that Vermillion has not left. We just did that before you arrived."

"All right, continue your watch. I want to get a closer look." Ori slipped away and was up to the front door of the cottage in seconds. She stood there, listening for verification that he was still inside. It didn't take long before she could hear a man snoring. Ori stood straight and let out a deep sigh. Ori thought to herself, maybe *I'm overreacting. I suppose it's possible that his story is in fact what happened. He must be exhausted, I think I'll let him sleep and wait to speak with him until morning.* She listened just a moment longer before leaving and headed to her own place for some food and rest. On her way, she passed by the tavern and requested food be delivered to her room as soon as possible. Ori entered the small home similar to the one they gave Vermillion to use and closed the wooden door behind her. She walked over to the small dining table in the far corner of the room and began removing her assassin's garb, placing it on one of the chairs. "What a day." She undid her dagger belt and laid it on the table. She was then removing her face covering when there was a knock at the door. Without turning towards the door and continuing to remove her armaments, she yelled, "Who is it?"

A young man's voice came from outside. "I'm here to deliver food and drink to General Ori."

"Come in and place it on the bench by the door."

The young man did as he was ordered. *Snap!* The sound made Ori pause, and before she could turn around, the young man's lifeless corpse smashed into the wall in front of her and crashed down onto the table.

Quickly grabbing two daggers from the belt on the chair, she turned towards the door and threw them with deadly precision. *Thunk! Thunk!* They sunk into their target. Ori slowly panned up to see a hulking, wolf-like creature standing in the doorway. *Clang, clang.* The two daggers were pushed out of the creature's flesh and fell to the floor. She looked on in disbelief as the wounds closed before her eyes.

"What the hell are you?"

The creature stepped forward and let out a roar before charging her. With speed the likes she had never seen before, the beast closed the distance and swiped at her with one of its large clawed hands. Ori already had another dagger and jumped over the creature, plunging the knife into the back of its neck. With a loud thud, the beast crashed to its knees as its spinal cord was severed. It slumped over in silence. Cautiously, she bent down to pick up the two daggers off the floor that she had thrown. Her eyes never left the still motionless creature. Then, the dagger in its spine began to slowly move outward, exposing more and more of the blade. Realizing she may need help with this, she bolted for the military quarters just up the street. *Maybe some magical fire will kill that thing*, she hoped, as she ran at a dead sprint. From the shadows to her left, something ran past and then a scream tore through the night's silence. Now more screams cried out to her right as something was ripping a person apart.

Just up ahead was the mage barracks, and two of them were wandering out front to see what was making that noise. Ori reached them a second later. "We are under attack by some sort of wolf-like creature, and normal weapons have very little effect!" She turned to look back the way she came, only to see the one from in her room barreling towards them. "Burn it now!"

One of the mages quickly launched a fireball from his hands while the other sent a handful of magic missiles at the approaching monstrosity. The missiles pierced its body and exited the other side just as the fireball made contact and exploded in a bright orange and red flame. The dim torchlight made it hard to see where it went and if it was dead. The three of them stood there, searching as their eyes readjusted from the light of the fireball.

"Send out a light orb," commanded Ori. The mage to her right made a gesture, and a six-inch ball of light floated from his hand upward and outward. The reflection of multiple sets of eyes looked back at them. Slowly, she backed up. "This isn't good."

From the shadows, one of those creatures grabbed one of the mages and quickly dragged him off into the darkness, oblivious to his screaming.

"What seems to be the problem?" came a familiar voice from behind. Ori turned to see Vermillion walking out from the office of Thadius. For just a moment, she felt hope before Vermillion transformed into one of those things.

"Run!" yelled the remaining mage as he unleashed a bolt of lightning at Vermillion. Ori turned and ran right into the open jaws of Timber. She struggled frantically, stabbing at the beast, but Timber sunk his teeth into her neck, releasing a spray of warm blood. Her body spasmed violently as her life slowly faded away. The last thing she saw were those cold, dark eyes of the creature that killed her and its crushing embrace around her neck.

That night, countless screams filled the air until they slaughtered every last human. By the time the sun began to rise, the town lay silent, like a tomb.

Arain rode slowly in through the southern gate with a wide smile across her face. Before her stood a legion of werewolves comprising those that survived the transformation. Those that did not lay dead, dismembered, and eviscerated in bloody piles of flesh. Arain dismounted her horse as Timber ran out from the pack to greet her. He was a normal wolf again as he jumped up on her, frantically licking her face in excitement. "Well done, my boy, well done!" Timber got down from her and turned to face the new pack. One by one, they bent the knee to Arain and the alpha wolf.

CHAPTER THIRTY-NINE
TALO'S GIFT

The horse's hooves clattered in a rapid cadence on the partially stone road as it carried its passenger. Talo Gray was hunched forward, tucking his upper body close to the horse to help cut down on the added resistance from the wind. He had been riding hard for the better part of a day now, and only stopped a few times to relieve himself and get the horse some water. The road from Angor to Kragg was in fairly decent shape, which aided them in their travel.

"I know I'm pushing you way too hard, but I must make it in time to receive that antidote," he said to the horse. Talo felt bad for the horse, knowing that this strain would probably end in the animal's death. His green cloak fluttered in the wind as it stretched out towards the rear of the horse. The air rushed by and made a low whistling sound in his ears. On and on they rode until the sun disappeared on the horizon.

That's enough, he thought, and he slowly pulled back on the reins, bringing the horse down to a canter. Just up ahead, he could see one of the small rivers snaking its way across the lands. *Perfect!* He pulled back a little more on the reins, bringing the horse to a slow walk. The animal's chest heaved as it breathed in and out deeply. Talo rubbed the horse's neck as he praised it for the day's effort. "Good boy, good boy. It's time to rest now."

They had made it to the small wooden bridge that spanned the little river. The surrounding area was mainly rolling hills covered in tall fields of various grasses. They stopped just shy of the bridge, and Talo jumped down. "I think we'll stay here for the night, is that all right with you?" he asked the horse. The animal cleared its nose loudly as if to answer *yes*. Wasting no time, Talo unsaddled the horse and removed its bridle. "There you go," he said as he set the gear down in a pile on the grassy ground.

The horse headed directly to the river's edge and began to fill its stomach with the cold, crisp water. With the last light of the day, Talo scoured the river bank, gathering just enough driftwood to make a small fire.

In short order, the crackling of the fire filled the air. "There we go, now I can work on my meal."

He plopped down with his pack in his lap. As he rummaged through it, he produced a water sack, an apple, and some slightly moldy cheese. The water and the apple were the first to go. Pulling a small dagger from a sheath on his belt, Talo scraped off the mold before devouring the remaining piece. After such a long day, just sitting down on the soft ground and eating his rations felt amazing. It was time to get some sleep, but first he tied a lead on the horse so he didn't slip away in the night. Talo chuckled at the thought of his horse deserting him. Quickly, Talo tied one end of the rope to the horse's neck and the other end to an old tree trunk that washed ashore a long time ago. He brushed his palms together, satisfied.

"Good night," he called to the horse, who was busy grazing on the grasses. Talo balled up his sack to use as a pillow and laid down next to the fire. Within minutes, he drifted off into a deep sleep. The insects buzzed and chirped in the tall grass while the gurgling of the river drowned out everything else.

The night was uneventful until just before dawn, when Talo stirred in pain. *My stomach feels like somebody just hauled off and punched me.* Sitting up made it worse, causing him to wretch beside himself. His lips felt tingly, and at that moment, he remembered the poison-soaked kiss from General Ori. *That must be it! What an evil woman to do such a thing to a complete stranger.* Looking over at the puddle he produced, he noticed patches of crimson visible in the mix of fluids. Talo was wide awake now, thinking of the agonizing death she promised him just one day from now.

It took little time to break camp and continue on towards Kragg. He felt like he had a nasty cold brewing, but knew it was the effects of the poison. The day's ride was horrible compared to the one before it. Besides being ill, dark gray clouds blotted the sun out early in the day. By noon, it was a complete downpour, which hardly relented the rest of the day. Talo's teeth were chattering and the comforting wind from yesterday was now freezing his soaked body. He had to slow down if he was to survive the entire day. His horse didn't seem to mind the slower pace one bit.

"I just have to keep going and I can make it to the castle by nightfall," he repeatedly told himself. Every second felt like a minute, and every minute felt like an hour traveling in these conditions. It took every ounce of Talo's being to hold on that day. The poison was moving quickly now and was making his vision blur. By some miracle, the two of them arrived at the castle just as darkness was approaching. A pair of guards in the castle courtyard stopped the horse just as Talo slumped off the saddle and slammed onto the ground with a thud. Though he was barely coherent, he was able to blurt out, "I come from Angor with an urgent message from General Ori."

The two guards hoisted him to his feet and carried him into the castle with haste. Once inside, more guards came forward to see what the commotion was all about. "Go inform King Malik that a messenger for Angor has arrived with news from General Ori!"

Off ran one of the guards to fetch the king.

The guards brought Talo to the castle's infirmary, where he was handed off to the healers. A wise looking old man with a bald head and short white beard took charge. "Let's get this man out of these wet clothes and into a warm bed immediately," he shouted to his assistants.

A much younger man and woman stripped Talo down naked. The woman gasped at the sight under his clothing. Large, oozing pustules dotted Talo's torso. The old man, seeing this, quickly headed off to the far end of the infirmary to gather two small vials, one green and one red. With inhuman speed, he returned to the bedside of Talo as the assistants covered him with thick blankets. He popped open and mixed the two vials together, making a new colored concoction. Gently, the old man slid one of his hands to support the back of Talo's head while carefully pouring the mixture into his mouth. Though he was almost unconscious, Talo could still taste the horrible fluid. It burned running down the back of his throat, which forced him to swallow.

"There we go, all gone," said the old man as he handed the empty vials to his young male assistant. He placed Talo's head back down onto the pillow.

"Will he live?" The sound of the king's voice came from the doorway.

"Ahh, your majesty, I think we may have gotten him the antidote just in time. This man hadn't reached the last stages of the verbane poison where blood leaks out from every orifice yet! At that point, nothing could have been done."

"Excellent work, Vazeer," praised Malik. "I wish to speak with him when he awakes."

"Yes, your majesty. He will be watched until he either wakes or dies."

"Sir," said one guard as he stood at attention holding Talo's pack in front of the king.

"What is it, soldier?"

"Your majesty, we searched this man's belongings and found this letter sealed with your royal crest." The guard handed over the letter from Ori. The parchment was damp, but the ink was still legible. It read:

"King Malik, I regret to inform you that the attempt to slay Arain Drake and her army has failed. Your soldiers were brave and fought hard, eliminating numerous enemy combatants. Vermillion and myself set a trap in the Stamrane Forest just South of Angor. We engaged her forces in the confines of the woods, which worked to great effect until a shock wave the likes of which I have never seen, extinguished the forest fire and laid waste to my troops. General Vermillion was most likely captured, or worse, killed by Arain Drake. What few of us survived fell back to Angor to regroup and bolster the city's defenses. We urgently require more troops if we are to have any chance of holding Angor for long. Until reinforcements arrive, each and every one of us that are still able will defend the city with our lives."

Malik's face contorted with fury as he crumpled the letter and threw it into the fire. Without a word, he stormed out of the infirmary.

"I told that woman to handle this matter and now Vermillion is gone! I will not let this charlatan insult me further by sacking another city and killing another one of my generals." Malik continued to vent to himself while walking towards the war room. As he passed a guard, he shouted at him to gather his generals immediately. The guard bolted in the opposite direction, heading towards the general's quarters. "I will deal with Ori if she manages to survive, that is certain." He flung the enormous iron doors open with ease and proceeded into the war room. Within thirty minutes, the remaining five generals had reached the chambers and were seated before the king.

Malik was so enraged he couldn't sit, but paced back and forth while shouting to his generals. "I have received word that the heretic Arain Drake has bested Ori and quite possibly killed Vermillion!"

Gasps of disbelief echoed around the table. "Almost all the troops she left with are dead and the City of Angor will probably fall within the next couple of days!" Malik stood facing his generals and bent over the table, placing his hands on its smooth, cool surface. "Hortus and Corwin, you will take ten thousand of your most talented troops and head immediately for Angor! Defend the city and obliterate that bitch Arain Drake! I want no man or beast under her command to be spared, is that understood?"

"Yes, your majesty," responded Hortus and Corwin. The two generals stood, bowed, and exited the room.

"As for the rest of you, I want this castle and this city ready for WAR!"

Pogo, Yuni, and Clink quickly stood from the table. "By your command it shall be done," they intoned, and the three of them filed out of the room.

Malik stood there silent and alone. No man or creature scared the king, but this threat had him worried. He stood there a few moments longer before heading out towards his personal armory just a short way down the hallway, to the left. There was an ornately carved wooden door with a gold-winged serpent signifying the king's standard on the front. There were no guards at the door, as General Corwin magically sealed the room. Malik was the only person alive that had the signet key to unlock it. He made a fist with his left hand and pressed his shimmering green jeweled ring into the serpent's eye socket. A click and a low whir could be heard as the door slid to the side. Magical light filled the room as Malik stepped inside. The room was deceivingly large, spanning some forty-foot square. All manner of beautifully crafted weaponry such as swords, axes, glaives, halberds, pikes, and crossbows hung on every wall. Racks filled with exquisitely made suits of armor were placed in neat rows down the center of the room. Malik walked over to the left wall where the daggers and smaller swords were hanging. "Ahh, that should do nicely," he murmured as he reached up and pulled down a razor-sharp short sword with silver inlaid runes along both sides from hilt to tip. The pommel and guard were designed to look like a bird with its wings outstretched and the blade coming from its beak. Below where the sword had hung was the scabbard that went with it. It was black with silver runes, much like the sword itself. With a satisfying *snick*, Malik slid the sword into its sheath. He headed off now to his bed chambers to get some sleep while the door magically resealed behind him.

***

Morning came and with it, good news. A *knock, knock, knock* cracked on his bedchamber door. Malik was already up and dressed. He never was one for sleeping the day away like so many others. "Come in," he commanded.

The door swung open with a creak to reveal Vazeer standing there. "Good morning, your majesty and my apologies for disturbing you so early."

"I was already awake. So, what news do you bring me?"

"Ah, yes, the messenger has just woken up and is recovering nicely."

Malik's left brow raised slightly and his mouth formed a semi-smile. "Very good, Vazeer, as always. Come, let us go see if our messenger has any other information about the battle down south."

Malik grabbed the sheathed sword from the night before and hurried alongside Vazeer towards the infirmary. They entered to see the messenger sitting up and sipping on a bowl of soup. As soon as he saw the king, Talo almost dropped the bowl and he sprang up out of bed to stand at attention.

"Please, please, there's no need for that. Lay back down and finish your meal."

Reluctantly, Talo did as he was told. Malik walked to the bedside and sat down in the chair that was next to each bed. Talo lay there, petrified. He had seen the king before, but never so close and personal. Just his presence exuded an air of power and respect.

"Let us start simple, shall we? You obviously know who I am, but I cannot recall your name."

With a slight stutter, he responded, "T-T-T-Talo Gray, your majesty."

"Well met, Talo. I would like to be the first to thank you for a job well done. I have received the letter and have acted on it accordingly. Your efforts may very well save the City of Angor." Malik picked up the sword he had brought with him and held it out to Talo. "In appreciation for your services, I feel it's appropriate to honor you with one of my personal swords. It is named Vixor."

Talo's eyes were so wide in amazement that they could have fallen right out of his head. "With great honor I accept this gift, oh great King Malik," he said as he reached forward to accept the sword.

"Now, let us get down to more pressing matters. What can you tell me about the battle to the south?"

Talo set the sword on his lap and cleared his throat. "They left me back in Angor with a fraction of our garrisoned soldiers to defend the city, while everyone else headed south with General Vermillion and Ori. Only a handful of troops and General Ori returned. They were pretty beaten up by the looks of them. One of the troops that returned was a friend of mine named Julia, and while I helped her to the city's hospital, she told me about what she saw during the battle."

Malik leaned in towards Talo with nerve-wracking intensity. "Go on."

"Julia is a fire mage specialist and was one of the many responsible for sending wave after wave of fire spells into the forest. The trap was working, she said, but then an explosion from inside the forest extinguished all the flames and knocked everyone flying. Many died from the blast, especially the archers up in the trees who were flung to their deaths. When she finally gained her wits, she could see the black-clad mages and assassins walking out of the smoldering trees, along with these giant frog-like creatures with spears. At that point, Ori and the few others that were still alive grabbed her and they escaped on horseback. That's all I know, your highness."

Malik sat back in the chair, processing this new detailed information. A moment later, he stood up and slid the chair back against the wall. He looked back at Talo. "That will do. Now get yourself rested. Your services may be needed again soon."

Malik walked out of the infirmary and headed to his dining hall for some breakfast. Talo now relaxed, letting out a deep breath.

Vazeer stood at the foot of the bed, smiling at the messenger. "Heck of a job, my boy. It's rare that I see the king hand out his personal arsenal as gifts."

Talo gave a slight shrug. "Well, it's not like I had much of a choice. Either I made it here, or I died."

"Hahaha, good point, Talo. No better motivator than death! Well, hopefully you learned your lesson and won't be kissing any strange women in the future."

"Yes, I do believe that is one lesson I shall never forget."

Vazeer headed off to his potions and concoctions at the other end of the hospital, leaving Talo time to think. He felt much better than the last day he could remember. He was still sore and a bit weak, but overall, he was feeling all right. His attention quickly turned from himself to the beautiful sword and scabbard on his lap. Never in his brief life had Talo seen anything so beautiful. As he grabbed the hilt, he noticed how warm the steel felt. *That's not what I was expecting, it's so light,* he thought to himself. With the slightest amount of pull, the sword slid from its sheath. There were no words to describe the absolute perfection he held in his hands. Talo sat there for some time, just examining every little detail. The feathers on the bird almost looked real, and only when he ran his finger across them did his brain realize they were not. He traced each rune, not having the slightest idea what they meant. "Vixor," he spoke under his breath. The sword glowed a faint bluish color.

"All right, all right, that's enough. Stop playing with that in here before you get yourself injured again," teased Vazeer from the end of the room.

"Oh, right, sorry about that. I just can't believe this is really my sword."

With that, Talo slid the blade back into its sheath and set it next to him on the bed. Vazeer walked over, holding a vial with an ominous purple swirling fluid in it.

"Here, drink this," he commanded, handing the vial to Talo.

Reluctantly, the messenger took the vial. "What is it?"

"It's to help your body recover from the damage caused by the poison."

Well, Vazeer saved his life, so as much as he didn't want to drink the liquid, he did so out of trust. Talo winced as he downed the contents of the vial. It tasted like cabbage mixed with chalk, and it made his throat feel cold.

"That was disgusting Vazeer," he informed the man as he handed the empty vial back.

Vazeer turned and headed back to the apothecary at the end of the infirmary while talking the whole way. "You know, this isn't the first time General Ori has used that poison to get men to do her bidding. Hell, I must have treated a dozen or so victims throughout the years, and let me tell you, the first two or three did not end happily."

Talo realized how incredibly lucky he was as he laid back down, pulling the blankets up to his chest. He was feeling rather tired from all the excitement. *I may as well get some rest,* he thought before falling back to sleep.

CHAPTER FORTY

NO TURNING BACK

The fascinating City of Tellium slowly faded from view as Seline, Uluck, and Sebastian continued on the road heading west. It would still take them around four full days of riding to reach their destination, and that was if they were unhindered. *At least the weather is in our favor,* thought Sebastian as he looked skyward to see blue skies with little wispy clouds scattered about. The sun's golden rays quickly burned off the layer of dew on the vegetation along the road while warming the morning chill away. Uluck was leading with Seline in the middle and Sebastian close behind.

"Seline, what should we expect today to bring?"

She turned her head to look back towards him. "We should make it to the Forest Town of Hemshir if we keep this pace."

"Why would they put the town in a forest instead of on the outskirts, like Addleberry and so many others?"

Seline paused for a moment before saying something rude. She reminded herself that this was all new to him, so these types of questions should be expected. "You see, the Hemshir Forest is the largest of its kind in Tauro, and as such, it is full of many of the animals we use for food, furs, and so on. King Elrick, in his wisdom, figured the resources would best be harvested by placing the town directly in the center of the forest. That way, the hunters employed by the king have a convenient place to return to with their spoils. Hemshir has everything you could need from taverns to blacksmiths."

Sebastian painted the visual in his mind. "It sounds like an interesting place."

"You could say that," responded Seline in a tone that made him a little concerned.

"What's wrong with that place?"

She shrugged her shoulders. "There isn't anything wrong with Hemshir, it's just a little different, that's all."

Sebastian got the feeling that Seline wasn't going to tell him, like she was having fun making him wait. *Oh well,* he thought, *I guess I will find out soon enough. I might as well enjoy this pleasant morning.*

The three continued on, passing the occasional merchant heading with their wares to Tellium. One group they came across steered a wagon full of furs guarded by the king's soldiers. Uluck and Seline were of higher rank, so the soldiers greeted them accordingly and wished them safe travels.

As the companions drew closer to Hemshir Forest, the landscape began to change. Instead of the flat shrub and grass-covered fields, more and more trees now came into view. By early afternoon, they were entering the forest. Trees so tall and green stretched to the sky some fifty feet up. Sebastian couldn't help but marvel at the beauty of it. This section of the forest seemed composed of only conifers, and the air smelled of pine. Sebastian was so entranced by his surroundings that he hadn't noticed that Uluck and Seline had stopped. Seline shot out an arm to get his attention. It did just that, along with nearly giving him a heart attack. The wonder of the forest turned to fear now as Sebastian looked at Seline for direction.

"Why did we stop?" he asked in a whisper.

"I don't know. Uluck must have seen something. Stay here and keep on the lookout for anything unusual while I go see what the problem is."

That sounded like a horrible idea, but didn't want to seem like a coward in front of Seline. He just simply nodded in agreement.

Seline, as quietly as possible, proceeded about twenty feet ahead to her brother. "Uluck, what is it?"

The massive warrior sat there looking off to his left.

"There's something over there! For the past hour, I've been seeing something black following us. There may be even more than one, but I can't be certain."

Just off a ways there stood a black, wispy looking animal staring straight at them. It simply stood there watching as the siblings stared back at it. None of them saw the others coming up from behind them until it was too late.

"Ahhhh!!" screamed Sebastian as one of them slammed into him, knocking the messenger sprawling onto the ground. His horse reared up and bolted down the path. The one in front of them was now closing the distance at incredible speed. Two more tried to remove Seline from her horse, but she quickly brought her war mace up to knock the attackers to the side. Now she could get a better look, and what she saw made no sense. They looked like some sort of dog or wolf, but dead and ethereal. She immediately looked for Sebastian. He was just now getting to his feet with his sword drawn.

"Hold on, I'm coming!" she shouted, just as one of the creatures latched onto her leg, pulling her to the ground. The pain was intense as those powerful jaws pierced her armor, driving its teeth deep into her flesh. Seline brought the mace down with bone-shattering force on the creature's head. Brains, or whatever the black ooze was inside its skull, came splashing out as the creature went limp. Its jaws were still firmly locked onto her leg. They could now hear snarls as more of these things emerged from the forest.

Uluck was already on his feet, laying waste to any that dared attack. He used his sword and shield with great efficiency. Uluck could see his sister was down, but reaching her would not be easy, as they now surrounded him on all sides.

Sebastian cleared his head for just a moment before setting on his attacker. His nerves faded and his adrenaline took over. Again, it lunged at him, but this time he was ready and drove his sword through its side and up through its spine. It crumpled to the ground, lifeless. To his side, he could see Seline struggling as she tried to get the jaws released from her leg. Two more of those things were preparing to attack her, but she was too restrained to properly defend herself. A fury boiled up in Sebastian at the thought of those things killing her. With a battle cry, he shot forward with his sword drawn back. They quickly changed targets and charged for him instead.

The first one jumped with jaws wide open, hoping to bury those long sharp teeth into his neck, but down came his sword, severing the creature's head clean off. The second one saw the opening and latched onto Sebastian's free arm. *Snap* went the bones in his forearm; his light armor offered little protection from the crushing force of those jaws. Fire shot through his arm as he screamed in pain. Violently, the creature shook him, trying to cause as much damage as possible. It took everything he had to fight back, and his blade finally found its mark, killing the horrible thing. Seline was now to her feet and rushing over to help Sebastian. The adrenaline was wearing off, leaving him tired and in pain. The weight of the dead animal clamped onto his broken arm caused him to kneel.

"Are you alright?" she nervously asked as she reached him. Sebastian could still see bits of the animal's head stuck in her leg. Streaks of blood ran down from the puncture wounds.

"I'm fine, but your leg looks hurt," he responded, knowing full well his injuries were much worse.

Seline placed the end of the mace between the jaws clamped onto Sebastian. "Okay, now this is gonna hurt, but breaking the jaw is the only way I can see to get it off you."

He took a deep breath. "Go ahead."

The bone splintered as she twisted the mace, snapping the lower jaw. The pain was like nothing he had ever felt. Specks of white light flashed as he almost went unconscious. Seline looked back towards her brother, who was fairing much better than the two of them. Black blood streaked his armor, as if somebody had dumped a giant ink pot on him. Uluck was slowly making his way back to his injured companions in between attacks.

"All right Sebastian, let's see what I can do to help." Seline was about to cast a healing spell on his broken arm when she noticed at least six more of those creatures closing in behind Sebastian. "Uluck!" she shouted. "More of them at our flank!"

For a brief moment, the warrior looked back to assess what was coming. "Shit, there's just too many of them, we need to get out of here!" yelled Uluck. The horses had long since run clear of the danger, but Sebastian and Seline were in no shape to do the same.

"Petre, Amindo, Mendosis," recited Seline while holding one hand above and one hand below his broken arm. A greenish hue radiated from her hands. Sebastian screamed as the bones realigned into place and his torn flesh fused back together. Before she could finish, the next wave of creatures were upon them. Quickly grabbing her war mace, she stood in a position to defend him. Uluck vanquished two more with a cleaving blow that sent arterial spray in all directions. Sebastian stood up and wielded the sword in his off-hand. His dominant arm was not fully healed, and he feared it would break again if he tried swinging a sword with it. He and Seline looked at each other for a moment before the first two creatures ran in to strike.

Seline managed to connect cleanly with the beast's head, slamming it into the ground in a fleshy puddle. Sebastian had much more difficulty trying to use his sword with his off-hand and only grazed his foe. The three of them, now winded and tired, stood back-to-back, trying their best to prevent anymore injuries.

"Guys, this is not looking good," remarked Sebastian, as if the other two hadn't noticed. Everywhere they looked, those things stared back.

"There must be fifteen to twenty more of them," counted Uluck. Slowly, the predators closed the circle around their prey.

"All right, boys, this is it. Make them pay for every drop of blood they spill!"

A loud hissing sound came from outside the ring of monsters. The sound rose from a group of small pine trees, and then a blinding white light followed. The beasts all stopped their advance and looked over at this new disturbance. In an instant, a streak of lightning struck the first one, incinerating it instantly before arcing in a full circle through all of them. Little specks of ash floated on the light breeze from what was once a pack of Morlocks. The three travelers remained defensive, but spots in their vision from the searing light now made it hard to see.

"Have either of you ever seen anything like this?" asked a considerably shaken Sebastian. The two siblings just shook their heads while trying to see what unleashed that blast. The small patch of trees where it came from was now quiet.

Seline turned her head and looked down at Sebastian's feet. "Umm, what is that?"

The two men looked down to see a striped white and dark blue creature resembling a fawn standing directly under the messenger between his legs. In a panicked tone, he asked, "What do I do?"

Seline knelt down on one knee and placed her mace on the ground slowly. The furry little creature cocked its head and looked up at her with big, blue eyes. "I don't think it intends us any harm. In fact, this little thing may have been what saved us."

Slowly, Sebastian stepped away so it wasn't beneath him any longer. Seline, not sensing any danger, extended out her hand like one would do to an unfamiliar dog. The little thing sniffed at the air as it cautiously approached. She hadn't noticed it before, but it had a long horn that ran from its nose up to its forehead. Unexpectedly, the little creature reached her hand and laid its head on it. On contact, Seline felt a small jolt similar to a static shock, and then it was gone. The only thing she felt now was the soft, warm fur of this animal. She slowly and gently rubbed its face and neck. To her surprise, it started purring, almost like a cat would. Seline couldn't hold back her smile as she stroked this incredible creature.

Uluck was still coming down from his berserker-like state and paid no attention to the little thing. "I'm going to scout the area and see if there are any more waiting to ambush us."

Seline snapped out of her infatuation with their new friend. "That's a good idea, brother. I will stay here with Sebastian and work on getting some of these wounds healed."

Without another word, Uluck disappeared into the forest. Seline turned her attention to the messenger, who was just standing there, amazed that Uluck had the energy to go off scouting when he himself could barely stand up.

"Let's have a look at that arm again," she asked. Her voice held a certain tenderness he hadn't heard before. Gingerly, he raised his right arm and pulled what was left of his leather bracer off. His arm looked a mess as some of the cuts reopened.

"All right, now stand still and keep a lookout for more trouble."

Seline again placed one hand palm up under the injured limb and the other hand palm down over it. She repeated the incantation from before, and the soft greenish glow returned. This time her eyes were closed, and she was clearly in a state of deep concentration. The pain began to fade as the spell mended his damaged flesh and bone. He even felt a little less fatigued once she finished.

"That should do it," she said as her eyes opened, and she let out a deep breath.

"I have never seen that done, let alone on me. That was incredible, Seline, thank you." He could swear he saw her blush at the compliment before she hastened on to care for her own wounds.

"It's getting dark, Sebastian, and we have no horses or a safe place to rest." She sat down on the soft ground a short distance away from the bodies. The wounds on her leg still oozed black and crimson. "I'll work on this. Why don't you go with Uluck when he gets back and find the horses, if they haven't run back to Trillium already?"

They both chuckled at the thought.

Sebastian wiped his blade off on a bed of moss close by before sheathing his sword. A few minutes later, Uluck emerged from the ever-darkening forest.

"I don't think there's any more of those things around," he told them.

Sebastian voiced what they all were thinking: "Good!"

"All right, I'll be safe here with this little fellow while you two go find the horses," Seline said. Uluck was about to go get some branches for a fire when a ball of light formed on the tip of the little fawn's horn. The immediate area was awash in white light. Seline shook her head in disbelief. "Well, aren't you just full of surprises?"

Luckily for the two that had to find the horses, the sky was clear, with two nearly full moons to help them see. They disappeared down the trail, leaving Seline and the light-emitting whatever-it-was sitting there. She took a couple of deep breaths before beginning the task of removing her leg armor.

"Mmmm!!!" she groaned through clenched teeth as she painfully worked the damaged sections free. "What a bite those things have," she remarked as she removed the last crushed piece. "I'm gonna need to visit the smithy when we make it to town."

Seline examined her leg, assessing how bad the damage was. An almost perfect pattern of the creature's teeth lay before her. A few of the punctures actually still had the broken teeth in them, probably from when she tried freeing herself. Taking breaks in between each tooth, she worked them from her flesh until just the holes remained, bleeding profusely. The little fawn scrunched its nose up when it leaned forward to sniff at the wounds.

"That bad, huh?" she asked. It was as if there was some kind of anticoagulant in the creature's saliva, causing natural clotting to not occur. *Smart,* she thought. All they had to do was bite their prey and wait for them to bleed out. "Not this woman!"

With her hands in position, Seline began the healing spell. The toxins oozed out, and one by one the holes closed, leaving just the slightest scar behind. By the time she finished, her companions returned with two of the three horses. Seline and Uluck's mounts stuck together, but the third one was nowhere to be found.

Sebastian checked his pocket for the king's letter and pulled it out. He noticed it wasn't as crisp and clean as it was when King Elrick first gave it to him. Nonetheless, it was safe, and back into his pocket it went.

Uluck walked over to his sister to make sure she was okay before helping her to her feet.

"Let us move on from here and make camp away from all this death," he proposed.

Seline and Sebastian couldn't agree more. Off they went down the path with Uluck in the lead. The little fawn creature walked next to him, lighting the way.

CHAPTER FORTY-ONE
REUNION

Where am I? Lucious thought as he opened his eyes, disoriented from the long sleep. He could see he was in a large, dimly lit room that seemed familiar somehow. He was in the most luxurious bed he had ever felt, and the air smelled like flowers. Lucious looked at the far end of the room and could see a smashed-in door and deep claw marks in the stone walls around it.

"That's odd," he whispered to himself. Just as before, his memories rushed back in a flood that made his head hurt. "I must be in King Elrick's meeting hall. Why would they put me here?" Turning over, he could see the reason and it all made more sense. There lay the gryphon alongside the bed. like some kind of dog. Its enormous chest heaved slowly with each breath. "It must have tried getting to me, so instead of it destroying the castle, they brought me out here to rest. Good choice."

His eyes drifted down to the sleeping woman next to him. Her smell was so invigorating. She looked so peaceful sleeping; he could just sit there and watch her for hours. Morgan was always close by, watching over him.

From what he could tell, it was either early morning or late in the evening, judging by the faint light coming through the many windows. Lucious knew the urgency of his quest would not wait, but he wanted to be selfish for just a little longer, lying there with the woman who meant the world to him. A short time passed as the room slowly grew brighter. Morgan's eyes opened to meet those of Lucious. What happened next caught him completely off guard; she embraced him with a passionate kiss. It was unreal how soft her lips were, and she tasted absolutely wonderful. This was his first kiss, and he never experienced a feeling like this before. Morgan pulled away and the two just lay there, looking into each other's eyes.

"What was that for?" he sheepishly asked, hoping he wouldn't wreck the moment.

Without pause she said, "I missed you."

"I missed you as well, Morgan. How long have I been asleep?"

"It's been a day and a half since you created that gryphon and collapsed."

Lucious almost forgot about the other two he summoned to get them out of that dungeon cell.

"Are the two Veassels all right?"

It took her a second to figure out that he was talking about Bibble and Bobble, the two thieves that released them.

"They're fine, as are Ulandra, Selim, and Stormy. King Elrick saw to it personally that everyone was brought to the castle. He immediately ordered by royal decree that all of us were under his protection."

"Does he know about you and the other Draconians?"

Morgan simply smiled and let out a little giggle. "No, we figured between the gryphon, the Arabis, and the Veassels that it was enough to take in already without revealing who *we* really are."

Lucious agreed, "That's probably for the best, at least until everyone can come to terms with the world they once knew is changing. There are always those that fear change and lash out violently at it."

Their intimate moment ended too soon; the gryphon lifted its massive head and looked over at Lucious. Upon seeing him awake, the gryphon let out an ear-piercing screech. Morgan and Lucious covered their ears, trying to block out the sound. Just like a dog, it jumped on the bed to greet its creator. The bed frame crumbled under the sheer weight of the creature. It laid its head on his chest and begged for attention. Morgan was quick and sprang from the bed before being injured by its talons.

"There, there, I'm glad to see you too," he said as he gently stroked the gryphon's head. It kept the bulk of its weight off of him, so Lucious didn't end up broken like the bed frame. What could he do but soothe the gryphon? He was pinned by its massive head, anyway. To be honest, Lucious didn't mind in the least. It was a unique blessing to have so many wonderful creatures devoted to him.

The door across the room was being unlocked, and with a few clicks it swung open. He couldn't believe his eyes when his father walked in. The gryphon quickly came about in a defensive posture, assessing the possible threat.

"It's all right, he's not here to harm me," Lucious reassured the animal just before he himself sprang from the bed and bolted towards Ezra. The cold stone floor on his bare feet bothered him little as he met his father with a bear-like hug that almost sent the two sprawling to the ground. Ezra returned the embrace to his son. "I thought I had lost you to those Morlocks, father!"

"Well, I tell you, it wasn't for their lack of trying, my boy." The two men released each other. Ezra looked at Lucious with a wide smile. "It's a relief that you are safe and well." As he peered past his son, he noticed the gryphon and a beautiful woman approaching. "I can see your powers are truly as magnificent as I had foreseen."

Morgan walked over to the two of them to introduce herself. Ezra's eyes stayed fixed on the beautiful woman before him.

"Hello, my name is Morgan Hunter. And you must be Ezra."

"Indeed, I am, Miss Morgan," replied the mage as he shook her outstretched hand. Lucious could tell the two were sizing each other up.

"So, Morgan, how is it such a woman has come to accompany my son?" Ezra wondered his entire trip who this mysterious woman was, and what she wanted with his son.

"It's all right, Morgan, you can show him," interjected Lucious. Ezra stood there, quite shocked, as Morgan shifted into her natural form.

"Your son created me."

The silence was palpable until the gryphon let out a screech like an eagle.

King Elrick and Queen Victoria walked into the great hall and towards the three of them. Morgan hurriedly began to shift back, but Lucious grabbed her arm.

"It's all right, Morgan, let them see who you are." The look he gave reassured her it would be all right.

"Very well."

The dark green velvet robes brushed the stone floor with every step the king and queen made. White fox fur adorned the collar and gold stitching ran around the edges. They truly looked regal as they walked over to greet the group. Lucious noticed how they didn't react as he expected when seeing Morgan's Draconian form. Both of them welcomed the group as equals

Victoria greeted everyone with warm hugs, while Elrick used a firm handshake instead. When he reached Lucious, his gaze went to the floor in shame. "I humbly beg for your forgiveness, King Lucious. I reacted too hastily when you came for aid."

"Nonsense. You acted as anyone would when presented with such an outlandish request. I'm just grateful you didn't have us bound and sent to the asylum for fear of us being mad." Elrick chuckled at the idea.

Screech! called out the gryphon, not wanting to be left out. Elrick, having spent much time with the creature, walked over to pat his lowered head.

"The King and I wish to welcome all of you into our home." The Queen's voice was so warm and inviting, making them feel truly accepted. With a polite bowing of the head, the three of them acknowledged.

"We are grateful for you and the king's hospitality, Queen Victoria," responded Ezra. Victoria looked over and could see her husband acting like a kid with his dog, vigorously scratching the gryphon's head and neck while he talked to the creature.

"Elrick, dear, when you're finished . . . ?"

Composing himself, Elrick brushed off the fine white feathers that had fallen onto his tunic before joining Victoria. "Sorry about that. I just can't help myself around such a magnificent creature!"

"The king and myself would like to invite you all to dinner tonight so we may discuss the encroaching threat we are facing from the west."

Bibble, Bobble, and the rest of Lucious' companions were now filing into the great hall, escorted by the king's guard. Lucious could see that Selim and Ulandra were still in human guise. Stormy ran up and jumped into Morgan's outstretched arms, where he snuggled lovingly. Morgan reciprocated, hugging the Arabis and rubbing her nose on his. All exchanged hugs and handshakes, as this was the first time they were all together. Selim and Ulandra looked at Morgan in Draconian form and glanced at Lucious for approval. He nodded his head.

"It's all right you two, this is a safe place." In a moment, both reverted to their true forms.

Ezra, who had been standing there silently the whole time, was just stunned with wonder and joy at what was before him. Four completely new species that never existed were all in one place. For the time being, the problems to the west were not at the forefront of his mind. The mage examined those in attendance, taking mental notes of their unique characteristics.

King Elrick cleared his throat loud enough for everyone to take notice. "Friends, myself and Queen Victoria must take our leave now to take care of matters of the kingdom. I will have my stewards planning and setting up for tonight's feast at the other end of the hall. Please feel free to relax and enjoy the castle as you wish, but for the safety of all, do not leave the immediate grounds. I have made all the guards and soldiers aware that their top priority is to keep everyone here safe."

Lucious stepped forward in front of Elrick. "We understand good king, and thank you both for your hospitality."

Everyone watched as Elrick and Victoria exited the great hall, walking hand in hand.

A few minutes later, the steward strode into the room and walked over to Lucious. This man showed remarkable focus as he ignored all the crazy-looking creatures behind me and went straight to work. "Good morning, sir. Would now be an opportune time to bring in tables, chairs, and perhaps some breakfast?"

"Yes, I think that would be great, and would it be possible to get a few bowls of water and some food for the animals?"

With a courteous bow, the steward promptly headed for the kitchen.

Looking back at his companions, Lucious smiled. Bibble was bouncing on the bed like a trampoline, while Bobble was atop the gryphon's back, riding it like a horse around the room. Stormy was now firmly attached to Morgan, while the Draconians conversed with Ezra.

This feels right, he thought as he stood there alone just watching. *I guess I better get myself a little more presentable*, he pondered, looking down at the pajamas he was still wearing. Walking over to the oversize bed he was just recently sleeping in, he found there was a small stack of new clothes, perfectly folded, and a fresh pair of boots on the floor next to them. With everyone distracted, Lucious quickly dressed, using the bed to separate them for at least a little privacy. As he finished pulling on his right boot, he looked up to see Morgan watching him. She turned away as soon as she realized she had been caught.

No less than ten stewards, cooks, and servants came flowing into the room with each carrying something. They set a long wooden rectangular table up first, followed by wooden chairs with green cushions for every spot. The kitchen staff set places in front of each chair, complete with cutlery, plates, and glasses. They brought in carts of food and placed it all down the center of the table, along with pitchers full of various drinks. So many tasty aromas filled the air.

Lucious was the first to walk over and take a seat. His stomach growled in anticipation. "This is the most glorious meal I have ever seen," he confessed to the person who was laying a cloth napkin across his lap. The serving girl just smiled and continued on with her work. As expected, Morgan sat down in the seat beside him and the rest of the group followed, taking seats at the table. Next, they brought in two large copper tubs. One they filled with water and the other with large chunks of various meats in a soup like broth. The gryphon impatiently waited for the servers to finish. Stormy received a much smaller water bowl and a heaping plate of greens. It wasn't long before everyone was eating their fill of the delicious breakfast. Once the last bite had been eaten, the small army of servers filed back into the great hall and cleared everything out, leaving only the long table and its many chairs behind.

Everyone spent the rest of the afternoon catching up on current events. Poor Ezra had the most to digest, as he was absent for most of the journey so far. Ezra, in turn, recounted the events after confronting the Morlocks and almost being killed. *It is surreal*, thought Lucious as he looked back at how much the world had already changed. Ezra meticulously documented everything in the red book he brought along with him. He even went as far as to cast a spell that would write and draw in pictures for him. It was a little odd at first, seeing the open red book floating next to him as the pages occasionally turned on their own.

Lucious spent a considerable amount of time with the vessels and the gryphon, seeing as he just created them before he passed out. The three were all too happy to finally get acquainted with their master. Bibble was the most talkative by far, almost like he was trying to impress Lucious with his skills. The Veassel's quickness of hand was almost imperceptible as he easily lifted items off of Lucious, only to hand them back seconds later. "I must say, Bibble, you could steal feathers off a bird and it would be none the wiser!"

"I'm as gifted as you have made me, master," he replied.

"It's just Lucious; you are your own masters."

There were a few moments of silence as Bibble and Bobble looked at one another, then back to Lucious.

"Very well then, Lucious it is," said Bobble.

"So, what can you tell me about your people?"

It was Bobble that did most of the talking now, as Bibble became distracted by the Arabis scurrying past him.

"From what memories I can recall, we hail from the land to the east called Dan'nar. It's a land full of lush green forests bordered to the south by swamps. I would say that most of us are hunters, tinkerers, and of course the occasional thief." Bobble shot Lucious a look of innocence as he said the word thief. Mischievous *was the word that came to mind,* thought Lucious.

Throughout the day, guards periodically changed out and the stewards would check in, bringing foods to snack on, along with pitchers of various drinks. As dinner time approached, they brought in a large wooden easel and set it up near the dining table. Next, a long cart with rolled up parchments was wheeled in and placed next to the easel. It took two men to unroll the first map and hold it up while a third quickly secured it down. The most beautifully detailed depiction of Tauro was etched on the parchment. Seeing it made everyone realize that their carefree gathering was about to end.

ACKNOWLEDGMENTS

To my lovely wife Jennifer and my beautiful daughter Aly. Thank you both for all of your countless hours of work helping me get this book up to its current level of polish. I couldn't have done it without you.

Made in the USA
Columbia, SC
29 August 2022

66022339R00186